The Witch's Hand

Wendy Joseph

ALL THINGS THAT MATTER PRESS

The Witch's Hand

Copyright © 2012 by Wendy Joseph

All rights reserved. No part of this book may be reproduced or transmitted in any form or by any means without written permission of the author and publisher and publisher.

This is a work of fiction. Any resemblance to actual persons, living or dead, is purely coincidental.

ISBN 13: 9780984721573

Library of Congress Control Number: 2012936178

Cover design by All Things That Matter Press

Published in 2012 by All Things That Matter Press

To the Mad March Hare

HISTORICAL SYNOPSIS

In the year 1206, King Philippe Auguste of France was busy taking French lands back from John of England, the unfortunate king who lost the crown jewels, was excommunicated, and in 1215 signed the Magna Carta. Innocent III, an idealistic cleric trained as a lawyer, and at age 37 when elected, the youngest Pope to occupy Peter's chair, dispensed a library's worth of edicts, condemnations, official pronouncements, and letters. He attempted to govern every monarchy and Church fief in Europe all by himself, down to matters of minor marriages and coinage. He called the Fourth Lateran Council which, among its other concerns, decreed that all Jews were to wear identifying yellow badges, and laid down the rules and procedures for what was to become the Inquisition.

Men, whole or not, straggled back from the disastrous Fourth Crusade, which had done nothing to free the Holy Land from Moslem domination, but had ended two years previously with the sack of Constantinople instead. The legendary Ailianor (Eleanor) of Aquitaine died in that year also, having outlived all her husbands and sons except her youngest offspring, King John. The throne of the Holy Roman Empire lay in a quagmire of contention. A curious movement known as the Albigensian heresy, both progressive and a pre-figuration of Puritanism, was spreading throughout southern France. The wandering trouveres and troubadours sang of love, chivalrous and otherwise, for their supper, and in the process created works of poetic complexity and simple melodic beauty. Francis of Assisi was 24 in 1206; a year later he would leave his affluent home for a life of poverty.

1206. A century before, an early renaissance in learning and enlightenment had been underway; two centuries later, Joan of Arc would be burned at the stake. Into this most middle place of the Middle Ages step our characters …

PROLOGUE: THE FOURTH CRUSADE

Lead lay molten in the small brazier. Its surface, dotted with flecks of black dross, cracked and wrinkled with iridescence; bright silver shone between the cracks. Two halves of a metal embossing mold, each the size of a flattened plum, waited on the table beside the brazier. Light from the candle heating the lead, and from larger candles ensconced on the walls, flickered over the table's dark polish.

Seated beside the brazier and oblivious both to the late hour and the simmering lead, a lone lawyer of divinity studied the parchment before him. Though the sheepskin had been cut from the underside where it was thinnest and most even, and had been scraped and tanned by Bello himself, the Perugian master, it was coarse next to the Moslem infidels' linen paper. He regretted that their craftsmanship and studies could not be turned to Christian ends, but that would come, with Jerusalem.

He had tried to regain Jerusalem for Christianity, had organized a Crusade seven years previously, a large but tenuously joined alliance. Spurred by the priest Fulk de Neuilly, whose eloquent fervor matched his own, a host of potentates from the Rhine to the Pyrenees, who were gathered for a tournament in November 1199, at Ecri-sur-Aisne in Champagne, had taken the Cross. Their leader, twenty-two year old Theobald, Earl of Champagne and nephew to both King John of England and King Philippe of France—could the boy have more unconvivial connections?—along with a heraldic roster of soldiers of Christ: Theobald's eighteen hundred vassal knights, his brother-in-law Count Baldwin of Flanders with his muster, Baldwin's brother Henry, Louis Count of Blois, the Anglo-Norman Simon de Montfort, Count Hugo de St. Paul, Boniface, Marquis of Montferrat, and the diplomat and negotiator Geoffroi de Villehardouin, who was Marshal of Champagne and chronicled the Crusade—a chronicle posterity should have raised *Te Deums* to—all swore to free Jerusalem.

Rome's requests for aid from the two crowns went unheeded. England's John and France's Philippe, the latter a veteran of the Third

Crusade some fourteen years earlier, were too absorbed in slashing away at a wary truce with each other to bother with the new Crusade. How could a model of God's kingdom be established on earth in the face of obstacles arising from personal vanity and greed?

Then, unexpectedly and discourteously, Theobald died in May of 1201. The Crusaders, whose growing ranks now included the Duke of Burgundy, the Count of Bar, and smaller contingents from Normandy, the Auvergne, Provence, Lombardy, and German baronies, elected Boniface of Montferrat as their new leader. And there began the trouble.

For Boniface was a nephew by marriage of Philip, King of Swabia, the pretender to the Western throne of the Holy Roman Empire, which rivaled the power of Rome herself. Its seat had been left vacant by the death of Philip's brother, Emperor Henry VI, in 1197. Philip was a powerful Hohenstaufen, and head of the German house of the Waiblings. His arrogance in claiming the title Emperor, against the rival Welf faction's recognized Emperor Otto of Brunswick, another nephew of King John, left the Church with no alternative but to excommunicate Philip in March 1201.

Neither Welf nor Waibling had recognized the late Emperor Henry's young son, the Sicilian Frederick, as Emperor. The Vicar of Christ at Rome succeeded in making the boy his ward, a shrewd move that effectively gave Rome control over any threat from the south. But the boy was unruly, titular King of Sicily and a troublemaker, and though his companions were rude, his education scanty, his spirit and pride were those of an Emperor, and he would bear watching.

Wax from the brazier candle dripped down its side. Disregarding his excommunicate status, the Waibling Philip had supported the Crusade, not in order to free Jerusalem but for his own purposes. His eye was on the East. With a large, well-equipped army of Crusaders near at hand, he had the means to enthrone his brother-in-law Alexis at Constantinople, the Empire's eastern capital. Alexis, nephew of the de facto reigning Emperor Alexis III, was in truth the rightful heir. But the road to that crown proved circuitous.

Originally, the Crusaders were to have taken ship from Venice to Egypt, saving them the lengthy and dangerous land route through

Romania, across the Dardanelles to Asia Minor, where decimating fevers and the Seljuk Turks waited, then across the Syrian desert to Jerusalem.

But Venice had betrayed them. Its crafty Doge, Enrico Dandolo, old and half blind, had arranged a nonaggression treaty with Egypt, consolidating Venetian trade with Alexandria; the Pisans and Genoans could take their cargoes elsewhere. No army could land in Egypt. Dandolo had thus put the interests of Venice above those of Christendom, God forgive the avaricious reprobate. He had signed the treaty, and the Venetian Council ratified it in July 1202—over a year after he and the Council had agreed, by treaty, to provide the Crusaders with ships, crew and provisions to Egypt.

Thus the expedition to fulfill Rome's prayers and regain her greatest hope foundered before it began, though no one had known of Dandolo's treachery at the time. The sword turned inward; insatiable, the Venetians demanded full payment for their ships from the Crusaders, who'd been gamely encamped on the Venetian Lido for nearly a year—payment they did not have for transport they could not take to Egypt. Disease and desertion had sapped their strength and numbers, and Fulk de Neuilly, who above all others might have been able to rally the disheartened warriors, was no longer with them. He had died in May, 1202. It was unconscionable, really; the propelling voice of the Crusade had never left France.

He must get back to the document at hand. The candle glimmering beneath the lead was half burnt down and would need replacing soon. It was already after Compline, and he had work to do until Matins. He hoped his secretary was keeping himself vigilant, and that he had enough candles to last until midnight.

Easier to replace a candle than to deal with the Venetians, or undo what had happened next. The Crusaders lacked a third of the money promised to Venice for transport, and Dandolo then offered them a means to pay: a politic, for Venice, expedition to Zara. Zara lay eastward, across the Adriatic from Venice, a competitor for and pirate of Venetian trade, and the spoils from its conquest could be used to settle the Crusaders' account with Venice.

The unavoidable dilemma was that Zara was a Christian city, placed under Rome's protection by her ruler, King Emeric of Hungary, who had himself taken up the Cross to Jerusalem. In vain were the protests of Cardinal Pietro Capuano, papal legate at Venice with the authority of Rome in his words. Venice used the Crusaders to eliminate Zara's threat to her own mercantile domination of the Mediterranean, made them attack the Church's ally in the alleged greater quest for Jerusalem. Four hundred and eighty ships crossed to Zara and besieged it for nearly a month, despite a ceaseless flood of letters from Rome holding excommunication over the heads of any whom should harm the city or its people.

Zara fell on—what had his chronicler Villehardouin written him?—November 24, and was mercilessly pillaged by Venetians and Crusaders alike. Then those uncontrollable *diaboliques*, Dandolo and Boniface, instead of releasing their armies, kept them at Zara over the winter of 1203 to help solidify Venice's hold on the city. The now excommunicated Crusaders brawled with the Venetians and deserted by the hundreds. They trusted neither Dandolo nor their own leaders, but one indisputable fact soon became apparent. Despite the spoils of Zara, they could not reach Jerusalem without continued help from Venice.

Into this rut of disillusionment stepped King Philip of Swabia, who through his proxy, Boniface, seized the moment to sway the cold, hungry and confused Crusaders into aiding his own ambitions. Philip compounded the Crusader-Venetian clash with the interests of the Empire. From the Germanic city of Hagenau, the still excommunicate king wrote, *Put my brother-in-law Alexis on the throne at Constantinople, and he will open the gates of that city to you. All her riches will be yours. From her stores you can provision yourselves for the re-conquest of Jerusalem. With Constantinople as your staging ground, you can mount an expedition all the Turks in Syria could not withstand.*

A fox's move. As an added inducement, Philip pointed out that Alexis, as Emperor, would be in a position to reunite the Churches of Rome and Constantinople, split since 1054 because the Eastern Patriarch had refused to acknowledge that the Holy Spirit came from both Father and Son, not the Father alone. And with Alexis as temporal ruler, East and West could finally wield the sword of Christendom against the Infidel, not each other. *Quid pro quo.*

The Witch's Hand

But Philip had failed to mention another possibility. With Alexis and the East at his command—willingly or not—what was to prevent Philip from deposing Emperor Otto, uniting the Empire's considerable forces in the West with those of the East, and marching on Rome? No. The Christian world had but one ruler, spiritual and temporal, and that was the Pope. No Waibling pretender could alter that.

The unraveling seams of the Crusade began to split. Through bribery and secret agreements, the party for Alexis, which included the Venetian Dandolo and the Crusaders' leader Boniface, won out over the opposing factions and diverted the Crusade to Constantinople. In a final outburst of anger and frustration at a winter's delay, and portent of things to come, the troops razed Zara to the ground before they left. It was then April of 1203.

The midnight cleric put his half read parchment down, rose and paced, candlelight wavering over his long white tunic and robe. The Crusade of his hopes had disintegrated from there. Joined by Alexis, the army reached Constantinople in June and bivouacked a mile from the city's triple walls. A month of preparations later, they attacked and were repulsed, but set fires as they retreated and a great swath of the city burned. The Emperor Alexis III, uncle to the Crusaders' Alexis, fled by night to Adrianople.

His brother Isaac, young Alexis' father and once Emperor in his own right, had been deposed, blinded, and imprisoned for eleven years. Freed, he took nominal command of the city. He admitted the Crusaders and, after a lengthy series of negotiations, he and his son were crowned as joint Emperors on August 1st.

Blind Isaac being sick and feeble, however, the real strings of power lay in young Alexis' hands. And those strings were controlled by Boniface, and through him by Philip of Swabia, who throughout the entire affair remained conspicuously absent.

By now the fractious hosts in Constantinople were Crusaders in name only. Embroiled and torn by the politics of Emperor-making, they had become mercenaries of the rightful claimant Alexis. And Dandolo. And Philip. And Boniface, the Crusaders' leader, who agreed to help put Alexis on the throne in exchange for 200,000 silver marks, provisions for a year, 10,000 knights and foot soldiers, and ships for transport. The silver was paid, and the Crusaders finally began to settle their debts with Venice and prepare to depart for Jerusalem.

But Alexis needed an army to consolidate his hold on Constantinople. The troops were forced to stay. Rioting broke out between Christians and Muslims, Franks and Venetians, and between adherents to the Roman Church and the Eastern Church. A second fire started and burned unchecked for two days and nights, destroying a larger, richer section of the city.

The new Emperor's dubiously held power began to slip away from him. Innumerable deceits, plots, counterplots, arguments, and splits between factions resulted in a reign of confusion. Alexis lost his hold over the populace, who had no reason to trust him, his doddering co-ruler father, or the troops in and around the city. The Western armies in turn lost their respect for the Emperor, as the fall of 1203 dragged into winter, and they waited in vain for the balance of Alexis' promised aid.

By this time, the plan to continue to Jerusalem was a chimera, and Rome's control of the Crusade had long vanished. Constantinople, with all her riches, beckoned to men weary with delay, want, and subterfuge. The queen of the East lay spread before them, a target for rape. Dandolo and the other leaders met, deliberated, and sent an ultimatum to Emperor Alexis: *Pay up or fight. We're coming to take what's ours.*

His Crusaders. In truth, they should have led the Cross to its greatest glory; they'd had all the necessary spiritual strengths, all the physical might, and what had happened? *Domine Deus*, Lord God, what had happened?

In the candlelit room the tonsured, pacing figure paused as he turned, and his ghostly garb continued to sweep the floor around him. Small but powerfully built, he stood, spread his arms and prayed for a true leader of holy warriors, one unswayed by personal gain. Avarice and the politics of Empire, earthly concerns, had undermined the Crusade. And part of it was his fault. He had sent armed men off, like a too trusting father, and like wayward children they had strayed.

"Father, forgive them . . . and forgive me also, for the mistakes I may have made." His grief, like a relentlessly throbbing wound, remained unhealed.

The Witch's Hand

At the end of January 1204, the situation in Constantinople collapsed. A revolution within the city overthrew the co-Emperors Alexis and Isaac, and the discontents' leader, an imperial relative called Mourtzouphlos, seized the throne. Isaac died from what were called natural causes a few days later, and shortly after that, Alexis also died, both most certainly murdered. You couldn't trust anyone in the East.

Civil strife erupted between the nobles and the people, and Mourtzouphlos had his hands full containing it. Dissension among the Western troops also kept them from storming the city. Dandolo and Boniface negotiated with Mourtzouphlos and each other for another two months, struggling to keep some order in the chaos.

Disgruntled men-at-arms readied battering rams and siege machines. The Westerners finally agreed on a plan to elect a new Emperor to replace Mourtzouphlos and divide the city's wealth, and if thoughts of Jerusalem remained in anyone's mind, nobody mentioned them.

On April 8th the assault began. Their first wave beaten back, the invaders regrouped and attacked again. And again. Constantinople fell on the 12th; a third fire destroyed an area the size of three normal cities. Mourtzouphlos and the Eastern Church's Patriarch fled.

The conquerors went wild. As madmen, they unleashed a three day reign of pillage, rape and murder. Women fell victim to unbridled lust; nuns were singled out for shameless handling. Men once sworn to chastity and continence for the length of the Crusade violated daughters of the Church, and enthroned a prostitute in the sacred chair of Hagia Sophia, Mother of the East, as they raided that church's altars.

Looting continued unchecked for days. Officers and men alike stripped altars of their rich cloths and jewel-studded chalices, melted down priceless plate and ornaments for the gold, and commandeered the most opulent houses for their own. Venetians hauled down some of the city's finest statues and shipped them home, to display atop San Marco Cathedral.

The few leaders who retained their fidelity to duty and discipline gradually restored order, by whatever means necessary. They hanged many Crusaders.

Constantinople's total wealth in hard cash and booty came to something close to twelve million marks; out of this, Dandolo took his requisite fifty thousand. Venice had been paid at last.

It was over. Three years of shambles, deception, defeat and disaster had ended with the shameless sacking of Constantinople and no palpable gains in the Holy Land. An expedition to Syria was decimated at Antioch. After Constantinople a handful of Crusaders continued to Jerusalem as pilgrims, but the Crusade itself lay in the dust. Throughout the following year its un-victorious survivors, maimed or whole, straggled back home.

The lone figure stopped pacing. He had done his best; encouraged, exhorted, threatened, and tried to salvage the great effort for God when it foundered. No one could have done more. In 1203 an outbreak of fighting between his mother's family, the powerful Scotti, and a host of other nobles had complicated his dilemma. The Christians immediately around him were not setting a good example for Crusaders or Muslims, and he had himself been forced to leave his home for a time.

He went back to the table and sat down, raised his hands with the fingers crossed at the tips and bent his forehead to them. He had tried, and tried. In retrospect, the evidence pointed to diabolical interference. The Evil One was a formidable foe, but the Church cried out for vengeance upon him, who had thwarted Her Holy Word. *Deo gratia*, God be thanked, he would be vanquished one day. But how many would go with him and what would the final tally be? Heresy was on the rise, practitioners of the dark arts increasing. *Quaestio primus*, the first question was how to most effectively combat the Serpent's insinuous ways of subverting the faithful.

The official mandate on the parchment before him was one tactic, and he returned his attention to it. In crisp, straightforward Latin it read:

> By Papal decree, all those suspected of
> witchcraft shall be formally accused, tried
> by an impartial court, and subjected to the
> prescribed tests for witches. The true
> witches shall be consigned to Perdition;
> the false, to Purgatory for a period of
> time determined by Jesus Christ, our

The Witch's Hand

Saviour and ultimate Judge, or to Paradise outright. As the book of Exodus commands us, "You shall not permit a sorceress to live," we have accordingly taken this measure. Given in Rome, St. Peter's, by his Holiness the Vicar of Christ, April 4, in the ninth year of our pontificate.

Pope Innocent III drew an intertwined length of silk, yellow strands twisted with red, through two holes at the bottom of the parchment. He laid the ends over one tallow coated side of the metal embossing mold, leaving enough silk hanging out below for a tassel. Then he took a dipper of lead from the brazier and, careful not to spill any on the table, poured a gently wavering and spreading globule into the mold. He waited a moment for the lead to cool and settle, then pressed the top of the mold, also tallow coated, firmly into the lead. When separated, the molds would reveal the heads of Saints Peter and Paul in shallow bas-relief on one side, and the name INNOCENTIUS III on the other.

It was done. The Vicar of Christ on earth had decreed the Church's future course toward one of her lengthiest and most troublesome threats, on this fourth night of April, 1206.

Innocent brushed a bit of lint from his linen sleeve, the cuff embroidered with fine gold crosses. He rose, strode to the door of the adjoining chamber and called, "Eminence?" Almost immediately a cowled figure appeared in the doorway—John, Cardinal deacon of St. Maria Cosmedin and head of the Chancery, the department of scribes, clerks and secretaries whose calligraphy and literary style were the envy of kings, emulated by their scribes.

"Your Holiness?"

"Excellent script on the witchcraft mandate. Please make copies for John of England—diabolical man; Philippe of France; Raymond, Count of Toulouse—he may well be a heretic, but we think he is with us in the matter of witchcraft; Frederick of Sicily—we must keep an eye on that boy; all the cardinals, archbishops and bishops; the Emperor Otto and Philip of Swabia—dealing with those two is like handling a two-headed snake. Have the one to Philip sent by unofficial means, he is still out of the fold; and copies to the Marquis of Montferrat, the ..." He continued, naming almost every potentate in the West. His Chancellor took no notes. He had a sometimes unnerving gift of word-for-word recall; speak a name or instruction and it was chiseled on his memory. A good man to have in legal matters.

"Have all copies ready for our seal by noon tomorrow." It was still Tuesday, however late the hour. By Wednesday night papal couriers would be far away in every direction with his mandate.

"Is that all, your Holiness?"

"Almost. Oh, we've restocked a fresh supply of ink; the quills won't be clotting up on you now."

"Many thanks, your Holiness. The Chancery staff will appreciate it."

"Convey to them the urgency of this work. It has escaped our attention for too long. And bring us the letters to Boniface of Champagne and the King of Hungary."

"The ink on the letter to Hungary was not dry when I left it, Holiness. It may be a few moments before I return."

"Blot it again, then. Don't be long; the matter of sufficient flour for the Host in Hungary gives us concern, great concern, and the coinage problem in Champagne could be disastrous for the Cistercian monks there." Innocent strode about as he spoke, his white habit swirling around him, and gave a short, explosive sigh. "Boniface! Couldn't lead a Crusade, can't handle money; the Knights Templars refuse to honor his latest mint. A banking system for them was a badly advised undertaking, an establishment of dubious worth; it has its advantages but also many perils. They've gotten far too independent, and meddle in matters better left to our Mother Church." He noticed his Chancellor still standing by the door. "Go, go; the ink must be dry by now." John nodded in reverence, his hood covering most of his features, and left silently.

Innocent III returned to the table and sat. Waiting for the lead in the mold to set and for his chief amanuensis to bring the letters back, the man who had once been Lotario dei Segni, nobly born, student of law at Bologna and theology at Paris, forty-six now and eight years Pope, rapped his fingers on the table.

1. THE CANDLE

Five hundred miles northwest of Rome, in the Gallic region of mountains and escarped plateaus called the Auvergne, the night was now nearly three hours past midnight, and silent. A woman's hand, manicured, patrician, moved along the top of a rough stone wall which was crumbling to the ground in places. The wall bordered a clearing amid deep woods, where a thatched cottage stood, a wood and stone box covered with bleached plaster. The door hung from worn leather hinges, and badger hides covered two minuscule windows. A plot of barely sprouted vegetables lay planted next to the cottage. In an open shed with a pen on the other side of the garden, a goat, a few sheep and some chickens dozed. Beyond that the woods began again, and a stream ran quietly through them.

I begin again.

The woman moved closer to the cottage, her hand still on the wall. A wide sleeve flowed from her wrist and fluttered over the stones. Her dress fell in silken cascades of deep blue and purple, loose here, gathered there, embroidered in places with intricate gold designs that were maybe Byzantine, maybe Celtic, but not anything conventional in this backwater. Over her shoulders she wore a light, finely woven purple cloak with more designs in silver tracery. A large gold brooch fastened the cloak, and a jeweled clasp held her dress in at the waist. For all the elaborate wear, she moved along the rough ground without snagging a single braided tassel or loose hanging.

All the powers.

She stepped through an opening in the wall, moved into the clearing and watched the cottage. Unhooded, an abundance of rich chestnut curls surrounded her brow and trailed past her shoulders. Her face was pale, a Visigoth's northern cast, and her eyes—in the darkness they were almost luminous, a translucence that varied between blue and gray, like icicles in moonlight.

And you?

No light shone from the one roomed cottage; no smoke rose from the chimney, its stones loose in their mortar and gone in some places.

It was in there. There. What she had come to find. Her eyes flickered, held on the right end of the straw roof, then moved dead center. She raised her arms—left thumb and forefinger out, right thumb and first two fingers out, all slightly splayed—and pinpointed the spot she sought within the cottage. With a master's assurance she quickly brought the extended fingers together without touching, and unleashed the collected force in a concentrated, invisible stream.

The center and left part of the cottage burst into flames. An object shot into the ground at her feet, and she knelt slightly to pick it up; it was embedded in the ground and she pried it loose, examining it in the bright flailing light.

It was a small wooden jar with a fighting boar and stag amateurishly carved onto its sides. The top was corked and she opened it to find crushed flower petals and herbs, the lemon-barbed rush of rosemary predominant. A periapt of sorts, though it would be hard to wear this one around the neck, a charm to keep the Devil and his tribe away. She smiled fleetingly, re-corked the jar and pocketed it.

She stood watching the flames, firelight playing across her face and silhouetting her against the burning cottage. From the shed, sheep bleated, a goat's bell clanked, chickens sent up a dry cackle. And from inside the cottage, a wail arose.

Liana struggled up from her pallet in the loft, straw clinging to her hair and shift. In front of her, flames shot through the rafters to the roof and curtained any glimpse of her mother and father's bed across the room. Smoke curled horribly against the roof, and parts of the thatch had already caught fire. She couldn't see her parents; wait, there—one, two figures moved, or writhed, a mixture of flames and confusion.

"No—no—"

Someone choked with a strangled sound, she couldn't tell who; she saw a hand, Maman's strong one, reaching through the flames for her, then a rafter crashed down, bringing part of the blazing roof with it in a cascade of sparks and smoke.

"Maman! Papa!"

Neither answered. Their side of the room had turned into a cauldron disintegrating into itself. A surge of heat before her drove her back and all the rafters were burning now: a bunch of squashes dropped with a

The Witch's Hand

thump at the other end of the loft, as flames ate its hanging line and the loft itself was ablaze, fire snatching its way along the straw toward her. Liana turned and fled to the wooden ladder by the loft's other end, but the fire had gotten there first and was devouring it from the ground up.

Another rafter fell, barely missing her. Its end clipped the edge of the loft and sent a shower of sparks onto the bottom of her shift, setting it afire. Beyond the fallen rafter was a clear space on the floor. Liana jumped.

She hit the packed dirt, stumbled, sprang up and dashed toward her mother but a whorl of heat and smoke drove her toward the door; only then did she realize her shift was burning. Beating at it, looking for a sign of her parents, praying no rafter would fall between her and escape from the running flames and burled smoke of the cottage turned crucible, she fell against the door, choked, called again, "Maman? Papa?" without hoping for or getting an answer, then the cracked leather hinges gave, and she burst outside as the loft crashed to the ground, its meager stores and straw blazing.

Barefoot and choking, Liana ran blindly out into the dark, and by feel more than sight she tore off the burning edge of her shift and threw it aside. Coarsely woven but thin with wear, the irregular tatter floated down, fire consuming it as it went. Liana tripped and tumbled to the ground.

Behind her, the cottage cracked like a split rock. Liana turned quickly and rose halfway as the rest of the roof fell in, taking parts of the walls with it. Clouds of sparks danced up and swirled into nothing. Only the chimney remained upright, though loose rocks dropped from its sides.

"Maman . . . Papa . . ." Liana sank to her knees and stared at the earth, her long dark hair falling around her. "*Requiem eternam dona eis, Domine,*" she breathed automatically, grant them eternal rest, Lord. She knew but the sounds; she could recite most of the Mass for the dead without understanding the Latin.

Firelight flickered over her as she fought to get air back into her smoke-filled lungs. The cottage, her home, was a ravaged wreck now, her parents indistinguishable from charred stone and burnt wood, her mother's outreached hand already haunting her. She turned away.

"Liana."

Lit by the dying flames, an apparition stood before her. Liana bolted backward, almost back into the flames.

"Child. Do not run."

Liana stopped, trembling and breathing hard. The phantasm spoke softly but with authority, her voice clear. She moved closer to Liana and quieted the flames with a calm gesture.

"I am Malaxia." The apparition was a woman in fantastic dress. From beneath a tasseled silk hanging, she drew a brilliant jewel the size of an acorn and held it up. It glinted with bluish light; a faint glow surrounded it. Riveted, Liana reached out to it but the spectre-woman quickly drew the jewel back and hid it beneath the hanging. Liana stopped with her hand out.

When the jewel disappeared it took its flash of moonlight with it, and light came again only from the smoldering fire behind her. Gold glinted off the ring on Liana's right hand, the only thing of value she owned.

Malaxia suddenly seized Liana's left hand. Liana grabbed her own wrist from beneath and pulled, but the woman's grip was too strong. Malaxia crossed her other arm over and took hold of both Liana's hands. A tingling began there and spread toward her elbows; Liana watched in disbelief, then horror as their four enmeshed hands began to glow like fire under goatskin. The tingling turned to pain and spread, through her arms, shoulders, up into her head; it filled both eyes and jabbed with every heartbeat. She could still see, but her vision was much curtailed.

Malaxia stood before her in the glow of their joined hands, her eyes calm, unflinching on Liana. Threads of pain encircled Liana's head, tightened, then shot like eagle talons through her. She shrieked and writhed but could not break free of Malaxia's hold. Authoritative but gentle, Malaxia spoke.

"It will not hurt if you do not let it." Liana, twisting like a landed fish, didn't understand. Malaxia continued, "You are my heiress now." Her tone would have soothed if not for the surge of pain, sharp and hot. Liana gasped and went to her knees, uncomprehending; she lost sight even of Malaxia's luminous eyes and heard only her voice.

"I will give you a power, to cherish." Malaxia released her hold on "cherish," and Liana crumpled to the ground, a singed rag before damask.

The Witch's Hand

She rubbed her hands and felt Malaxia's fingers, strong but sensitive, around her head. The searing fire began to subside.

"The pain will soon cease." Liana looked up at her. Malaxia's eyes, drilling into her a moment before, were softly composed now. "You will understand, later." With a rustling sweep of her dress, Malaxia turned and moved toward the woods, her cloak gliding along the ground. At the open section of the wall she stopped and looked back at Liana. "And you will see me again."

She went on into the woods. Liana lowered her head a moment, then looked up. Malaxia had disappeared. Not a shadow moved to give away her path. Liana looked around; she couldn't have vanished that quickly, but Malaxia was gone.

The cold caught up with Liana and she shivered. Behind her, the embers of the smoldering tomb still glowed faintly; loom, cooking pots, bedcovers, clothing, traps and snares, herbs, dried meat, and her parents, her staunch ones, all lay charred, half melted or in cinders, surrounded by ravaged walls, the blackened chimney standing like a diabolical sentinel. Of Liana's possessions, only her dirty, burnt white shift and her ring remained.

A last timber broke and fell into the embers, and one of the sheep bleated. The goat clanged its bell. Liana looked up past the trees and saw that of the two circling Ladles, the Big One to the left had dropped beneath the Little One; past Matins but a long way till dawn and Prime. Maman would be up then, slicing goat cheese, the first sunrays lighting the creases about her mouth as she smiled at—no.

The only way to warm herself here was to huddle with the sheep or draw near the dying fire, and the latter she would not do. She would walk to town; Peranville was not far, she could make it by sunrise. She rose and went to the shed. Kneeling by one of the sheep, she buried her hands in its fleece and rubbed warmth back into them.

"Don't stray too far," she whispered. There was only a little of last year's barley left in the bin, but with forage and the stream nearby she didn't think they'd wander very far till she got back. With help. She couldn't sort through what the fire had left in the cottage by herself, and her parents needed a priest for a ... for a proper burial.

May the angels lead you into Paradise. And may the martyrs meet you.

The martyrs and the other children before her, the ones her parents had lost, though Liana didn't know how many; they'd never talked much about it. Liana left the shed and headed toward the woods.

"*Salve Regina, mater misericordiae, vita, dulcedo et spes nostra* . . ." The words came automatically through her numbness as she walked and this time she knew what they meant. "Holy Queen, mother of mercy, our life, sweetness and hope." The mumbling monk, a fixture on the steps of Peranville's cathedral had taught her. Branded mad by the Bishop, his eyes glazed over with the egg white blindness, he'd nonetheless had a dignity, of sorts. Liana had once gotten close enough to listen and realized he was praying, half in Latin, half in her own words, Auvergne's langue d'oc, the language the rest of the world spoke. She had listened and repeated it enough to get the Salve Regina in both tongues. Six months later, on another visit to town, the monk was gone.

Liana hurried; walking wasn't doing anything to ward off the cold. She had to go to the cathedral and ask to have a Mass said to make sure her parents got Heaven and not Purgatory. It would cost two sheep probably, and maybe a couple of chickens. Also, she would need more hands to help bury Maman and Papa, if the fire had left anything.

Liana stopped short and leaned against a tree. She had banked the fire the evening before. A piece of wood must have rekindled and fallen out.

"*Mea culpa, mea culpa,*" she whispered. My fault, my fault. When she reached Peranville and confessed, the penance would be horrible, probably torture with coals, but she had no other hope and no place to go. Her father had been a game watcher for the Bishop; in return for acting as a beater on the Bishop's hunts and keeping poachers out of the forest, he held hunting rights for small game, deer and boar excluded. She might hope for the Bishop's favor. Liana hastened through the woods, her feet unerring on the irregular path. *Help me, Papa. Make the Bishop remember what a good game watcher you ... oh Papa, I'm sorry ...*

The full moon still held the western sky and the light from the stars was dim. Liana peered through the trees into the uneven shades, and her eyes were good but she saw no sign of Malaxia. Was the woman a demon, sent already to punish her?

The path dropped abruptly into a narrow freshet. Liana leaped across and scrambled up the steep opposite bank. Halfway to the main road to Peranville now.

2. OUTCAST

Dawn seeped through the trees and lit bushes from beneath. Dewed leaves turned translucent green with crisp silvered outlines, and out of the gray meadows, faint gold shone. The sun cleared the horizon and filtered its sheen through soft violet, a pale ball in a pale sky. Shadows became hills, both rolling and sharp, and out of the shadows trees rose, of varied height and shape, each merging into another. As the mist lifted, interchanging hues of green began to flood the countryside. Shocks of white and pink tree blossoms broke the greens, and wildflowers lay violently scattered; the Auvergne was in bloom.

In Peranville's market square a loose chicken squawked, flapping its wings, and loose feathers flew as its keeper chased it. The sun had been up for less than an hour, but the guild merchants—cobbler juggling his hammers to draw customers, a draper hanging out his cloths, purse maker eyeing him to make sure he didn't hide his own wares, goldsmith bending to polish a piece, lace maker working hurriedly to mend a tear, bloodied butcher, his brother-in-law the fussy sausage maker, furrier laying out pelts, glass blower harrying his assistant not to break his jars, parchment maker with sleep puffy eyes, chandler, in the shade where the sun wouldn't melt his candles, and firing up his forge with a bellows, a blacksmith—already were doing business, bartering and cajoling, breathing garlic on prospective customers and waging verbal wars with each other.

Along the wall that bordered one side of the square, flies buzzed over a confusion of chickens, pigs, cows, horses for the rich, goats, sheep, oxen, and their steaming fresh droppings, while their owners haggled over trades. And haggled. And *haggled*. In a corner beyond the animal market, dismissed servants and runaway peasants offered themselves and their skills to any who could afford them. Two women with shark's eyes and low slung shawls lingered in the shadows.

The Bishop of Peranville stood on the cathedral steps, looking out over the square. The stink of the market place was not as great in the early morning as it was later in the day, when only animals and beggars were unaffected by it. The ground was still damp and had not yet risen in clouds of rose-gray dust. Right now the vendors' and buyers' voices reigned, a babble and chatter of jays. The swirling stew before his Excellency was a mélange of colors bright and dull; earthy brown and green, yellows—*what did they dye it with, manure?*—a liberal working of blue, with fur, jewels and embroidery marking the occasional titled money, and here and there a flash of garish red, rather like the wounds of Christ and it intrigued him, the notion of the rabble as one bleeding Christ. But he shook it off.

The Bishop waited to hear petitions from a straggling line of farmers, peasants, beggars and criminals. Though it was only Wednesday, he wore his white holy day vestments and stood out like a firefly above a swamp. It was good practice to appear thus before the mangy to demonstrate God's concern for them. The Archbishop had advised him on this. He therefore gave a quarter of an hour every morning after Mass to hear pleas and requests. "It is a great mystery," "The Lord hears you and will answer in His own time," or "Pray for strength," were his most frequent replies.

Two guards in gray cloaks throated with black rabbit fur flanked the Bishop. The Lord of Heaven was also Lord of earth and needed watchmen for its valuables; besides the august person of the Bishop, there was the barley and wine stored in case of famine or extra taxes from the Archbishop. More guards moved through the market. Brawls over prices and cheating were not uncommon, and the people needed to be reminded that their beneficent God was also God of justice.

The Bishop noticed a handful of strangers in dark garb, who took no part in barter but drew a merchant aside and spoke with him in low tones. Heretics from the south, likely; his guards had orders to watch these folk and overhear their talk whenever possible.

A pilgrim on his way to the shrine of St. Jacques de Compostelle in Spain knelt before the Bishop and asked for his blessing. The man stank and the Bishop drew back slightly, trying not to breathe through his nose. His blessing was wide and generous as he attempted to clear some of the rancid smell away. Absorbed in his duties, he did not see Liana enter the square.

She slipped in from a corner street, her half burnt shift disappearing and reappearing through the crowd like a duck on rough water. A

The Witch's Hand

weaver thrust a bolt of cloth into her face as she went by; she shied around it and headed for the motley sunrise-and-gray stones of the cathedral, at the opposite side of the square. Liana plunged through the crowded market.

She bumped into one furrier haggling with another, and was jostled between the fat chandler who smelled of wax and the cobbler brandishing a hammer.

"You're taking up my space!"

"*My* selling space!"

The tanner next to them flapped a large cut of cowhide out; she veered to avoid it, veered again sharply to dodge a scythe a woman raised to examine, then she tripped and grabbed at a hanging string of sausages. The line broke and she crashed into a trestle table piled high with sausages, upending it. Sausages large and small spilled into the dirt but Liana kept going, while the sausage maker dashed out crying, "Hey! Come back here, you little pig thief!" Liana, intent on getting to the flash of white that was the Bishop, didn't hear him. The vendor looked at his wares on the ground, wailing, "My sausages," then got his feet tangled in a coil of links and fell into them.

"Serves him right," growled his brother-in-law the butcher. "Always skimps on the pork." Three weeks before, the Merchants' Guild had forbidden the Butchers' Guild to make sausages, ruling that it was a separate craft.

Liana struggled through the last of the crowd and ran up the cathedral steps; help was finally at hand. "Your Grace!" He took no notice. "Your Excellency!" He turned at the proper form of address. Liana stopped, seeing his elaborate array, and wondered if it were a saint's day. She didn't notice the guards moving in closer to the Bishop. He looked down at her, annoyed.

"What are you doing here, before the house of God, in that indecent clothing?" he demanded. Liana suddenly realized how she was dressed, fingered her ragged, scorched shift, saw her dirty legs, the knees cut and bruised, and couldn't answer.

"Almswoman!" the Bishop called.

An old woman came forward from her place beside the cathedral steps where she had been standing with her cast off wares. She herself wore what looked like a patched tent.

"Find this child some suitable apparel," the Bishop ordered. He glanced at Liana's feet. "And shoes."

Liana's eyes shot down to her bare feet, then back up at the Bishop. But he had already turned away, back to the line of waiting petitioners. The rabble stank more and more as they proceeded, and his responses grew correspondingly shorter. *Gratia Deo*, thank God, the fifteen minutes were almost over.

Liana followed the almswoman down to her pile of rags, where after observing the girl with a practice-worn eye, she dug out a long sleeved tunic, forest green, faded and oversized, of wool, darned, patched and stain splotched, and pulled it over Liana's head. It fell loosely to her knees. Her shift hung down several inches below the tunic. The almswoman took a knife and sheared the extra length off, tore it into two strips and knotted it for a belt. As Liana tied it around herself, the almswoman found a pair of dusty brown hose and dubiously cobbled boots, and helped her into them. The girl was seventeen maybe, no more than twenty, a beggar headed for a convent or a brothel, probably the latter. But that was not her business.

Decently attired at last, Liana said, "Thank you," to the almswoman, who crossed herself and replied automatically, "You're welcome, God be with you," and returned to her disarrayed goods.

Liana started back up the cathedral steps toward the Bishop. A man in rough clothes, with a rougher face, came toward her and barred her way. He stank of soured wine and old rank sweat. "Bit young to be out wandrin' the world, aren'tcha?"

Liana recoiled; seventeen was not that young and she was not wandering the world. Instinctively she put her hands up to ward him off, then started back as a light flashed and the grubby man flew backwards like a rock from a catapult. He landed hard on the stone steps and tumbled to the bottom. Next to him, the almswoman looked in horror at a scrap of Liana's shift she was holding and dropped it as though it had the plague.

The Witch's Hand

Astonished, Liana stared at her hands, not hearing the scattered mutters and whispers of those who had been close enough to see.

"Witch . . . witch . . . witch," the words circled, rising into a chant. "Witch! Witch! Witch!" The crowd began to close in on her. She turned to the Bishop.

"No, your Excellency! I am not a witch!" She dashed for the cathedral doors and sanctuary. The Bishop, impervious, made a small gesture and the two guards blocked the doors with their halberds, each one crowned by a wickedly sharp spike atop a double headed axe, ready to spear her on command. Liana spun back toward the menacing crowd, then again to the Bishop. She fell to her knees and clutched his embroidered vestments, soiling the white linen.

"Witch! Witch!"

"Please, let me inside," she implored, desperate. But the Bishop stepped back, pulling his surplice away from her, enraged she had dared touch it. Outwardly he was unmoved; one brow flinched, but his voice remained calm.

"The holy Church offers no sanctuary to witches." He saw the small wooden cross on a chain Liana wore, broke it from the chain and pocketed it beneath his vestments. He turned to the guards. "Seize her." Each reached a burly arm out for the girl.

"No!" Liana jumped back, hands out. Both guards doubled at the waist and fell as if pummeled with a pike, though this time no light flashed. The crowd around the cathedral steps went silent, and slowly began to draw back. Some crossed themselves. Liana, frightened, turned and looked at them, unaware they were more afraid of her. Haltingly she descended the steps and moved through them; they parted like the Red Sea, though she expected a blow at every step. Wary, fearful eyes followed her but none laid a hand on her. The entire market was hushed. She reached the end of the square, hurrying now, passed the huddle of beggars and ran down a narrow alley.

"After her!" the Bishop barked. The two guards rose and looked dubiously at each other. Impatient, the Bishop shoved one against the other to get them started, adding, "And if she reaches another parish by nightfall, then it is their affair." Relieved, the guards trotted off through the crowd after the ragged witch girl.

The Bishop watched them go, then turned toward the dark arch of the cathedral doors, ignoring the cries and protests of those petitioners he had not yet heard. On the top step, a wizened old man in a bloodstained leather apron faced off with a large woman, red in the face, who held up a plucked dead chicken by the neck and bawled, "Cheat! Cheat! Your scales are off! Cheat!"

"My scales are true weight, they're balanced, the Guild checks them once a month—"

"Cheat! Your Excellency! I've been robbed by this man, this excuse of a man, who doesn't know hen from cock! Sets his scales off and has been doing it six months now, here, under the nose of the Virgin! Guild be damned!"

The Bishop disappeared into the darkness. The two imminent pugilists tried to follow him inside, but another guard stepped forward and barred the door with his halberd.

"Bishop's orders. Come in to pray or back off."

The red faced woman slapped the chicken against the stone balustrade, spewing out bloody insides. "Cheat!" She shook the fowl with its dangling entrails in the old man's face, and stomped off.

***

Liana raced down the alley toward the road out of town. The way bent erratically, and rounding a turn she found herself face to face with an oncoming oxcart. Double yoked and loaded with milk buckets, there was no room to squeeze by on either side. She pulled up, panting, looked behind her and saw the two guards coming up fast. She set herself and ran straight at the oxcart.

Before the driver could check his team, Liana dove under the yoke tree between the oxen and skinned along on her elbows and knees, in as narrow and straight a line as she could to avoid the immense cloven hooves falling on both sides. Past those, she ducked a trace strap and crawled under the wagon till the solid wooden wheels and rumble were behind her. She looked sideways and up to make sure she was clear, scrambled to her feet, and dashed on.

The Witch's Hand

The guards barged up to the oxen, seized their harness and tried fruitlessly to shove past them.

"Cow butt! Out of the way! Move your damned cart!"

"Use the main road!"

"My milk! You're spilling my milk!" Overturned buckets dripped white puddles onto the ground.

Liana had disappeared around the corner. Marais, the first guard, reeased his hold on the ox and jerked his head.

"Come on, Boulon. The main road."

They doubled back up the alley toward the square, then turned off into a narrow byway that paralleled it.

Liana followed the twisting alley till it hit a rough path along the inside of the town wall. Another turn and there was the main gate, past it, the road.

Marais and Boulon burst out of a passageway ahead, spotted her and rushed up. Liana skidded to a halt. Marais drew his dagger and it slammed into a doorframe beside her before she knew he had thrown it. Pursuit was one thing, knife attack another; she seized a rock from the ground and hurled it at Marais. It hit his leather covered shoulder and bounced off. Seeing him unfazed, Liana turned and fled alongside the wall till she reached a broken-topped section, stones to rebuild it piled neatly to the eaves of the building opposite. She climbed the stones, jumped from there to the wall and dropped to the other side. Across a newly plowed field stood a copse of trees, very dense, and she headed for it.

Marais yanked his knife free from the doorframe, and he and Boulon raced up to the pile of stones. Boulon put a foot up to climb them, but Marais grabbed his arm. "Ah, porkpie, you'd never make it that way." He pulled Boulon over to the wall.

"Up, idiot." Marais clasped his hands for Boulon's boot. "Come on."

"Why me?"

"Because I'm bigger. You can give me a hand from the top." Marais boosted Boulon, who managed to get a handhold just below the top stone. He scraped and hauled and kicked and made it up with the help of one boot on the wall and one on Marais' shoulder.

"Ow!"

"Sorry."

Boulon reached down from atop the wall and Marais handed him both their halberds, which he dropped on the other side.

"No! Boulon! You should have kept one and helped me up with it. Ahh! Don't go down for it. Just give me a hand."

Boulon hung over the wall as far as he dared, which wasn't much, his legs dangling on one side, his arms reaching for Marais on the other. Marais jumped, grasped Boulon's hands, and half pulled, half walked himself up. Boulon dug his knees into the wall and felt the stones cutting his stomach in two while Marais attempted to pull his arms off. He began to slip down the wall headfirst.

"We're—both—going—to—go!"

"Hold on, idiot."

Finally, hand over hand on Boulon's shoulder and back, Marais climbed high enough to swing a leg over the wall and straddle it. He slapped a deflated Boulon on the ass.

"Uhh."

"Shut up and get down. You look like a dead rat." Marais vaulted from the wall and picked up his halberd. "Come on! I can still see her!" Across the field, Liana was just entering the trees. The much stretched Boulon slid off the wall in a heap, staggered up clutching his halberd and followed Marais. Marais pulled his knife out again, but Liana had disappeared into the woods before the guards were halfway across the field, which was furrowed and broken up into uneven chunks.

"If she's a real witch, how come that rock didn't turn into poison or fire when it hit you?" Boulon panted.

"She's a witch." Marais held up his knife. "I don't miss, not at that distance. I can peg a rabbit to the ground from farther off." He shoved the knife back into its sheath.

"This one's fast as a rabbit. Wha'd she do back there? Felt like a war horse kick."

"How the Madonna do I know? Witches make pacts with the Devil. They copulate with him and he gives them different kinds of powers." Marais rubbed his shoulder. "Maybe she can't do things to rocks."

"Is it bothering you?"

"Shut up and come on." They entered the woods.

The Witch's Hand

"Marais. What's copulate?"

Marais groaned. "What do you do with Claudette?"

"Oh. Maybe we should go back for horses."

"If we're out past Nones, they'll send a mounted patrol. Where the Devil did she go?" The copse of woods was deeper and thicker than it had looked. Marais drew his sword and slashed at a tangle of bushes. Boulon waited till the way was clear, then trudged after Marais.

"My luck to draw early duty today. How come Valère never has to stand morning watch?" Boulon grouched.

"His cousin's a cardinal, that's why."

Marais caught a flash of something moving ahead to their left. "Wait." He halted and peered through the leaves. "There she is!" The hounds charged after their rabbit.

Liana bolted out of the woods into a field. A thatched hut stood next to a low stone wall with a gate midway through it. Liana dashed toward the wall as the guards burst from the woods. She glanced behind her and made for the gate, shoved it open and, bent low, scurried along the wall in the opposite direction. The two guards ran past her on the other side. She ran behind the hut without being seen.

Marais and Boulon reached the gate at the same time and slammed together trying to get through.

"Damn it, Boulon, she's not important enough to break ribs over, the little wretch!"

"Witch."

"Shut up."

They rebounded, went through the gate one after the other—and the girl was nowhere in sight.

Liana stopped behind the hut and fell back against the wall to catch her breath. Immediately a clump of loose thatch fell from the roof on top of her. Choking on the fine chaff, she batted away the straw and took off again, this time toward another stand of woods. As she reached the edge, Boulon saw her and pointed.

"Over there!"

Liana ducked under a branch. She didn't know how long she could evade them, but she was quicker through the woods, made no more sound than a deer, and despite being numb from last night's and this morning's events, she did not run blindly in a straight line but dodged and weaved, crouching when the bushes offered too little cover.

"Branches," Boulon muttered. "Why are there so many branches in the woods?"

Expecting a knife in the back at any moment, Liana slid down an embankment to a stream some five sheep backs across. Submerged rocks formed a rough dam that made a pool, but enough stone showed above water for her to cross and she stepped nimbly over, leaping twice at wider gaps. On the other side, she slipped into a tangle of brush and briars that caught at her flying hair and scratched her arms and face.

The guards, not wood haunters, sloshed through the pool one after the other. Marais was nearly across when behind him, Boulon caught his foot on a root and fell, drenching himself and sending a shower of water over Marais.

"Idiot! You jackass!" Marais roared. He helped Boulon up the opposite bank. "I'm putting in for another partner."

"So am I."

Marais halted and studied the bushes before them. "She could be anywhere in there." He pointed in one direction as he started off in the other. "Go around. Look sharp and listen."

The two guards began to encircle the stand of brush. Slowly and warily Marais moved around his side. A shadow there? A twig snap—no, it was that ox Boulon. The girl was in there, no doubt of it, making her way her way through the dense growth. Another shadow moved. She would come out there—no, *there*; he drew his knife and leaped as the girl broke out of the brush before him, but she shied away like a weasel and he collided head on with Boulon. They both fell back flat. Before they got all their senses back, Liana had vanished again into a further stand of trees. Sprawled on the ground, Marais and Boulon glowered at each other. Boulon spoke first.

"I think this is the next parish."

"For once I think you're right." Marais got to his feet and hoisted Boulon up. "Let the priests chase this one. Come on, my brother-in-law doesn't live far from here. Hoards his wine, but he's been known to have charity for those in God's service. Particularly when there might be an indulgence in it for him." The two servants of God headed off through the woods, opposite the direction the damned witch girl had taken.

Evening sun rays, barely lengthening now in April, shone through Peranville's mostly deserted town square and turned its lingering dust to a subtle rose gold. The market stalls were shut and only a few beggars remained in the shadowed corners near the cathedral. Marais and Boulon turned into the square and trudged toward the arched doors. As if on cue, the Bishop appeared there, still looking as though he could step out at the head of a holy procession. Marais threw down the sprig of rosemary he'd been chewing to get rid of burgundy breath, clumped up the steps and bent his knee in obeisance. Boulon, a little behind him, did the same.

"We could not find her, your Excellency," Marais said.

Boulon, drooping, added, "We looked everywhere."

The Bishop contemplated them a moment. Marais was a staunch enough fellow, one to be trusted in matters of duty, while Boulon was too new to have proven himself valuable in anything but reporting for duty late, at which he excelled. But the Bishop saw their muddy boots and sweat lined faces; both had done their work today.

"Come inside and I will absolve you of any evil the witch has put on you," the Bishop said. The cathedral bell started to ring the twelfth hour, six p.m. "Vespers is about to begin." Leading the way into the darkness of the cathedral, the prelate added, "And I will send a messenger out with news of the witch. We cannot let this go unnoticed, unpunished."

Behind him, Boulon muttered, "I hope he sends Valère."

The Bishop chose not to hear him. He was more concerned with the southern heresy at the moment, but reports of witches and their malevolent acts filtered in continually; a stack of newly inscribed incidents lay upon his desk. He would get to them tonight.

3. *JETTARET*

The next morning's sunlight leaped through the new greens of spring, shimmering down the hills and over an outcrop of lichen decked rocks. Beneath them huddled Liana, barely awake, cramped and cold after a chilly night, and hungry. She heard something, or felt it rather, and put an ear to the ground. Hoof beats. One horse, at a fast walk, and coming closer. She squeezed back into the rocky enclave, jabbing her shoulder and knocking pebbles and grit loose. They fell down the slope before her and the hoof beats stopped. There was a silence, then two footsteps of someone dismounting and the *whhsssh* of a sword being unsheathed. The footsteps approached.

Liana tried to jam herself further into the uneven rocks, which stuck into her back painfully, and her movement knocked more grit loose. It skittered over the old rotted leaves and new grass sticking through them. Then a pair of well made but travel worn boots stopped before her. She looked up at a brown, weather stained cloak, and beside it a long shining sword. Holding the sword and looking straight at her was a man with dark rough hair and deep eyes, which filled with puzzlement as he saw her.

"Well, well, what's this? Chicken feed? Raven meat?" His tone was quizzical but not a peasant's. Liana looked past him and braced herself for a wild break from the rocks. He noticed this but did not move.

"Oh, no need to fear me." He sheathed his sword. "Or I you." He knelt and regarded her closely, but without suspicion. Pointing to his ear, he asked, "Are you deaf, girl?" Liana shook her head. He indicated his mouth. "Mute, then?"

With a voice she could hardly hear herself, Liana said, "No."

The stranger rose, his feet in a wide stance. He was only a few years older than she but had the bearing of a sergeant at arms; a knight maybe, despite his shabby clothes. Hands spread out, he queried, "Am I that frightening, then?" He seemed about to laugh.

Liana jumped, bumping her shoulder against the rock again, then shook her head. "Did you …" she managed, then her steadiness returned and she looked at him, resolved. "Did they send you to kill me?"

"What?" If she had turned into a winged serpent and bitten him, he couldn't have been caught more off guard. "What for? You wouldn't make a good meal for a meadowlark—come to think of it, you look like one. Tell me, do you eat?

The girl crouched in the rocks looked Hunger up at him through translucent wood-green eyes.

"Yes, and you're starving. Hold on." He turned and strode briskly back to his horse, a black Andalusian mare, fine boned and more streamlined than a war horse but sturdy, with long legs and a nose that curved in instead of out. He took a round of bread from one of the saddlebags and returned, tearing off a crusty chunk. He held it out to Liana. "A bit stale, but no bugs yet."

She hesitated, then took the bread and started to devour it; Maman's fresh from the hearth had never tasted better. Her server sat, tore off some bread for himself and handed her the rest.

"Well, and what did you do to come to be out here?" he said presently. He glanced at her rags. "Queen of some forgotten country?" She didn't look at him. "Heiress to a stolen fortune?" He snapped his fingers; he had it. "Abscond with the parish collection." Liana's eyes flashed but she remained silent. "Seduce the Bishop? Steal his plate?" Liana shuddered at the mention of the Bishop and stopped chewing.

"Take your time; you needn't answer right away." He cast a glance about the surrounding country, devoid of other people. The path he'd been on was a short cut only those who knew the area rode. "Hmm. No inns about, and there are a few beasts in these woods that just might find you tasty." Liana lowered her bread and looked around. He laughed. "Ho, never mind; you're with me." He laid a hand on her shoulder and she shrank away. A runaway peasant, young as she was?

Peasants were bound to the land, whether it belonged to a lord or the Church. If an incorrigible one bolted and managed to reach a town far enough away, apprentice himself to a trade and remain uncaught for a year and a day, he was legally free. But times had to be rough in the extreme for anyone to risk that; fines, torture and death or maiming were the consequences for an apprehended runaway, and this part of the country was peaceful, productive. Neither famine nor plague had scarred it for some years, and the taxes of Church and noble were not overmuch;

he could attest to that. The girl shivering in front of him couldn't have a trade yet, and the thing to do was get her home or to a convent before her eyes went dead and her voice hard, hawking women's oldest wares.

He noticed her fingers, clutched around her knees, were bluish white. "I'll build a fire. Wherever you're going, you won't get there dead." He got up and gathered what kindling he could find, piled it up, dragged a fallen dead branch over and set it on top, then took flint and steel from a leather pouch on his belt and went to work. Sparks landed on the still moist wood, glowed a moment, and went out.

"Damp in these parts," he muttered. "Ah, I've got a good flint." He continued striking it but the kindling refused to catch.

Liana watched the shower of sparks and saw again the flash of light when she'd thrown the man in the square back. She looked at the place where the sparks were falling, instinctively raised her left hand toward it, hesitated, then pointed her thumb and forefinger out. Slowly she brought them together. It was like trying to squeeze a chunk of hard clay. She lowered her head a moment, concentrated, and fixed her eyes on the unlit branch. When her outstretched fingers were as close together as she could get them without touching, a jolt left her hand, and a small flame flared up, but died quickly. The stranger kept on sending a shower of sparks down.

Liana then tried with her first two fingers and extended thumb. When she got them as close together as she could, a second jolt threw her hand back and flames exploded from the branch, much bigger than she'd wanted, driving one startled would-be fire maker back. He deftly swept his cloak away before he tripped over it, and stared at the flames but only remarked, "Must not have been as damp as I thought."

Liana also watched the burning branch, which smoked and steamed like a normally lit piece of undried wood, its flame the same color and intensity; watched with mingled awe and pride. She had done it. It was her first controlled spell, more or less. At least she hadn't blown them both up. She caught sight of the traveler looking at her. His cloak showed fur at the throat, ragged, but only nobles wore fur. A bandit then?

"You're shivering," he said. "Come over by the fire." He went to his horse again, adding over his shoulder, "I've got an extra cloak." Liana stayed where she was. He returned with a dark, heavier cloak and draped it around her. She pulled the hood up and it fell over her face.

"If you don't feel like talking, that's all right; I can talk enough for a convocation on St. Augustine." He laughed and took her hand, drawing her toward the fire. Strength went out from his hold, but Liana pulled back.

"Huh?" He dropped her hand. "You haven't got leprosy, have you?" She shook her head. "You're to wear a red hat if you do." She wasn't wearing the leper's required cap, but the laws were uneven from duchy to county and unevenly enforced. He observed the back of her hand and saw nothing unusual, then nodded up sharply. "Both hands." Liana held them out. He motioned for her to turn them over, and though the palms were scratched and grimy the fingers looked normal enough, all there and untwisted.

"No. Well. You can sit on the wet, cold ground, and no doubt chatter your teeth loose, or you can sit by the fire with me. I'm not such a bad sort. There are many worse than I." With that he turned and sat by the fire, his back to her. Liana hesitated, then the draw of warmth won out and she followed, but went past the bandit and sat on the other side of the fire.

"There," he remarked dryly. "Not so hard, was it?"

Liana shook her head, the movement barely perceptible within the hood. "Thank you, for the bread. I have not eaten nor slept in—I don't know how long."

"Yes, well, that is a sure way to die, you know." He looked away toward grass and shrubs filtered with sunlight, then back to her. The fire crackled. "I believe you have just spoken two complete sentences. Keep it at that and you will be a most attractive woman."

"Please, don't make fun of me. The Devil honors me with trouble—"

The bandit was unconcerned. "We all have troubles, my girl. I am about to be married. Betrothed at nine to a woman I have not seen since. Have her picture here ..." he fished out a miniature portrait on a wooden oval, looked at it with a noncommittal "Hmm," and turned it toward Liana. The paint was faded and she couldn't see it well, but gold rays shone around the face as it did around the saints' faces, all of which looked the same, in the cathedral windows. Solemn eyed, she said nothing. The bandit tucked the miniature away, then suddenly turned back to her.

"Oh, by the way, Michel Antoine Jettaret, Vicomte de Solignac."

A vicomte. Liana didn't know what to do. She mouthed "vicomte" and stood, confused as to why this one was traveling alone in the woods. Nobles hunted with hawk and hound and had a covey of servants about them always to carry out orders; they lived in castles big as a town and wore clothes like Malaxia's. They made the laws and had you punished for breaking them. Awakened early and hastily dressed to hunt for the witch, had he only been amusing himself with her before he took her back to Peranville to be burned?

Whatever the event, you didn't offend nobility. She stepped back.

"Uh ... um ... your Lordship ... your Respect ... I ... I ... Sir," she implored, "what do I call you?"

The Vicomte de Solignac sat back and laughed. "Jettaret will do. I may be an aristocrat, but I assure you, I get cold and hungry like anyone else. And your name?"

"Liana," she halted, trying to think of what to add. From the game watcher's cottage? Second stand of trees after the stream? "Liana de—" Turn off the road between the big myrtle and the rock? She drew herself up and put her hood back. "Liana de Peranville."

"Liana," Jettaret repeated. "Lovely name." She stood waiting, wondering what to do next. Bow and back away? Ask if his Lordship wanted more food and drink? The fire crackled. Finally his shaggy Lordship asked, "Are you going to sit down or not?"

Liana dropped like a stone. Jettaret went on, "I have several days' travel to Lyon ahead of me. Where are you bound?"

Away from the Bishop and guards and witch hunters, to ... She said, "I don't know."

"You intend to wander the woods for the rest of your life?" He shook his head. "Wouldn't recommend that. Dirty. Lonely. Unhealthy. Know anything about hunting, fishing, which berries are good and which are not?"

Liana held her head up. "I was raised in the woods. My father is—was a game watcher for the Bishop." Her voice remained steady. "I know something of all that." The verses came automatically.

Rosemary tea for headache and rheum,
Comfrey root for colic and gout,
Bedstraw for goiter,
Nettle to blister,
Egg white and cobweb to stop a wound,
Yarrow and thyme for pains of the spine,
And myrtle in summer, till the harvest comes.

Jettaret looked at her and didn't miss a beat. "Easy to go mad all alone," he said dryly. "When I want medicine I'll ask for it." A flirtatious gleam lit his eyes. "I suggest matrimony," Liana stared at him," with someone of your own station. Or, if that doesn't suit you, or your family perhaps—"

"My mother and father are both dead," Liana interjected. She looked through the fire to the darkness beyond.

"Ah. So that's it," Jettaret muttered to himself. To Liana he said, "My sincere condolences in your bereavement." His voice was deep and quiet. She was not the first to be driven into the wild by grief. "Well, there is a convent of nuns some three days' journey north of here." He saw her shudder again. "Not the religious type. Not the marrying type." This was getting unfair. "A little batty in the head maybe. Of all the women in the world, I have to run into— " he met the hurt in Liana's eyes and sighed, "a girl. And an orphan."

"I can't marry anyone and I can't go to a convent." She stopped, then leveled her gaze at him as staunchness outweighed fear. "They say I am a witch."

Jettaret choked. "If you're a witch I'm the Pope." He leaned back, amused. "Well, do something. Show me your magic. I don't believe in it, by the way, or witches either. Come on. Turn into a cat. Turn *me* into a cat ... no, a rat. Make something vanish." He threw his hands up. "Poof!" Liana jumped.

"Stop it!" she cried. "A vicomte should be well behaved, and even if you aren't," she fought through fright, "you should know, have the sense, they *burn* witches!" Her rebuke brought her close to tears.

"So they do," Jettaret acknowledged. A cold dissonance crept into his voice, tempering his levity. "I am aware of that little atrocity. All this witchcraft business ... it is a way, I am afraid, of people saying they don't like what you think, what you believe, what you look like, what you do," Liana caught the awful implications of his last three words; Jettaret did not notice, "and gives them an excuse to seize your land."

"I've no land to take."

Jettaret was thinking. "They would not burn you if you took another identity. My future wife will doubtless need more servants after we are married. I shall pass you off as a lady-in-waiting from my own household, presented as a nuptial gift," he concluded briskly. "Would that suit you?"

Liana was at a loss. "I don't know how to be a lady-in-waiting."

"Just curtsy and apologize when you bumble something and you'll do fine. Either that or burn."

Liana looked out at nothing, her voice low. "I saw them burn a witch once. It was winter. First they took her to a lake and dropped her through a hole in the ice ... her face turned all blue ... she was almost dead when they pulled her out. Then they tried to put her hands into a pot of boiling water but she started to scream and so they held her down in the snow and ... and—"

"And poured molten lead across her throat." Liana stared at Jettaret; how did he know? He shrugged. "It's a common practice."

"And then they burned her. She was already dead, but the smell ..." She sat still, remembering. A rotted deer carcass in a plaguey swamp hadn't a fouler stench.

"What did they accuse her of?"

"Consorting with the Devil. I've never done that," Liana added hastily.

"I believe you." *But then, you're consorting with me,* he thought wryly.

Liana rose and walked off to one side, her tunic hanging from bony shoulders. Jettaret watched, puzzled then amused, as she stuck one foot out, then the other in an awkward attempt to curtsy. Wobbly and off balance, she stopped in consternation and called, "Which foot do you use when you curtsy?"

Jettaret the Vicomte looked at his feet. He rarely bent the knee anymore; homage was due to one's liege lord, who could be of the same rank but with more power, and in ascending order, to a comte, called an earl in England, though on his one visit there years ago he hadn't been there long enough to meet one, only scholars, and on up to a marquis, duke, prince or king. All the ranks overlapped in de facto power; Raymond, the Comte de Toulouse, wielded enough authority for a king, enough to trouble the Pope, and homage could be owed to more than one lord, as well as to prelates of the Church. This could lead to difficulties over whom to fight for if any of them went to war with each other.

But Jettaret's allegiance was solely to King Philippe in Paris. His bow, when needed, had always come automatically and he puzzled over his feet a moment; which went forward and which went back? Men did it differently than women anyhow. Then he said to Liana, "A bit of triviality not included in my training. Just try not to kick anyone."

Liana glared at him and went on trying. Finally, with one knee bent behind her, she managed an unsteady curtsy.

"Brava!" Jettaret applauded. Liana curtsied again, more sure of herself this time.

"But that's easy!" she exclaimed. "What else does a lady-in-waiting do?"

Jettaret started to answer and stopped, tried again and couldn't. It was outside his experience; he had no idea what else a lady-in-waiting did, other than help the lady of the castle give visiting lords a bath and sometimes share their beds. They couldn't spend all their time doing that. Liana was watching him expectantly. He cleared his throat.

"That I assume you will learn as you go," he said, rising. He stomped the embers of the branch into the dirt, mixed them well, and stomped on it all again. Liana kept her hands down at her sides until the fire was out. Jettaret started off toward his horse, then halted abruptly and looked around.

"You don't have a horse," he realized. Liana shook her head. "You do know how to ride?"

"Yes."

"Pasquale isn't going to carry us both to Lyon. I'll go back into town and get you one. Here." He unsheathed his dagger, flipped the blade end into his hand without looking, and tossed it end over end toward her. "Use this on anything that isn't me." He aimed a little short and to one side, but Liana was there and caught it by the hilt. Jettaret stood still a moment, then broke his eyes away. This girl knew knives.

"I'll whistle," he whistled four notes, two high, one low and one high, "when I get back." He checked Pasquale's girth and glanced up at the sun. "Shouldn't be too long."

Liana practiced the whistle a couple of times and nodded when she had it.

"Good," Jettaret said. "Stay here." Liana sat crouched by the rocks. Jettaret swung up and reined the mare quickly around. "Come on, Pasquale." Dirt and leaves spurted from beneath her hooves as she spun and galloped off through the trees. The sound faded rapidly, and the woods became silent again. Liana waited, Jettaret's knife ready in her hand.

4. INTO THE BOAR'S TEETH

Peranville's market square swelled with its ruckus of livestock and hucksters. Entering at the end furthest from the cathedral, Jettaret was confronted by a smelly gaggle of beggars who reached out with dirty, skinny arms, imploring him; their voices, dry and broken, merged into one shrill drone that rose and fell.

"Bread! For the love of Christ, bread! Alms! For God's sake, alms! For the poor! For the poor! Sweet Mother of God, have mercy!"

Seated, some half rising, were bald old men and bald old women indistinguishable from them, toothless, wrinkled, some so disfigured they were more akin to the cathedral's gargoyles than human beings. Mothers, young perhaps but with lined faces and shriveled breasts that held no milk, sat holding their squalling infants in soiled swaddlings. Whining toddlers, not much older, wore little, and a few wore nothing, as they pestered boys and girls of ten or so who had dull, unfocused eyes. The older ones reached out grimy hands from habit, not from the hope of getting anything, and a girl younger than Liana pulled up her torn skirt for Jettaret as he passed. The blind, those with stumps for arms and legs, a stinking variety of the skin diseased, half-wits and a contingent of malady fakers added their cries, though some sat silent.

Jettaret reached beneath his cloak and pulled his money bag forward on his belt. It was a noble's duty. He undid the tie on the flap, untied and pushed open the thick leather folds strung together underneath and took out an assortment of gold, silver and copper coins. These he tossed at the beggars in a horizontal arc, aiming at the worst off, who dove after them. None thanked him. Duty. Not an unpleasant one, this. But they would still be miserable. He pulled the drawstring tight and rode on.

"Feather of the Angel Gabriel! Feather of the Angel Gabriel!" Before a two story house fronting the square stood a relic seller, a goose down feather in his hand and assorted relics about his boney knees: lint from Mary Magdalen's dress, a tooth of John the Baptist, the dice the Roman soldiers used to gamble for Christ's robe by the Cross, hairs from the tail of the ass the Virgin Mary rode into Bethlehem, and the ever-present piece of the True Cross. The relic seller's wide black eyes were filled with innocent conviction, his voice with a hawker's mechanical rhythm. He held the feather up as Jettaret approached. "Feather of the Angel Gabriel!"

Jettaret rode past, noting other relics in the spread array: a swatch of cloth from St. Anthony's cloak, an assortment of pig and goat bones for the bones of the Apostles, a lock of white hair from St. Elizabeth. He didn't see the ass's jawbone Samson had used; some other relic seller must have that. On closer inspection he saw that the wood from the True Cross was a piece of fresh cut birch, the sap still oozing. Demand must be good.

On a narrow balcony above the relic seller a woman built like a hefty ham beat dust, lice and fleas from a feather pillow. It burst suddenly and sent a cascade of downy feathers around the seller who choked, floundered in a swirl of white and came up with feathers clutched in both fists. He held them high in triumph.

"*Feathers* of the Angel Gabriel!"

Jettaret rode on.

"Fresh killed pig! Slaughtered this morning!"

Blood dripped off a piglet's little snout into the street as Jettaret passed by. His jaw grew tight and he searched with narrowed eyes for the horse market, finally spotting it across the square.

Jettaret dismounted by the horse barterers and handed a scrawny boy a copper obol. "Hold my horse." You didn't tie up a horse here and leave it. The boy's eyes were expectant. "One more when I get back."

"A Pegasus, sir! A Pegasus!" Jettaret regarded the horse trader's touted Pegasus, of dubious breeding and more dubious feeding. He shook his head at others, too old or broken down to last a day on the road—not a war horse among them—spavin hocked, over at the knees, one bony ribbed misery, and a huge chestnut whose own weight looked like it had splayed his hooves out sideways.

He moved further among the stock with a frown, shutting out the traders' cries, and spotted a dapple gray mare that looked sound enough. She was smaller than Pasquale. He stepped closer, stroked the mare's head—eyes alert, deep and bright, no sign of cloudiness in them—and waved his hand behind each eye to check her rear and peripheral vision. She blinked. Good. To test her hearing he snapped his fingers by each ear, and she flicked them but was not head shy. Good. He pulled her

The Witch's Hand

mouth open and rolled her lips back for a look at her teeth, and judged her to be about seven; little wear on the back teeth yet.

"Won't pull a plow. Too small." Another buyer moved on. Jettaret ignored this, and went over her with his hands, paying careful attention to her legs, which looked clean, no white on them anywhere, and found no lumps or swelling, no tender places to make her flinch. He slapped her along the withers and back, found her sturdy, and ordered the trader to trot her away and back. Kneeling, he watched the action of her legs from the rear and head on, saw she neither paddled in nor out with her hooves and showed no signs of lameness. Her wind seemed good as far as he could tell from a cursory listen.

The gray stood quietly as Jettaret stroked her head again. Gentle, nice arc to her neck, not too broad in the back; a decent mount for the girl back in the woods, if she was still there. If not, he was out a good Venetian dagger and the price of a horse.

Jettaret nodded the horse trader over and paid more than he would have liked but did not belittle himself by bargaining. He stopped at a saddler's close by and bought a used but serviceable saddle and bridle. Looking over the gray's back as he saddled her, the girth snug but not too tight, he noticed two guards in their black furred gray cloaks talking to a cutler at his stall, some ways off. Jettaret could not hear what they were saying, but one guard held his hand out at Liana's height and drew the other hand down as through long hair; the other made an explosive gesture, throwing his hands out to both sides.

They were still looking for her. Jettaret gave the stable boy his second copper, mounted Pasquale and led the dapple gray alongside, walking till they were out of town, then broke both horses into a gallop.

"Get up. Whoa. Get up. Whoa." Liana's voice was intense with concentration. Jettaret reined in before he could see her, approached cautiously without her noticing him, and when he came in sight of the clearing he did not whistle.

Liana sat astride a fallen log and pulled on invisible reins. "Get up—no." She loosened the reins and shook them on the log. "Get up." She pulled the reins in. "Whoa," loosened them again, "Get up," pulled them in, "Whoa."

Jettaret watched, amused, as she tried to figure out how to turn her log horse. Then he whistled. Liana started and turned to see him riding through the trees toward her. He halted in front of her.

"Here's your horse." He dismounted and handed her the reins. "She's very gentle. And I'm pleased to see you know how to ride."

Liana's eyes did not waver, but her jaw flinched and a blush tinted her hunger blanched cheeks. She handed Jettaret's dagger back and touched the little mare's neck.

"What's her name?"

Jettaret thought a second, looked at the bluish cast of the dapple's coat and her hard dark hooves, and replied, "Bluestone." A peasant girl's palfrey didn't merit much of a name, but then peasants didn't usually merit palfreys.

Liana looked up at the saddle, then at the stirrup. Jettaret smiled briefly, shook his head and bent over with his hands clasped. "Here. Put your foot here." She stepped into his hands and he boosted her into the saddle, nearly throwing her over the other side. She picked up the reins.

Jettaret mounted Pasquale with careless ease. "Use one hand," he said, holding the reins in his left hand for Liana to see. She did the same. "A little looser . . . there. All right?" he asked. She nodded. He raised the reins imperceptibly, touched Pasquale's side with his boot and the horse started off. Liana watched, then lifted her reins an inch and urged softly, "Get up." Bluestone moved forward, following Pasquale rather than her command.

They rode in silence for a few minutes, Bluestone moving up beside Pasquale. Jettaret glanced over at Liana, down at his rein hand, then at her again.

"They were looking for you in town." Her fear returned visibly, like a fast tide. "Don't worry; I know this country. We'll take a few short cuts. They won't find us."

"It's not the guards I'm afraid of."

Jettaret checked Pasquale. "Who then?" He chuckled. "*Did* you clip the Bishop? Seduce some wandering saint, and now he's out for revenge?"

"No! It, it's someone, something else." Jettaret waited, but Liana said no more.

The Witch's Hand

"Well, if you are a little criminal, I have no intention of being hanged or tortured for helping you."

"Please. I didn't do the kind of things you said." She turned to him in earnest. "I won't hurt you."

Jettaret laughed. "I'd like to see you try. Witch." He shook his head and rode on.

Liana looked down at the pommel of her saddle, touched her fingers to it gingerly but nothing happened, and held on for security. After a few strides she started to look at the leather more closely. It was rough and coarse grained, goat rather than sheep or cow then, stained and cracked; it needed sheep fat rubbed into it. She tried to figure out how they had stretched it to fit the high wooden pommel and how they'd shaped the wood. The seat was made of curved lengths of wood covered by worn sheepskin, the fleece side turned inward. It was not thick fleece, and her bottom and legs were starting to hurt; she had not yet begun to learn the automatic way a rider moved with his horse.

They climbed a series of ascending ridges. Liana's forebodings welled up, as though Malaxia might appear beyond the crest of every rise. But each time, there was nothing.

Pasquale reached the top of the last hog backed ridge and slid in gravely dirt down the other side. Bluestone scrambled gamely after, Liana holding on with both hands. The slide ended in a trail cut into the side of the hill and they headed northeast along that. It was narrower than a deer trail and Liana, though she could have walked it, didn't see how the horses could. She looked ahead to Pasquale's hooves and saw the shiny black was placing them almost in a straight line, swinging her legs out and around slightly to do it. Bluestone would be picking her way in the same manner then.

The trail descended into thick woods at the bottom of the ridge and they rode through them, not following any path that Liana could see. At Sext they halted briefly for a midday meal of sorts—bread, wine and dried sausage that chewed like wood bark. As they continued the trees thinned out, broken more and more by meadows in soft bloom, and Liana's thoughts of Malaxia vanished. When the sunrays were slanting low from the west, and Jettaret judged they were well out of the way of any searchers from Peranville or chance wanderers, they stopped by a spring to make camp.

Liana slid off Bluestone and found her legs unsteady and very sore, both shoulders stiff with kinks. Jettaret uncoiled a long line of rope, looped it twice around a tree trunk near the spring, tied Pasquale to one end and motioned for Liana to lead Bluestone over. It hurt to walk. Jettaret said nothing but turned his head to hide a smile as she approached. He tied Bluestone to the other end of the line, looking to make sure there was enough forage for both horses within the lines' length.

"Here," he started to unfasten the girth on Pasquale's saddle," undo the knot like this." Liana watched and undid Bluestone's, using her teeth to help get it loose. Jettaret helped her pull the saddle and blanket off so they wouldn't fall on her, and placed them beside Pasquale's, propped up on a rock to dry their undersides. Liana stretched and tried to work a kink out of her shoulder, then rubbed her left leg, which hurt more than the right. This time Jettaret didn't try to hide his smile.

"First day's ride is always hard," he commented. "Particularly when it's also your first ride." Liana was too spent to be embarrassed. "Walk around in the sun a little, and get some kindling together. I'll see to the horses." He rubbed their legs and sweat-darkened backs with a piece of rough cloth, checking for tenderness or sores.

At least the girl, like his horse, didn't complain. He wondered how he'd introduce her to his bride and in-laws to be. "Picked her up on the way"? "Won her in a wager"? Maybe not. He'd ride into Lyon without her and have someone else bring her in.

Liana wandered about their campsite, picking up what dry sticks of wood she could find. Then she wondered what they were going to cook; Jettaret had no fresh game that she could see. They needed a snare. She put the sticks down, went over to her saddle, knelt and tried to work free a number of leather lashings knotted on it, meant to tie bundles behind. There was only one bag behind the high cantle, and it was empty, but all the remaining lines were fastened on too snugly and teeth didn't help this time. She lowered her hands, considered other ways to go at it, then re-determined, put her hands to the lines again.

The Witch's Hand

Before she touched them, several came loose and slithered into the grass below. Liana's hands flinched back, and she sat still a moment, poised where she was. They had been tightly tied before. She looked toward Jettaret to see if he had noticed, but he was bent over examining one of Bluestone's hooves. She closed her eyes, rubbed her hands, and didn't notice the air above her wavering the way it did above a fire. Then she picked up one of the fallen lines, noting the twisted narrow place in the middle where it had been tied.

I didn't touch them. Or did I? Her hands again, and the inexplicable.

Doubt and apprehension aside, she had enough lines now for her purpose. Swift and deft, she tied them into a rabbit snare, got a dried crust of bread from one of Pasquale's saddlebags and crawled into a large tangle of bushes and briars, already damp with dew in the fading light. She pulled a handful of the crushed looking moss that rabbits favored and placed it and the bread crust in a large leaf for bait. Then she set her snare around it, hung the jerk line over a low briar stem above, backed off to the end of the line and waited. Half hidden in the underbrush, she lay unmoving and might have fallen asleep if her tightening stomach had let her.

Jettaret had the fire going and cut chunks of bread, setting them on a rock next to strips of dried venison. He hadn't planned to live out in the wild completely, on rough way-fare; there were inns and acquaintances enough through the Auvergne for him to have food and lodging almost every night, but he hadn't counted on stumbling across a runaway peasant either, with the Church after her. Not that another heretic at the stake mattered much, but civilization, or what passed for it, needed grubby hands like hers, enough to work the land and serve in the household; they were vital for a lord like himself to keep his holdings productive and secure, and invaluable in a war as initial attackers with their pikes, protective buffer pawns for the knights who did real battle. A noble could never have too many peasants in fealty to him, and the girl was of childbearing age, a definite plus.

The one reason Jettaret didn't list to himself was that he could not let her die.

He dismissed Liana's claim to be a witch as an inventive ploy. She had committed a petty theft out of hunger and would be better off among nuns than in a vicomtess' train of attendant ladies. But once married, his wife's ladies were hers to dismiss or retain, and this one probably would be relegated to scullery work or sent to tend goats.

Beyond that, he had never cared for the Bishop of Peranville, a man of low birth and high ambition, principally for land and fealties traditionally belonging to the Vicomtes of Solignac. Frustrating the Bishop's search for one minor criminal put a little sauce in Jettaret's pot.

He looked toward the tangled bushes where Liana had disappeared with her snare. She was used to the woods all right, but you could wait all day with the best bait and catch nothing. Bread, dried meat and one wineskin would serve till they reached an inn or town.

Jettaret rose and headed toward the brambles, peered into them but caught no sign of Liana, and wondered if she'd fled after all. Peasants were unfathomable; God knew what went on behind those blank sheep faces. He couldn't account for this one at all. Less than a woman yet, she still had sense, certainly imagination, but the rest was inscrutable. She was from the Auvergne and of low birth; her speech and accent gave that away. But those deep, grave eyes held intelligence along with apprehension. Not mad, not an idiot—and not here.

"Well girl, you can starve if you want, but I'm having supper. Now." He sat by the fire and started in on the bread.

Liana held the end of the snare, ready, hardly breathing. A rabbit hopped toward her bait, paused, sniffed with a quick tremor of its nose and hopped forward again. One small jump more and he was in the trap. Liana waited half a breath, then snapped the snare up tightly round its neck.

Jettaret heard the rabbit's high squeal cut short, and a moment later Liana emerged from the bushes, the rabbit in her hand dangling from its broken neck. He rose and pulled his knife to skin it but she took the knife from him as she walked past, and sat by the fire opposite him. Taken aback by her effrontery, he shook his head and sat down.

With quick strokes Liana cut the rabbit's throat, slit a straight line down its belly, and had it skinned and ready for the fire in less time than it took to peel an apple. Glancing up as she worked, she caught a bemused Jettaret watching her with growing admiration.

"I'm hungry," she said simply.

The Witch's Hand

Jettaret smiled. "Only one other person I know could dress a rabbit like that."

Liana stopped working and stared at him. "You knew my father?" she asked, blood dripping from the knife.

"No," he said wryly. He looked past the fire. "No, it was somebody else."

The next day the hills flattened into rolling stretches of rises and shallow valleys, scattered with a patchwork of trees amidst tall grass, which rose until it began to brush against the horses' bellies. They rode through it one behind the other, Pasquale breaking trail for Bluestone. Liana, saddle sore, watched the rises on either side for Malaxia and the Watch, while she tried to find better ways of keeping her seat. Jettaret gave the immediate terrain only a casual scan. The grass around them was too high and thick to see more than a few feet into it, making low-boughed trees look as though they didn't have trunks. The horses would be aware of any humans or animals near before he was, and anyone coming over the rises would be in silhouette, easily spotted.

The day warmed till foam rose beneath the reins on the horses' necks. Liana's knees, now raw against the saddle through her thin pants, stung with sweat. Toward noon the grass began to alternate between tall stands and shorter clumps, interspersed with patches of dirt and rock, and even the latter looked to her like inviting places to stretch out and rest for a while.

Jettaret finally stopped by a curled wire of a stream, next to a grove of squat chestnuts and birches thin as Liana's arms, for a midday meal taken cold. There was enough wood for a fire, but when Liana bent for wood Jettaret shook his head.

"No fire." He indicated the heights around, good vantage for pursuers. "Anybody could see the smoke." Liana looked through the trees, listened; then back at the grass—there was nothing—before sliding off her horse.

When they finished, Jettaret got up and studied the surrounding hills for any sign of movement. Liana went over to Bluestone with the wineskin and the end of a crust, put them in her one saddlebag and turned to wait for Jettaret. She still couldn't get on without a boost. He stood where he was, his back to her as though waiting. She started toward him, then halted.

The horses' ears pricked forward simultaneously; Pasquale's nostrils flared wide and Bluestone snorted. Through the grass came a *whhssshh*. Jettaret about-faced and strode quickly up to Liana, scooped her up and threw her into her saddle, cut the tie lines and mounted Pasquale. Another *whssh*, ahead and to the left. Then a low snuffling grunt. Jettaret reined in a dancing Pasquale.

"Wild boar," he said in a low voice, watching the grass and listening. Liana nodded; she knew boar. She struggled to keep her seat as Bluestone jumped and skittered in a half circle. Another grunt and a snort ahead, this time to the right. Jettaret brought Pasquale alongside Bluestone and with leg and rein forced both horses sideways, away from the boar. The grass rustled behind them. Bluestone shied, there was a snort and a snarl much louder, and the little gray reared and bolted. Liana tumbled off into the dirt. The boar snuffled through the grass, coming toward her; Jettaret swung down and with one hand on the rein of a plunging Pasquale, dashed for Liana.

"Are you all right?" Liana nodded. He helped her to her feet and handed her the reins. "Hold Pasquale."

Jettaret drew sword and dagger and faced the stand of grass, turning, listening. For a few moments there was silence. Then the grass rustled again. Jettaret advanced toward the sound. The boar snorted, louder, coming closer. Cold steel waited to meet him.

The boar burst out of the grass directly in front of Jettaret, snarling. Jettaret shifted his feet quickly for a better stance, but one boot met a loose rock and slipped; he fell backward, losing his sword. He shielded his face with one hand and clenched his dagger. The boar was upon him.

Liana dropped the reins and flung both hands out at the boar. "Uhh!"

Pasquale and Bluestone shied violently as dirt and shimmering lights exploded between Jettaret and the boar. Its attack bellow broke into a short high squeal, then a dying gurgle. The multi-hued dust and lights faded, revealing Jettaret sprawled before a disemboweled, dismembered and cooked boar. He stared at it, drew himself up and slowly turned his eyes to Liana. She took an involuntary step back, trying to hide her hands—she didn't know what to do with them—stood there hopelessly and met his gaze.

"I *am* a witch."

"Thank God." Jettaret sounded dazed. He glanced at the boar again. It was still dead. He rose, picked up his sword and dagger and faced Liana, motioning toward the blasted boar

"Suppose you tell me how you did that?"

Liana dropped her eyes and looked back up like a thief run out of alibis. "Can we get away from it first?" she countered.

Jettaret nodded assent, sheathed his weapons, and made his way through clumps of thick grass to fetch a still quivering Pasquale. He soothed the horse with low words while Liana followed uncertainly and stood off behind him. She looked around for Bluestone but the dapple gray was nowhere in sight. "Bluestone? Blue?" she called out anxiously, and waited. There was a clop, a snort, and Bluestone appeared out of the small thicket, splashing through a gully the creek had carved. Liana's relief came out in a child sized sigh, and she went to get her horse.

5. *MALAXIA*

Liana walked up to the little mare and caught her bridle. Bluestone's sides were streaked with sweat and her dark pointed ears flicked nervously in different directions, but she seemed unhurt.

Jettaret came over with Pasquale, and a quick appraisal told him the gray was all right, though as frightened as his own horse. He stroked Bluestone's neck and murmured, "All right, it's over now," but he didn't believe it. The girl beside him was more than unschooled runaway.

"One horse rarely goes far from another," he remarked. He led the way up a rise to a large chestnut tree standing a little apart from the rest of the woods, and they tied the horses to a low branch. Jettaret set his sword against the trunk and settled beside it, expectant. Liana remained standing for a moment, still, half turned away from him, then sank in the shade, her head down. He watched her with severity and sympathy mixed.

"Now . . ." he said. She looked across the waving grass below, silent.

"I was asleep," she began. "There was a fire, in the cottage—"

"Your parents?" Jettaret knew the answer. Liana lowered her head again.

"It all ... it—"

"I have seen cities burn, my girl. You needn't go on."

She had to. "It all fell, and I couldn't reach them ... Maman—" she choked. "I banked the fire that night; I did it—"

In back of them, out of peripheral view, Malaxia emerged from behind a tree, the wisp of a smile on her face. Liana started to speak, faltered, sensing her presence, looked about and saw nothing. Jettaret too looked but saw only the girl. She regained herself and continued.

"I ran outside, and a lady, a strange lady, was standing there. Malaxia," she whispered it, "that was her name. And she ... made me into a witch."

"Oh no," Malaxia spoke unheard, though Liana felt the wind rise behind her. Malaxia moved closer. "Not yet." The horses grew restless. Liana lifted her head, disconcerted. She fingered her ring. Jettaret watched her, waiting. He noticed the gold on her right hand.

That sinks it; no peasant wears gold. This girl was not what she was. In a casual manner he asked, "She gave you that ring?"

Behind her, Malaxia moved away.

"No." The presence vanished. "This was my grandmother's ring, and then my mother's, and then mine. The Duchess who was Queen of France and then England once came here, and threw it from her horse when she rode by."

"Eleanor of Aquitaine. Went on a Crusade herself once. Died two years ago."

"They said there were counts and cardinals and lords in the procession, throwing money and jewels to people. Grandmaman caught this. Maman gave it to me last Candlemas. She always said it was a sign, and that rings like this were dipped in holy water when they were made."

Earnest, straightforward; devil's horns, the girl was bewildering. Liana did not notice Jettaret's bemused countenance at her words. Such things were possible though; in the heat of an excited celebration, with the standard largess in tossing alms to the poor, a noblewoman or churchman might easily throw away a valuable piece of jewelry, and regret it afterward. The mystery of the ring was solved, at any rate.

Shyly, Liana continued, "I've often dipped it myself, when Father Trebonious wasn't looking. I didn't know if it was right or not." She twisted the ring and tried to take it off but couldn't. "That's funny, it always came off before . . ." She pulled and twisted at it some more.

"Maybe your magic, or Malaxia made it stick—"

"No! She never touched this;" Liana covered her ring with her other hand, "I had my fingers around it like this, but maybe she burned through it, when everything was burning—" The shock that had carried her through three and a half days cracked and wrenching sobs broke through. But she did not wail. Tears ran down her cheeks and fell on the ground, she held her knees and rocked back and forth, but made almost no sound.

Jettaret moved closer, put a hand on her startlingly thin shoulder and waited till her rocking slowed to a halt. Liana, still choking back sobs, ran shaky fingers over her ring. He eased her left hand away and looked at it. Dirty and tarnished bands of thick gold were worked into an open spaced, four strand weave, evenly, all the way around. It was stuck tight.

"Maybe your finger swelled up then; I wouldn't worry too much about it, you've got enough worries—"

Far off, from over the hills, a church bell rang nine times for Nones, the ninth hour, three hours past midday. The monastery of St. Basil—they were closer to discovery than Jettaret wanted, but the church itself was still out of sight. Liana listened to the bell as Jettaret thought.

"Kyrié elé . . . Kyrié . . ." she began automatically, but the words suddenly stopped and her face went into confusion as the rest of the litany left her. *I can't pray.* Jettaret glanced at her. Lettered or not, most people knew the only Greek words of the Mass: *Kyrié eléison, Christé eléison, Kyrié eléison*; Lord have mercy, Christ have mercy, Lord have mercy. But he was not concerned over why she had stopped. The echo of the last bell ended.

"This Malaxia," he spoke up, "have you seen her since?"

"No." Liana sounded as though she'd just realized it.

"If you do, just point her out—" he caught himself quickly, "no don't point," he jerked his head, "nod; and I'll do the rest."

"She is strong, very powerful; and the Devil knows what she could do."

"I've taken my chances with the Infidel; I'll take my chances with her."

Liana's swollen eyes went wide with respect. "Infidel—you went on the Crusade?"

"Yes," Jettaret replied shortly.

"You saw Jerusalem?"

"Yes. A dusty old city that was hardly worth the trek to get there. Not to mention the ... carnage."

"But Jerusalem is the City of God."

Jettaret looked at Liana and realized it was useless to argue with her. "The New Jerusalem perhaps. Not the earthly one."

Liana lowered her head, then asked with renewed hope, "Did you bring anything back?"

"A splinter from the True Cross perhaps? A relic from the Holy Sepulchre? No." *Just memories no confessor has been able to bury. What did I know, I was eighteen then.* "Don't ask me any more about it."

"All right." Liana drew with a finger on the ground, subdued.

"Liana." His voice softened "If there is a New Jerusalem, we carry it around with us. That's as far as my theology takes me." *And behold, you were within me, and I sought you outside myself.* St. Augustine. He ran his hand along the sheen of his sword. "I will not kill on matters of God anymore."

Above them a finch broke into song. Making a lot of noise for a little bird, it warbled roulades up and down, sweeter than my armor was strong, Jettaret thought. A second singer joined in, weaving its notes in and out of the finch's, but not the same song. It rolled and swelled in continuous alteration, like rain on leaves or glass hitting against glass, and finally overpowered the finch, who faded out. The second song, soft and deepening, moved closer and continued just behind Liana, then stopped.

"How pleasant you've found a traveling companion," Malaxia's voice caressed. The deep glass-on-glass bell sound chimed as she laughed again. Liana turned, saw nothing, put her hand out and felt nothing. She turned back quickly toward Jettaret, but he had walked over to see to the horses, deaf or oblivious to Malaxia's voice.

"I will not be far, child. When you need me call; let your wishes ride the wind, as you will someday." Malaxia took a veil from her dress and drew it slowly and gently over Liana. Liana felt a light waft of air, first from one side, then the other. She looked at the leaves above her but they were still.

Malaxia continued, "I will show you such visions, such dreams, as you never had. You will know what it is to be the scent of the flower, the topmost branches of the tree. You will play with lightning, speak with thunder." Her voice began to change subtly into another's, from beside the hearth at home. "You will know, and understand, and all the power and beauty of the world will be at your hand. My child . . . my child . . ."

Liana spoke from a trance. "Maman?"

The voice was in her ear as Malaxia leaned close. "Malaxia." It began to move away. "I am preparing a gift for you. But you must be strong enough for it, and ready." Liana followed the voice to where it faded out behind a tree; beyond it, a faint breeze ruffled the grass and stirred the leaves.

The Witch's Hand

Liana shivered out of her trance. She stood and searched the woods behind her; there was nothing. She looked over to Jettaret, but he was standing with one arm raised against a tree, his back turned, head bowed. Closer by, his sword caught her eye. It rested point down against the chestnut tree where he'd left it, the crosspiece angled toward her. Sunlight slanted off the blade. She reached out to touch the sweat-stained leather wrapped around the hilt, and saw the rounded pommel was of solid steel and held no ornament. The crosspiece, also steel, flared out at both ends, and squarish letters she could not read were cut into it. As for anything more ornate, this was a war sword and no fine etching or jewel bedecked it.

Liana put her hand around the hilt and pulled the sword toward her. It was lighter than she'd expected. She lifted it high and turned it, looking like a dark cormorant trying to swallow a shining silver fish. The blade was almost as long as she was tall. Running a finger along it, she felt the bite and knew a little more pressure would bring blood. A few nicks marred the edges; though filed down and re-sharpened, they told what letters did not.

Liana shifted the sword from one hand to the other, held it up with both, then whirled to meet an imaginary foe. This sword could have handled the boar, if Jettaret hadn't tripped. She tossed it, caught it, drew the blade back and cut the air, tossed it up again; it sprang higher from her hand. She ran a few steps to catch it, turned the flat edge sideways and swung it up whistling into a high arc. The momentum carried her and the sword around and it clipped a low leafy branch. She did not see the branch glow and redden as it fell, but spun again, the blade flashing in the sun. Then she rested the point on the ground, and didn't notice Jettaret had turned back toward her and was staring at her. His eye went to the steel in her hand.

"Liana, that sword is far too heavy for you, and it takes a lot of practice to handle right—huh?"

Liana had not heard him. Once more she was wielding the great sword deftly with both hands, flipping it into the air where it glinted like a spinning dazzle of sun. The blade became alive, trailing streams of silver fire, of incandescence and sparks. Where these hit the ground or trees, leaf, blade and branch changed color; pale blossoms withered or turned deep green, bark was splattered with light-shot purple, fall's reds and oranges glimmered amidst the show of spring.

"Ho, whoa." Light played over Jettaret's face. Liana was nearly lost amid the pyrotechnics which set nothing aflame, but left a seeping mist that drifted through bushes and around trees. Determined, he said, "I don't believe in magic. I don't believe in witches." He watched some more. "I don't believe in this—you want to watch the edge there?"

Liana was suddenly aware of his presence again and stopped her display. The lights faded, the mist dispersed, and she handed the sword back with an abashed smile. Jettaret examined it distrustfully.

"Fortuna Domini," he muttered its name under his breath, "what has she done to you?" To Liana he asked, "You haven't hexed this, have you?"

"Oh no, no." Her barefaced honesty was direct, guileless. "I never got to hold a sword before. How do they make them this light?"

"They don't." His eyes flicked to a freshly hewed branch, normal looking now, both it and the trunk above still oozing sap. Liana saw the round, scar-white slice on the trunk and stood still regarding it, then at the places the sword's trailing fire had hit. The consequences of her untrained exuberance hit her. Quietly she said, "I hope that is all I do with a sword."

Jettaret ran Fortuna Domini home in its sheath. "The next smithy we come to, I'm getting you one; this *is* bandit country."

Liana held her hands out and smiled. "I don't need a sword for bandits." Her eyes were strange, and her voice sounded intangibly different. Jettaret looked at her.

"No, I guess you don't. Come here." Liana approached but he had to take the last step to meet her. He took both her hands, small and grubby, in his own; they felt warm, normal, neither unusually hot nor cold, and he didn't turn into a smoking boar at their touch. They looked ordinary. He tried intently to see what was different in her eyes, and she, surprised but controlled, pulled away. He shook his head. There was no witchcraft therein; only Liana had looked back at him. All mysteries are known to God, the family priest Jehan had intoned at difficult questions, and only God knew the answer to this one.

"Liana, let me build the fire tonight. No help; no—" Jettaret attempted a clumsy imitation of the three fingered fire spell.

The Witch's Hand

"Like this—" Liana raised her left hand confidently, extended her fingers and began to draw them together.

"No, no!" He grabbed her hand before thumb and fingers could touch. "Why not?"

Jettaret let her hand go. She stood there puzzled while he searched for an explanation. "Your power," he tried, "it's growing. It's making you ... different. I don't know how, but I can see it. Even if I don't believe it."

Liana looked at her hands, and fear surged up and hit her in the ribs as she realized what he was saying. She took a step back.

"Different?" she whispered. "How?"

"Not on the outside. Not very much." A breeze fanned the grass and fluttered leaves past their feet.

"How am I different?" she persisted. "What's changed? Oh *Deo Domine*—" Lord God—

Behind her a twig snapped and she whirled in rising recognition. "Malaxia?" No one answered. "Malaxia!" Liana dashed toward the sound of the twig. Jettaret leapt after her. She was quicker than a rabbit and dodged him twice; he caught a glimpse of her face and again something not Liana was there. *I don't believe in witches.*

He tackled her from behind and she hit the ground hard but scrambled sideways, almost getting to her feet again. He kept one hand on her ankle, brought her down and her other foot jabbed him in the face. She kicked, squirmed, hit him harder than she looked able to, grabbed a fallen branch and swung it at him. He warded it off. She fought like a cornered badger, and Jettaret felt like letting her go, crazy peasant; he was getting tired of holding onto her and was also getting just plain tired.

Liana flayed a hand out; he grabbed it and promptly got a solid whack in the jaw from her other hand. He twisted the arm he held, forcing her over face down, turned her wrist into her back and managed to grab her free hand, which was out scratching and crawling on the ground like a spider trying to go up a strand of web.

"Uh-uh. No hand stuff." He pinned both arms to her back and covered her hands with his own. "Understand?"

Liana, gasping and still squirming beneath him, nodded. She bobbed her head up and asked, "Where is she?"

Jettaret looked around. "I don't know." From the trees above them came laughter mingled with the rustle of leaves. Liana erupted into a new struggle and Jettaret set his knee into her back. He steeled himself, kept hold of both her hands with one of his, and slapped her face hard with the other. Liana cried out, but was Liana again. She lay limp as an empty goat bladder, breathing in sharp, tired rasps. Jettaret let her hands go with caution and she didn't appear to notice, but he kept her pinned with a leg across her back just in case. Liana lifted her head and propped herself up on her elbows.

"What's this lady got over you?"

"She told me . . ." Liana hesitated, "I was her heiress."

"You would be like her?" Liana nodded. Fortuna Domini rang in its sheath and he held it up. "She'll have to go through this first."

"It ... it's a matter of will. Right now the power is mostly in my hands. If I can keep it there ..." She fell silent. "If it should spread, I—" She shook her head. "I don't know. But I can still control it, now." She rubbed one hand against the other. "I think." When she spoke again she sounded lost. "Say a prayer or something; I don't know them anymore."

Jettaret thought a moment. It had been a long time since he'd prayed. "Uh, Lord, uh . . . 'Fight against them that fight against me . . .'" Liana looked at him expectantly and waited. "That's all I know; Psalm something or other. Can I let you up now?"

"I think so." Liana listened. "She's not here anymore." Jettaret released her and she sat up wearily. He took one of her hands and scrutinized it.

"Looks normal enough to me." He let it drop, rose and regarded her from a pace back. She sat with her head on drawn up knees, hands joined around them. *Fortuna Domini,* he silently addressed his sword and the air, *Fortune of the Lord, what have you sent us now?*

Liana raised her head and caught his eye. Her voice was troubled but steady. "You build the fire."

Jettaret looked down the grassy slope. "We'll move further in first. I don't want anyone from St. Basil's to find us, and we're in plain sight here. Come on."

They untied the horses and rode deeper into the woods, where spruce spires dominated other greens and the shadows grew darker. They reached a clearing surrounded by thick brush and rocks, overhung with branches, and halted there. Jettaret chose two trees close to each other around the perimeter, as posts for the horses. They unsaddled them, Liana struggling with the awkward weight, and Jettaret tied each horse to an overhead branch, leaving enough slack so they could stand nose to tail alongside each other.

Jettaret searched the ground for dried wood. While he was gathering it, Liana untied the heavier cloak from behind Pasquale's saddle, shook it out and wrapped it around herself, then tried to get as comfortable as she could beneath an overhanging rock. Jettaret put an armload of wood down nearby and started arranging it in a cross thatched square. He stuck twigs and the driest small branches in the inward facing cracks and went to work with flint and steel.

When the fire caught he looked over at Liana but she was already asleep. One hand had lost its grasp on the cloak and lay curled outside it. Her dark hair swept across her face which, though softened, remained sad.

St. Basil's, out of sight in the distance, tolled the twelfth hour, six p.m. Vespers; night was falling. Jettaret looked into the fire. A mad peasant was a useless peasant, and this one was both mad and dangerous, a magician of the Eastern science maybe, despite her youth. The Saracens hadn't gotten their flying fire as refined as hers, but it looked to be the same stuff. This girl was one of his own, moreover; by her word a vassal of the Bishop's but from his part of the country all the same, and thus falling under his protection. Still, if she really was what he suspected, she deserved the same sentence as a maimed wolverine. Killing magicians had its risks. Letting them live could be riskier.

Jettaret shoved a half burnt branch further into the flames. The girl might be an agent of the Devil, or she might merely be suffering under demonic infliction; he still believed in that. He looked up at the first stars. *If she is wounded beyond repair, let me do what I have to do.*

Behind him mist began to fill the hollows of the ground and rise from the shadows. He stood to stretch and listened. The day sounds were quiet, and the night sounds had not yet begun. The horses tore at and munched new grass. A cricket chirped once, twice, and was silent. Jettaret stomped his feet. "Cold up here . . . we're higher than I thought." He strode over to the horses, rubbed Pasquale's nose as she curved her neck up and around to greet him, and checked that the tie lines for both horses were secure. He brought his saddle and the other cloak over to the fire and, with the saddle as a makeshift couch and the cloak for a blanket, settled himself in for the night.

Jettaret woke out of an uncomfortable doze. A charred branch had fallen from the smoldering pile and rolled against his foot, trailing ash. He pushed it away, shivered and pulled his cloak closer around him. The saddle dug into his back and he shoved it around trying to get more comfortable, but its builder had made a saddle, not a couch.

He looked over at Liana. She slept peacefully, her left hand still outside her cloak, motionless and slightly curled. He eyed it, then the dying fire, raised his left hand and tried to make the three-fingered fire spell. Nothing happened. He regarded Liana a few moments longer and noticed her hand was white with cold, the fingertips blue. He got up, went over to her and stood there a moment, shaggy vicomte above wayward peasant. Kneeling, he put the cold hand under her cloak, taking care to turn it well away from him. He drew the edge of the heavy wool out on the ground, doffed his own cloak and spread it over hers, then crawled under them both beside her. He put Fortuna Domini between them; he wasn't going to touch this one. Two cloaks over two warm bodies worked better, that was all.

***

Night retained its hold on the hills to the north. In a clearing far from the sound of St. Basil's bells, the stars and a past-full moon lit an odd house, half dwelling, half fortress. It emerged from the base of dark cliffs made of multi-sided basalt columns, which continued upward in staggered levels behind it. Three round stone towers dominated the house itself; a broad, squat one in front and a little to the right, a tall narrow one further back to the left, partly against the cliffs, and between them, further back still and rising directly from the rock, a medium wide tower, shorter actually than the others but taller due to its high roost.

The three towers formed an uneven triangle; between them, and connected to them by parapets and covered passages, stood two adjoined cottages of stone and thatch. The one to the front was smaller and attached directly to the rear one, which in turn was built right into, or rather projected from the stone columns behind.

Begun over a century before and abandoned after the First Crusade had taxed pockets and stomachs past further work, it had been given up as part of a ransom package for a count, to another who had neglected it. There was no entry barbican, no main gate; no crenellated walls protected the two cottages, neither did moat or ditch surround the stone conglomerate. Half complete it remained, passed over by marauders who chose lower, more remunerative paths, a bastion without a garrison. It crouched, an unfinished sculpture ready to spring from the rocks or crumble and erode back into them. This was Malaxia's house.

Mist drifted and turned before the ground level stones, played upward on the towers and vanished. High in the narrow tower, light shone from a narrow slit of a window.

Malaxia stood at the window staring out. Behind her sat a small table and ornately carved chair, a Syrian trestle chair with curved arms and legs, a narrow backrest tapering inward toward the top, and a deep red Persian cushion, richly embroidered. Intricate mother-of-pearl and wood inlay gleamed on both table and chair. On the table a thick, half burned candle flickered in a silver holder of Thracian design, with two flared handles; it glistened with rubies, rich blue lapis lazuli, and diamonds that sparkled irregularly.

Light fell across Malaxia's face, setting her straight fine nose in sharp outline. She glanced down at a slant-roofed shed that leaned against the tower below, and saw where the mist had congealed into dew on the straw. It glittered hard as the stars. She looked back out into the night.

Five hundred years I have waited. I have seen kingdoms, empires, practices come and go. I attended at the court of Charlemagne; stood watch at the gates of fortress, field, and monastery. None brought forth whom I sought. She turned away from the window. *By my arts, wisdom, and looks* — she placed a stray curl behind her ear — *I rose above the common lot of women in those times. I was counselor to Guido d'Arezzo* — she touched a woodcut of Guido hanging on the wall, with a memory of rapture long vanished — *musician, genius; advised Otto the Great, Holy Roman Emperor. He had not the hot knife.* She allowed herself contempt for a sorry lover, Guido's opposite there, superb ruler and man that he'd been otherwise. He'd been dead two hundred thirty-three years now and his Empire lay in the hands of incompetents. *But I abandoned all that long ago.* She'd dismissed him along with other men when stronger, greater passions overpowered the transient ones.

She went to the table, fingered the silver candlestick. Books and scrolls lay on a wall shelf above, in the dim light beyond the table. *I have studied the knowledge of East and West, of Egypt, the Kaldeans, what remains of Greece and Rome,* under which empire she'd been born, *and those islands to the north where the guardians of all that is aether clear and true, proof adamantine, powerful and beneficial, where those such as I stand watch with the old gods.* Malaxia looked out the window again, past the creeping ground mist.

I have perfected my art. I brought it to countless leaders, of state, of religions, principalities, Vandal bands, households;, but none would accept the knowledge I offered. It mattered not which guise she had taken; beggar or noblewoman, no one had listened and most had laughed, derided her. They had paid. *Pity; they could not learn the powers contained in the old works, which are now banned, and burned.* She moved about the circular floor, gently crushing the rushes spread over the stones to absorb the damp. She stared into the candle's flame. *It was time, I realized, to wait.*

But I had time. And, after much thought, I knew it was not a king or pope or bishop, or great power wielding beauty or withered hag or virile warrior that I needed, but a child, of no lineage, no importance, no apparent worth. She took a fresh sprig of rosemary from a bunch lying on the table, its pairs of rind shaped leaves curving up in subdued green from the stem, and twisted it in her hand. Regarding it dispassionately, she pressed hard. An aroma of bitter lemon filled the round chamber.

And I have found her. At last. A protégé, a daughter I may teach, one who will learn all I have to offer, receive all I may give her, if she but comes to me of her own accord. She held the rosemary out. *An orphan who has nothing to lose, one who already knows the basics*—she flicked it into the air with her fingers, and it flamed and sizzled into dust—*herbs, the uncultivated fruits of the land, and with much watching, the birds of the air and beasts of the fields, also those of the waters. And the action of water itself; the play of stream against rock, the fall of rain upon ground. The movement of stars at night*—out the window she sought and found her star Al Nasr Al Tair, the Flying Eagle, brilliant white, smiled—*and their groupings in the sky, those that are constant and those that burst and fade.* From a vial on the shelf she took a pinch of magnesium powder. She tossed it into a bowl of pale yellow liquid on the table and a sudden flash lit the room. *Unlettered, untaught, but rich in knowledge already and yearning for more. The letters I can provide. The talent, the ability, but most of all the strength to withstand trial and onslaught, are already there.*

Malaxia sat in the chair, curled her fingers over the ends of the armrests, and closed her eyes. *I have found my heiress. At last.*

6. MAGIC STORM

Crickets broke the night where Jettaret and Liana lay curled beside each other under their cloaks, like a couple of crescent moons facing the same direction. Liana stirred, opened her eyes, and realized she was not alone. She moved her shoulder and felt something behind her, slowly turned her head and came face to face with a sleeping Jettaret, one arm stretched over his head, the other holding Fortuna Domini's hilt close to his chest. Liana snatched up her cloak and bolted straight back like a shot from a crossbow.

"Ahh!"

"Ahh!" Their cries overlapped as Jettaret woke, up on his knees with his sword at the ready instinctively, trying to focus through sleep and hair that fell over his eyes. Tangled in the heavy, flopping wool, Liana crouched, her heart racing, ready to jump again. Jettaret came fully awake, saw the white-faced girl staring at him from under her cloak and realized at once what had happened. A surprise bedfellow was, after all, a shock. He lowered his sword. A moment passed while he thought.

"As a Catalonian lo—" he caught himself before saying 'lover,' "comrade of mine one said, 'It is better to be warm together than to freeze apart.'" Liana remained apprehensive. "Oh. You are still a virgin." She closed her eyes with a relieved sigh. "If you were before." Fuming, she glared at him, raised her hands and it was Jettaret's turn to back off, half springing to his feet, Fortuna Domini up to ward off whatever was coming. "Whoa, no!"

"Oh!" Liana realized what she was about to do and lowered her hands. "Oh . . ."

"I won't touch you." Jettaret's voice was strong. "I am on my way to my future wife, remember? Who is beautiful, has money, the last I heard, land, goats; I assume we'll get along, produce an heir or two—" he yawned, "it's the way of things—"

"Is that what being noble is?"

"You *are* from simple folk." Jettaret shook out his cloak, cast it around himself and stretched out again, cold hard ground be damned, away from her. "Well, some things are hard to understand. I don't understand witches, don't understand women—" he pulled the cloak over his head and his voice was muffled, "don't understand men, or hard ground, what I'm doing out here ..." he trailed off, dozing. Liana pulled a burr from her hair, crouched back against a tree with her knees drawn up, pulled her cloak close around herself and fell asleep watching Jettaret.

In the long, dead hour before dawn, Malaxia stepped silently into the clearing, regarded the two sleepers a moment, then went and stood beside Jettaret. She waited, her eyes on Liana. The girl moved under her cloak and began to murmur.

"Ma ... mal ... Maman ... mal ... ax ... Malaxia? Malaxia!" Liana started up, knowing who was there before she met the sorceress' luminous gaze. "Aah!"

Jettaret was awake again and found the girl staring fixedly at him. No, through him. He looked around behind and saw nothing.

Malaxia raised her left hand, curved her fingers down slightly and flicked them out. Light flashed without thunder. She swept her right hand around, and from the rim of a circle around Liana the grass rustled and trails of mist rose, slowly and sporadically at first, then like steam from under the lid of a boiling pot. The mist grew brighter, shining with its own light. The leaves and mulch beneath jumped and sizzled and started to fade, turning from deep earth to dark green, from that to light green, yellow and glowing white, till Liana sat surrounded by a ring of light. The mist swirled upward and vanished.

"Do not leave the circle," Malaxia warned quietly. Liana, sitting in a half trance, showed no signs of leaving. Malaxia raised her arms and extended the left toward the trees, her right out toward the ground, both palms down. She spoke words too low to hear and every night sound became silent. Jettaret stood looking warily about, Fortuna Domini in his hand. He saw neither the ring of light nor Malaxia, only Liana motionless on the ground, staring at nothing. Malaxia forced a tremor out of her hands, then flipped them upward, and instantly the night burst around them.

Geysers of blue fire shot from the ground, tops of trees exploded into splinters and chaff, out of the sky came an unearthly wail. It shrieked in vicious blasts, tore bushes to shreds and chased them wildly about. Tree trunks burst like split ice.

"*Ave Maria,*" Hail Mary, Jettaret ducked, Fortuna Domini out, but a blast threw the sword from his hand and he went to his knees.

Luminous translucent spheres flew haphazardly about, and shivered into streams of fire when they collided with themselves or anything else, shooting silver, purple and blue sizzling trails out in all directions. The air crackled, whined, the earth pulsed in quick vibrations, as the fiery explosions left the clearing in alternate light and darkness.

Mist and smoke rose in puffs, jets and fountains, drifted through the woods, circled bushes and spiraled upward along tree trunks. Mist cascaded around Liana like entwined curls, though none fell within the ring of light. Misted light spun around Malaxia, who stood now with outspread arms, directing the chaos with subtle gestures, a raised finger, a nod. Mist wound about and enfolded Fortuna Domini like a scabbard. It spread in shifting layers on the ground, bobbed in tufts out of the clearing and hung in shimmering curtains above.

Jettaret threw himself flat on the ground and tried to see Liana. She sat amidst the blasts of fire and debris in unruffled wonder at first; then a flaming chunk of earth scorched toward her and she flinched away, her hands up as fear returned. The chunk pinwheeled and disintegrated into a dozen pieces. The storm increased. Liana shrank from the explosions, her hands frailly warding off assaults of flame, spheres and flying rock. Then she straightened—and began to return the attack in kind. She threw her hands out and streams of fire issued forth. Malaxia looked almost startled as Liana shattered a glowing sphere. Slowly, though, the girl's hands took on a will of their own; in whatever direction she turned them, a concussive blast or blazing shaft of bluish white flame hurtled off, whether aimed at a target or not. She could not control the outbursts. Dodging in one direction, scrambling back in another and twisting away in order to avoid both the storm and her additions to it, Liana left the ring of light.

Immediately the frenzy struck anew. An icy scythe of wind hit the clearing and whipped it into fresh pandemonium. Arcs of fire met in midair, split into hissing ribbons and caromed off in all directions; demolished trees turned into a crossfire of hail. Through it all ran the disembodied scream.

St. Michel the archangel, get down here, I could use you— His sword beyond reach, Jettaret heard the mares' terrified whinnying and he flung grit into the teeth of the wind. *You're not going to kill the horses, you're not going to hurt the girl—*

The redoubled storm seized Liana and she writhed in tortured helplessness. Between flashes of light so bright they blinded, she made out the figure of Malaxia standing untouched amid the fury, sovereign, one arm raised to shoulder height, the other higher, palms up, the embodiment of the elements around her. Liana tried to crawl toward her.

"Ma . . . Mal . . . Maman!" The storm seized her again and threw her back. Malaxia lifted her head in concern, watched Liana a few moments, then nodded and silently left the clearing.

Head down and arm up as a shield, his knife in the other hand, Jettaret made his way to the plunging horses and cut them loose before they could cast themselves in their lines. They bolted at another burst of light. Jettaret threw the pieces of line over his shoulder and started back toward Liana.

Dirt splattered in his face and scatter-shots of light forced him to his knees. He continued, dodging blasts that Liana unleashed, still out of control. When he reached her she was shaking in violent spasms, her eyes lost. Careful to stay out of the path of her hands, he seized them both and pinned them to the ground above her head, whereupon she thrashed and knifed a knee into his ribs. Jettaret lashed each hand to the opposite elbow and, keeping them above her head, bound her forearms together. Liana twisted convulsively and kicked him once, twice, three times, hard.

"I'm trying to save your life!" he shouted. "If you were a Saracen you'd be dead by now." With that he tied the long end of the line from her arms to a tree, a still solid tree, returned and grabbed one of her ankles. He bound it with the second line while she kicked away with her free foot. Her heel landed on his ear.

"Ow!" Jettaret shoved himself back, one hand to his ear, the line from her ankle still in his other hand. He gave up on her other foot, and tied the line to a tree opposite the one trussing her arms.

Abruptly the storm subsided. Fires went out like snuffed candles, glowing spheres vanished and the mist dissipated into the night. The ring

The Witch's Hand

of light on the ground faded, the wail died away, and all was still except Liana. Jettaret went back over to her and knelt.

"Liana? Liana!" Caught in warping convulsions, she did not hear him. The lines drew tight around her arms and ankle as she twisted to one side. Jettaret tried to hold her down but it was like grabbing a net of flapping fish. He sat back.

"If you're going to go on like this I can't wait for you." He rose to his knees, put both hands together, and two-fisted Liana just beneath her breastbone. Her breath came out in a strangled *whoosh* and the convulsions stopped as she choked for air. Jettaret weighed the confusion in her face. Slowly he drew his knife.

He turned it in his hand, looked up at the night, closed his eyes briefly and steeled himself. Liana lay with her head to one side, incomprehension wavering with clarity. Her breaths began to draw out and deepen. She moved her head back toward Jettaret and met his eyes as he put the blade to her throat.

"Jetta—" Liana cut herself off at the touch of steel on her neck.

Jettaret's hand froze; he leaned closer and found recognition there. "Liana?" Her eyes went to what she could see of his dagger, then back up to him.

"What?"

Jettaret sighed with a relieved smile and sheathed his dagger. Liana tried to bring her arms down, but the rope stopped her and, surprised, she saw how she was tied.

"Why am I bound—?" Realization drove out puzzlement. "She was here. What did I do?"

"You don't remember?"

Liana shook her head, suddenly noticed a shattered branch and pieces of strewn carnage that faded away into the darkness, and looked around in horror.

"What did I *do*?"

Jettaret rose. "Well, no damage that a little time won't fix. He walked about. "The trees should grow back in a hundred years—" he stooped to pick something up, "and you've even gotten us breakfast." He held up a charred pheasant, its long tail feathers singed away down to the shaft. Liana stared, unbelieving, and dropped her head back.

"Please. Leave me here to starve."

Jettaret shook his head. "I can't do that." He set the pheasant down. "If I tied you with the Gordian Knot she'd cut you loose."

"Then kill me." Liana looked straight up at the fading stars. "Please. *Please.*"

Jettaret went for his dagger again, saw the welling shine in her eyes and stopped. "No. If I did, I'd be killing the heiress to God knows what, and then what's to prevent Malaxia from coming after me with some sweet vengeance? Like throwing around more of that Greek fire." He glanced about at the ravaged clearing. "I'd need a few more blades. And I'd like to know what she looks like first. Besides—" his voice took on a different tone; if you killed a witch there was some debate on whether she would stay dead, "I don't think I, or anyone else, can. Not now."

Liana looked at him with despair and realized he was right. She stretched weakly against the ropes.

"Here, I'll untie you—" Jettaret bent over her hands.

"No. Not till daylight. Malaxia might come back."

"Are you sure?" She couldn't be comfortable as she was.

"Yes."

Jettaret covered her with her cloak. "Try to sleep. I'll watch." *Eius non timebis a timore nocturno, a sagitta volante in die, a negotio perambulante in tenebris,* he thought Compline's Psalm 90 for her, 'You will not fear the terror of the night, nor the arrow that flies by day, nor the pestilence that stalks in darkness.' With drawn sword across his knees, he sat to wait for dawn.

The tangle of dark, silhouetted branches slowly became more prominent against the sky. A shadow moved behind them. Fortuna Domini in his hand, Jettaret rose, followed the shadow's progress and finally beheld Malaxia as she stepped into the clearing.

Her smile was part seduction, part maternal wrath. She extended a graceful right hand toward Liana, whose left hand began to flex and curl against her bonds; she shifted awkwardly but did not wake.

"I do not allow others to treat my daughter thus."

"*You* do not—! Jettaret looked at the carnage of the magic storm, some of it still smoking, then at Liana. Malaxia advanced toward the girl, her

The Witch's Hand

cloak a shimmering exchange of blue, silver and violet. Jettaret leaped between them and planted his feet, sword point at Malaxia's eyes.

"By all that is holy, leave this girl alone!"

"Holiness? From you? Tell me, St. Antoine of the desert, how many children *did* you butcher? Were they Infidels or Christians—or didn't you ask?"

Jettaret shook with rage and crucifixion from within, and lunged at Malaxia, who laughed and flicked her right wrist. Fortuna Domini fell from his hands. In sheer frustration he tore his cross from his neck and hurled it at her. Malaxia recoiled as if stung.

"Viper!" she hissed. "You will die, at her hand!"

Jettaret snatched two charred sticks from the dead campfire and placed them in a cross over Liana. Malaxia stood there a moment, her eyes a cold blue-white glow, then swept out of the clearing and passed behind a tree. Where she would have reappeared, leaves blew along the ground.

Jettaret picked up Fortuna Domini and slid it home in its sheath. "If a viper bit her, the snake would die." He sank down against a tree and closed his eyes.

Birds chirped; far away a cock crowed. Jettaret forced one eye open. "Oh, no." The eastern sky was getting inexorably lighter.

Morning light began to fill the area. Liana stirred. Jettaret got to his feet, found his cross in the dirt some distance away, undamaged except for the broken chain, and pocketed it. He picked up the charred pheasant lying a little further off, eyed it to see if it showed any signs of coming back to life, then tore a strip from the wing to eat and returned to Liana. The pheasant tasted normal, if burnt.

"You're not a bad cook." He knelt and held out the blistered wing. She tried, with difficulty, to eat it.

"I can't eat lying down."

Jettaret hesitated, then put the pheasant down and cut Liana's ankle tie. "Scoot up."

As she did, the cross of sticks fell off her and she looked at them in surprise.

"You needed a little more protection than I could give you."

Liana stared at him. "She came back."

Jettaret nodded. "I saw her," he said quietly. "I will do anything I can to keep her from you." He pulled out his broken cross chain, bent a link open with his bare hands, and squeezed it shut around the next good link on the other end. He slipped the chain over his head and dropped the cross—gold, small but ornate, with *fleur-de-lis* at the tips—inside his tunic. "And I will not leave you."

"Then you will die. She, or I, will kill you. If I tell you to leave, please, go. You must."

"An Auvergne aristocrat never goes back on his word. I swore to go to Jerusalem; I got there. Getting you to Lyon won't be half the trouble. Come on, now," he tried to pull her upright, but Liana shook her head, resisting.

"No. The greatest favor you could do me is to find a fast river and throw me in."

"If I did that you'd probably turn into a fish. Come on, up." He drew her up and she brought her bound arms over her head, in front of her. They came face to face for a moment, and behind her fleeting loss of guard he saw again a steadiness, even curiosity. Then she sat hunched over and began to shake with her nearly silent sobs.

Jettaret reached into a tunic pocket and pulled out the linen rag he used to clean his knife, saw how filthy it was and tossed it aside, than leaned over and wiped Liana's eyes with his sleeve. Suddenly he jerked her upright.

"Don't sit like that, you'll turn into a hunchback."

Liana stared at him. "That's the least of my worries," she managed faintly, then started to laugh in spite of herself. Jettaret leaned back, amused; it was the first time he'd seen her laugh.

"Ow." His hand went to his ribs. Liana's levity vanished.

"Did I do that?"

"Neither one of the horses did. And it wasn't the Angel Gabriel." He tore off some more of the pheasant for her. "Eat."

Liana turned away. "I'm not hungry."

Jettaret took the piece of pheasant back. "*I* am starving." He chewed on it, watching her hands, and presently asked, "Can I untie you now?"

Liana nodded. "I'm more in control in daylight."

The Witch's Hand

Jettaret bent and began to loosen the ropes around her arms, but he'd lashed them too well and the knots became snagged. He worked the lines down to her wrists and stopped.

"Hm." He stepped back, drew his sword, and raised it high. "Hold still." With one slash he cut the rope between her hands.

Liana sat immobile looking at her hands, then up at Jettaret, who smiled slightly and sheathed his sword. She rubbed her arms and stretched them, grimacing.

"Hum. You can still feel human pain," Jettaret offered helpfully. Liana flashed him a look, half provoked, half grateful.

From the woods a horse neighed. Jettaret strode off and disappeared behind thick boughs, as Liana rose. Morning light showed what she and Malaxia had done. She walked slowly about the clearing, surrounded by scorched trees, fallen branches and withered roots where clumps of bushes had grown, steam still rising from some. Rocks had cracked and crystallized in stained glass hues—dark blues, amber, deep red and amethyst, with arresting emerald fissures—more brilliant than Peranville's cathedral windows. A sparkle on a blasted trunk caught her attention; she went up to it and saw what looked like infinitesimally small particles of silver, ground in where the bark had been blown away.

Here and there a flower still stood upright amidst the chaos, throwing a fragile arrogance to the sun. But most of their leaves had withered or turned queer shades, and other flowers left standing had changed colors. White petals had turned blue, yellow to scarlet, pink to parchment. She fingered them, troubled.

Jettaret returned leading both horses. He checked their saddles, lying upended on the ground, to make certain they were usable; they were unseared by the storm. He still didn't want to call it magic.

Liana hesitated a moment before she walked back over to Jettaret, her eyes down, her countenance grave as a Good Friday penitent's. She took Bluestone's reins from him in silence, stroked the mare's neck and pressed her head against it, stayed by its warmth, its softness over taut muscle. Then she turned and looked slowly around, like a new-caught slave at auction, a hare that doesn't understand why it is being hounded. Jettaret had an impulse to hold her, but he couldn't. They both scanned the ravaged clearing.

"I did that?" It wasn't a question.

"Yes."

"*No!*" Anguish shrank Liana's voice, soft and small. "What else am I going to do?"

"I think it's more a matter of what Malaxia's going to do," Jettaret pointed out quietly. He laid his hand on her shoulder. "Come on." She did not move. "Come on. I know what this is like for you—"

Liana spun round. "How do you know?" she cried. "You don't believe in magic, you don't believe in witches—" Shots of blue flame spurted from her left fingers and she crumpled to the ground in horror, shivering.

"Liana." Jettaret knelt, put a hand over her fire hand, and faced her. "I helped burn Constantinople. Come on."

They saddled the horses, rolled up their cloaks and tied them on behind the saddles, Liana watching Jettaret to make sure she did it right. He handed her the roasted pheasant.

"Here, you carry this. And don't make it too well done." His drollery threw her off guard, and she was caught between an impulse to laugh and revulsion. But food was food. Liana put the pheasant in her saddlebag and mounted Bluestone without Jettaret's help.

7. LEPERS AND WATCH RIDERS

Vicomte astride black and peasant on dappled gray, they left the thick woods behind at mid-morning and rode uphill toward a bare, serrated ridge. As they approached, a crow started upward with a raspy caw and Liana listened for it to turn into Malaxia's voice, but all became silent. They crossed the ridge between two high dark rocks, wedged nearly together at the base.

Jettaret led the way down the other side, along a steep switchbacking path that turned into a straight slide at the end. The horses scraped their haunches as they plunged through loose gravel; it splattered out ahead of them in cascading fans and rebounded off rocks. Liana held hard with hands and knees till they reached level ground, where Jettaret dismounted to examine the horses' hindquarters. Liana looked backward, almost straight up, at the ridge.

"Who uses this trail?"

"Wild goats mostly." Jettaret ran his hands down Bluestone's legs. "And us." He stepped back. "A few scratches. Nothing bad." He picked up each of Bluestone's hooves and carefully dug out a few stones with his knife. "Walk her around." Liana rode Bluestone in a circle, and Jettaret noted that her seat was better as he watched the little mare's strides. "Looks all right. Feel any catch, any unevenness?"

Liana shook her head. "No." She walked Bluestone away and back in a straight line to make sure. Then another thought hit.

"Oh, no."

"Now what?" He was picking out Pasquale's hooves.

She turned to him in consternation. "I forgot to milk the goat."

"What?"

"Before I left."

"The goat." Jettaret put Pasquale's hoof down. "We are not going back for a goat. Either it's gotten out or someone's come along and taken care of it by now. Don't worry about it." Jettaret led Pasquale about, watching her gate, remounted and walked her till he was satisfied there was no lameness.

They continued around hillocks lush with green till they reached a river, not wide but fast moving and nearly flooded over with spring runoff. Jettaret turned east and they rode upstream alongside as it wound and rose steadily through a narrow valley. Surrounding mountains plowed into the valley's bottom, which rolled and dipped but continued to climb.

"Jettaret." Liana had not spoken since they'd halted at the ridge. "What's the Gordian Knot?"

Jettaret smiled; well, she wouldn't have read Xenophon. "It was a knot tied by King Gordius of Phrygia. He said whoever could untie it would be master of the East. Nobody could do it. Then Alexander the Great rode up, drew his sword and cut it with one stroke. Cutting the Gordian Knot means a fast solution to any problem." He cast a sidelong glance at Liana's hands.

"Who's Alexander the Great? Is he still alive?" There was hope in her voice.

Jettaret's eyes went to the sky. "No." He let out a deliberate breath. "Lyon. I'll tell you in Lyon. It's a long story and I'd have to look at the histories to make sure I don't leave anything out."

Toward noon the river curved past a series of bluffs, then a higher peak appeared behind them, a rounded surge of white streaked with dark gray where the snow had melted. Jettaret reined in.

"We turn north here. Further east there's a town, and I can't take you through towns, not yet anyway." He rode a little ways further along the bank, muttering, "Witches," as he searched for a place shallow enough to cross. The water ran swifter up here but was far less deep.

"I can hide in the woods if you have to go into town."

Jettaret turned in his saddle and looked at her. "What an unassailable proposition. The consummate arrangement. Ride off and leave you alone for Malaxia to find. Then have both of you come after me with some variations on that Turkish fire stuff? Blast another forest, a mountain maybe, and one stupid vicomte? No, thank you." He turned back around and continued searching for a place to ford.

Liana looked down at her hands. He'd known, and she had forgotten, how witches were different. She urged Bluestone forward.

The Witch's Hand

Jettaret chose a relatively calm crossing and they splashed through without mishap. On the other side he glanced at the sun, pulled up and dismounted.

"Heat up the rest of that pheasant—no." *Careful, Antoine.* "We'll eat it cold." Liana remained astride, not reaching for the pheasant behind her. Jettaret walked up to her and stopped with a hand on his sword.

"I've been in some strange company, but I never rode around with a witch before. I don't know your protocols. I don't want to get you angry, believe me. But it's a long way, and it's going to be longer if you take offense at everything I say." He dropped his hand. "Don't look at me like that." Her gaze, though unreproachful, had not left him. He paused and sighed. "Liana. We're going to Lyon, and if I get there you'll get there. So, don't mind any wrong things I may say, I don't mean them. It's only a way to shorten the road a little. All right?" Liana nodded. "Good. Can I have the pheasant?"

"It's in the right hand bag, behind me." Liana dismounted. "I don't want any."

Jettaret took the pheasant from the saddlebag. "I've got some bread, a little sausage—"

"Just bread."

"Don't play starving saint with me. We have a long way to go yet." He got out the bread and sausage.

They ate quickly. Jettaret finished off most of the pheasant, and threw the unsalted remains into the bushes for scavengers. Then they rode on through flatter terrain, following a faint trail that wound northwards through dense woods. The high snowy bluff receded behind them. To their right, Liana sometimes caught a glimpse of rolling green hills she would have called velvety if she'd known what velvet was.

A dry rattling broke the quiet ahead. Jettaret halted, listened; the rattle was approaching them. Without a word he turned abruptly off the path into the woods, beckoning Liana to follow. They dismounted in the cover of thick bushes and held the horses, Liana not sure of what was going on.

"Down!" he hissed. Liana crouched beside him, anxious, trying to construe what would make Jettaret so wary. He peered out through a tangle of foliage and briars as the rattling grew louder. Then, from behind the trees, a slow procession emerged.

Nine people, singly and in pairs, filed along the path. They wore nondescript cloaks drawn closely around hunched shoulders, and red hats pulled low. Each carried a pair of dried bones hanging from either end of a leather line, and these made the rattle as they dangled and struck each other. One of the nine, a hunchback, served as a crutch for a tall scarecrow of a man, and as they got closer Liana saw the scarecrow had only one leg. A woman who might have been young but was worn and beaten with suffering carried her bones over one elbow; she had withered stumps for hands.

A child followed another shuffling woman, and when they passed the bushes where Liana and Jettaret were hiding he turned a horrible face toward them. It had the features of a gargoyle, both eyes askew, off center, with a craggy misshapen brow and jaw, and a flattened sniveling mistake where its nose should have been. Green mucous ran from two irregular holes beneath the eyes and mixed with drool from its mouth, all of it darkened with dirt into a muddy slime. He did not see the two watching him.

One man wore his hood hung low over the red cap; Liana suspected he had no face. Holding onto a rope tied to the hooded man's waist, a boy her age groped his way along behind, his head up in a horizon gazer's tilt, blind. He used a wooden stick as well as the rope to find the path ahead, and his bones clattered against the stick, like a third bone.

"Who are they?" Liana whispered.

"Lepers."

Liana started up toward them but Jettaret yanked her back.

"No! You can't help them, and we can't have them telling people where we are. Stay here."

The lepers passed, slowly making their way southward. Their bones continued to rattle long after they had disappeared into the woods, then they too faded. Jettaret waited some time before he led Pasquale back to the trail. Liana followed and stood looking after the lepers, Bluestone's reins loose in her hands, as Jettaret mounted and checked the fastenings on his saddlebags.

"You can't want any more trouble, unless you're weirder than I thought. Come on."

Liana swung up and rode silently for a few minutes, then said, "They were going toward my home."

"Home is where they're waiting to burn you. And those people won't get much of a welcome. The Bishop issued an edict last year banning lepers from town; they have to stay outside the walls."

"I wonder if anyone's buried Maman and Papa yet."

Jettaret looked back and drew Pasquale up till Liana was beside him. "When we get to Lyon I'll send someone to see about it."

"Thank you."

They halted around Nones, beside a shallow stream where water pooled behind a fallen log and fell in a thin, lively wash over it. No church was close enough to ring the hour, but the sun was approaching the western treetops. The horses dropped their heads to the pool to drink, their necks forming long, arced bows, black arc next to a dappled one. Then Liana turned Bluestone aside and urged her across below the fallen log, where the stream was shallower and the mare could see to pick her way through the rocky bed. Jettaret followed and dismounted on the other side.

"We'll stop here a little while. There are two ways to go from here, and I haven't decided which is best yet."

Liana reined Bluestone around, and slid off onto a alluvial bank of sand. "What are the two ways?"

"We can follow the stream, which has its disadvantages—some bad sections, tight places where there's no path—or we can cut northwest to a road not far from here, which would be faster but more dangerous. It's a main road."

"I could tie my hair back, put up my hood, and say I was your brother." Jettaret raised an eyebrow at her. "Cousin?"

"Possibly. There's not enough woman on you for anyone to notice. I'll think about it." With that Jettaret led Pasquale up the bank to a level place, soft with low growth and moss. Growling, "Witches." he cast himself down beneath a smooth-barked tree and leaned against it, one knee drawn up. Liana tied Bluestone to a bush, walked upstream to the pool and stood looking down.

Her silent opposite stared back at her with steady, unflickering eyes. Long dark hair, stringy here, tangled there, with briars caught in it, fell around a frail looking figure in earth-stained clothes. Liana searched for the demarcation between witch and girl and found none. She bent to drink and her somber twin wavered and dissolved as the tips of her hair hit the water and slid in, swallowing themselves. The water was icy in her cupped hands, and it had a bite; there was mint upstream somewhere. Then she rose and turned toward Jettaret.

Jettaret's head had dropped to his knee. She halted, seeing how weary her escort was. A warrior, a Crusader; the great sword's hilt gleamed latent at his side. And a vicomte, who dressed like a peasant. What was his canon, his set of rules? She had never been this close to nobility before and couldn't figure out what was different about them, definitely different about this one. He had been to Jerusalem; he was closer to God than she. But it was more than that. He didn't seem like a pilgrim, a holy man. He didn't seem like a peasant or a vicomte, a priest or a butcher or the Wandering Jew either for that matter, but again, what did she know about nobility?

This noble's duty-fueled fortitude looked spent. Whether asleep or not, she didn't disturb him. He was more tired of her probably than the journey, and there were still nearly three hours of daylight left. She thought about the western road. Quietly she untied Bluestone and led her away, over a muffling shroud of moss, under a banked rock that leaned out over them like a chunk of overgrown turf, and passed into the trees.

When they were far enough away to make more noise, Liana mounted and urged Bluestone up a wooded rise. At the top she checked and searched the country. They were alone. A rough jumble of crags and trees rose to her right, the way they would go if they followed the stream. To her left the lowering sun stretched shadows over smaller hills, with fewer trees. Liana shaded her eyes against the sun, which seemed abnormally bright even as low as it was to the horizon, and spotted the main road winding through the shadows, its glowing dust undisturbed, empty. Behind her the woods remained silent; Jettaret had not followed her. She couldn't tell if anyone else had. She nudged Bluestone down the slope.

The Witch's Hand

Though there was no trail, the undergrowth wasn't dense, and Liana and Bluestone dropped into a gully and splashed through a shallow brook. She wasn't sure if it was an offshoot of the stream where Jettaret had stopped. She entered a small copse just short of the road, where she and Bluestone would be out of sight from anyone passing by, dismounted and tied the mare to a tree. A sudden wind lifted her hair from behind and blew it out in front of her, snagging it on the bark. She pulled it free and turned; there was nothing there. She sat facing away from the road, into the wind, and after a few seconds it calmed.

Liana sat for a while in silence, tracing a line in the dirt without looking at it, without looking at anything. Her hands could unleash powers terrifying, immense, but as yet she had no idea of their extent or uses, beyond destroying things. Could she control them? How much of a witch was she? She was an annoyance and a burden to Jettaret. He would be relieved to get rid of her, and her magic. She didn't know where Lyon was, much less how far, and Jettaret hadn't mentioned how long it would take to get there. She could take the road and be someplace where they didn't know who she was before sunset, maybe.

Across the clearing, fallen blossoms lay over last year's leaves and mulch. Tentatively she raised her right hand and drew a circle in the air with her forefinger, then another. The blossoms and leaves stirred. They began to move in a circle, slowly at first, then faster and with purpose, and swirled into a whirlwind. Liana lifted her hand and the whirlwind rose as if growing from the ground. She held her hand level; the whirlwind remained steady. Then she began to feel off balance, even sitting as she was. She swept her hand down and the whirlwind collapsed, scattering leaf and blossom haphazardly.

To her right a stone the size of a round of winter cheese lay embedded in the dirt. Liana extended her right hand again, palm up this time. Slowly she brought it higher; her hand began shaking with the effort. The stone trembled in its place and turned up, the underside dark with wet earth. Its dry top thudded into the ground.

The right hand could move things and set the air astir, then. What about the left, and fire? Liana stretched out her left hand at a clump of bushes. Nothing happened. The fingers, wait, the same as for the campfire—thumb, first, second—she splayed them out toward the bushes and tried to bring them together. Again it felt like squeezing thick clay. Just before her fingers touched, her hand jerked back with a recoil that threw her backwards; there was a flash and a *hsss* and the bushes were aflame. Bluestone started, snapping her tie line straight out, but it held. Liana hurried over to her.

"Whoa ... whoa ... it's all right ..." But it wasn't. The fire was bigger than she'd expected or wanted, and it wasn't burning like a normal one. It wavered and glowed with a queer light. Liana struggled to untie Bluestone and led her further away from the fire, calming the little mare as well as her own fright would let her, and re-tied her at the other end of the clearing. Then she turned back to the fire.

The flames were rising but hadn't spread to anything else yet. She had nothing to beat them out with, and there was no water. But she had started this fire, stranger if smaller than the one that had burnt her home, more menacing in its unnaturalness.

Her right hand. It could move air into a wind, and a strong enough wind could hit things with explosive force. If she concentrated it right and aimed it dead center, she could blow the bushes apart and stamp out the scattered pieces. She lifted her right.

The left hand—it could make fire, and though she hadn't put one out with it yet, she might be able to control the flames' height and bring it down a little, maybe extinguish it. She brought her left hand up shoulder high, level with her right.

Now she faced the fire and concentrated, her breath short and shallow, sweat and the fire's heat stinging her eyes. Holding both hands out, palms down, she spread her right fingers wide, half curled those of her left. The fire began to diminish. Then she curved her right fingers down, not quite as much as the left. She blinked the sting from her eyes and prepared.

Simultaneously she brought her left hand down into a fist close to her waist and flung her right hand out, straight at the flames. The fire vanished in an explosion of dust and light that flared through the clearing and set every leaf in sharp outline. Bluestone went frantic.

Liana found herself on the ground with her hand shading her eyes, which hurt from the light. When she could look again she saw there was nothing left to stamp out; blackened scraps and pieces lay about, spread

The Witch's Hand

like rays from a flattened sunburst, but the fire was gone and nothing identifiable remained of the bushes. Liana went over to Bluestone, held the gray's head and leaned against it, as much to steady herself as the horse. She untied Bluestone and led her out of the clearing, toward the road. Then she heard hoofbeats, walking. Two sets. And voices.

"It was over here . . . this way . . . careful . . ."

"Careful of what? She's a witch, she might be anything. Look like a magpie, sound like a goat; she might be invisible. She might be behind us."

"Shut up and ride."

From the road they had seen the explosion's flash and cloud of dust rise out of he woods to their left, which had made Bernard's horse rear. The cloud had quickly dispersed; under the place where it had been, an unnatural green afterglow lingered. Bernard had drawn up his fractious mount and pointed.

"That's witchcraft, Jean. Come on." He'd spurred off the road into the trees. Jean had followed him, glum.

Liana stood, pressed back against Bluestone's chest and shoulder, listening. They were coming closer, slowly. If she stayed still and kept Bluestone quiet they might not see—

"Damn. Why did it have to be in our neck of the woods?"

"That's why we're out here, instead of patrolling in town. Better to fight her here than there. Less property damage. And you have to admit the road is cleaner. Beats slogging around those stink-rot streets."

"I'd rather patrol in shite and have a tavern nearby, all right?"

"All right. Let's get this job done, then. The Watch rides until the witch is killed, or until we determine there was no threat."

"It's all a bunch of rumors. Rumor can turn a moth into a dragon."

Bernard nodded at the glow over the trees ahead. "That was no rumor."

"I wish it were. Messing with witches can make you weird yourself. They're dangerous, tricky; I'd rather face a charge of Anjou knights. How do you handle a witch? You can't tell what they're going to do, nobody even knows for sure how to kill them—"

"No. If you're on speaking terms with the Virgin today, ask for some help."

"I talk to her. She never talks back."

"Good habit in a woman. Careful now. We're getting close."

Liana held Bluestone's nose and watched, not breathing. *Wait—maybe they won't*—no, they were too close, she needed a better place to hide, but there weren't enough tall bushes or low-boughed trees to conceal them both. Liana scrambled up into the saddle. She legged Bluestone around and took off at a gallop, back toward their camp.

"There! To the right!" Jean shouted.

"I see her. Let's go!" The Watch riders jabbed their spurs in.

Bluestone dipped her head under a succession of branches hanging at staggered heights; Liana ducked and crouched low on the mare's neck. Black mane stung her face. Behind her the Watch's larger horses swerved around the trees but couldn't avoid all the branches, and horses and riders got smacked in the face again and again.

Jean closed on Liana. She heard him coming up behind and feared a long arm reaching out to grab her. Then Bluestone brushed under a thicker branch. Liana flattened herself enough so only the leaves swatted her, but Jean was almost unhorsed as the main branch swung back and hit him hard. He fought his way back up and let Bernard pass as he tried to clear his head and watering eyes. *Witches!*

Bluestone broke into open ground, raced through and was into the woods on the other side before Bernard entered. The small mare's size was an advantage in close growth over uneven ground, but after the clearing the underbrush thinned and the going, though uphill, got fairly smooth. Bernard and Jean were beginning to catch up when the ground dropped slightly, towards the brook, and their horses' weight gave them more momentum.

"Come on, Blue, come on!" They'd walked through the brook before, and Liana didn't know if she could stay on in a mad splash over rough footing, but if the riders behind caught her they would burn her. She wouldn't be caught.

The ground fell away sharply at the bank. Bluestone half slid down and bunched herself; she wasn't going to be able to stop. Liana held onto her mane tight and closed her eyes as the little mare sprung, nearly bounding from beneath her. She cleared the brook in one leap. Liana

The Witch's Hand

landed off center and grabbed at anything to stay with her horse as Bluestone surged up the opposite bank in short, strong bursts.

Bernard thundered up. Frothing hard, his horse charged the brook and only extended his stride to get across, but covered twice the distance Bluestone had. Behind him, bent forward, hands high on his horse's neck, Jean was close enough to catch spurts of dirt from the take-off. But instead of duplicating the leap, his water-shy mount balked and almost sat on his haunches in a violent halt. Jean flew butt over head into the brook. He landed face down near the opposite bank, splashing out a mantle of white spray, and, his hose torn, his wind stricken and knees bruised, struggled up and yanked his horse across.

His pride hurt more than his cuts. He had the faster horse and Bernard knew it. Remounting with a wet splat, he lashed his horse into full stride after his partner, some five lengths ahead.

Through a break in the trees Liana saw the leaning rock by the stream, where Jettaret had stopped. Bluestone was holding her distance ahead of Bernard; Jettaret's judgment about the mare's sound wind had been right. Then Jean, though chilled stiff from the air blowing through his wet clothes, felt a grim satisfaction as he finally passed Bernard, and closed ground.

Liana rounded the overhanging rock and pulled up short. Jettaret was nowhere in sight. Pasquale had also vanished, and the riders were coming on fast. "Jettaret?" Bewildered, she turned Bluestone about in a half circle. Jean rode into her line of vision, heading straight for her. He was only a few trees away from the rock when a dagger thunked into his chest too quickly to see where it had come from, and, vacant eyed, he somersaulted backward over his horse's tail into the dirt.

Close behind, Bernard reined around Jean but didn't check his horse. As he passed under the last tree before the rock, a shadowy form with a flying cloak dropped from the branches above him, and they both careened to the ground. Jettaret rose first, sword ready. Bernard disentangled himself from Jettaret's cloak quickly and threw it aside as he got to his feet. They faced off, sword to sword, circling warily.

Liana started to raise a hand. *No magic. No magic!*

Jettaret feinted high; Bernard reached for it with his sword and Jettaret kicked him in the stomach, Fortuna Domini drawn back. Then he swept the blade diagonally up and hewed off Bernard's head. Blood spurted from his neck. His body crumpled erratically to the ground, while his face, not having had time to look surprised, concentrated dumbly on nothing as his head thudded to the ground and rolled. Dirt and blood mixed on his face, matted his hair.

Jettaret went over to Jean and pulled his dagger free. He wiped it on the dead man's tunic before sheathing it. Then he snatched up his cloak and threw it over his shoulders, wiping off his sword with the edge of it. He strode coldly past Liana.

"Welcome to the Crusades." Jettaret sheathed his sword and disappeared into the woods. Some moments later he returned leading Pasquale. "I had to take a chance she wouldn't make a noise and give us away." He faced Liana. "I found your tracks heading toward the road. I thought you were off catching another rabbit." He paused. "You weren't after rabbit. Then I heard you coming back—Bluestone's never moved that fast—and I wasn't sure how many were behind you. But even the Knights Templars run or play dirty when the odds are more than three to one. The tree was the prudent place."

Liana was staring at the two lifeless riders on the ground, pooled in blood. "Did you have to kill them?"

"Would you rather I let them take you back? Or wound them and let them die slowly? Maybe just scare them off and let them raise the alarm all the way home?"

She was silent a moment. "They're not from Peranville." She'd noticed their cloaks.

"No. These are from the north. Word of you seems to have gotten around." He straightened. "Well. We can't take the road. All of my weighing and measuring and considering the odds, and you decide for us. We can't risk the road now, it's too dangerous. All the Watch around here will be on it when these two don't come back."

"But there are only two of them. And no one will be expecting them back for a while."

"You don't know when. No. We take the stream." Jettaret mounted and reined Pasquale around toward the bank. Liana remained where she was, still looking at the fallen riders.

"May the angels lead you into Paradise."

The Witch's Hand

"Yeah, right. And may the martyrs meet them." Jettaret caught her glance. "I'm not going to waste time burying them. When their horses go back without them—and they will, there's not enough grass here—they'll send more riders out. Come on."

He rode upstream. Liana did not follow. After some yards he looked around, saw she hadn't moved, and rode back to her. Controlling his ire, he spoke.

"Liana. These . . . witch powers of yours, or whatever they are, Malaxia wants you because of them; I don't know why or what she would do to you, and the Church would burn you for them. You're in a lot of danger, besides being dangerous yourself. Do you want my help or not?" He waited. "Well?"

Silent tears began to work their way down Liana's face. She turned away.

Jettaret sighed. "Now what?"

"I'm frightened."

"I don't doubt that."

Liana wiped her eyes unmindfully. "What can you do?"

"Keep you out of sight, away from witch hunters."

"And Malaxia?"

"I don't know." He could promise nothing there. "I'll do my best."

Jettaret led the way further upstream, a good deal further, till the light was fading and they had to stop. They made no fire. Jettaret sat up long against a tree, watching.

The wind changed suddenly, from fair to whipping. Water sloshed in through the open hatch, along with great bunches of grapes that fermented as they fell. Choking on water and new wine, Jettaret tried to right himself in the pitching hold. "Jehan! Alberge!" Alberge growled something from above, but Jehan was still lost somewhere below and Jettaret went back down for him when a huge swirling funnel rocketed him to the surface with a howl—

His ears rang with his own cry as Jettaret woke. Near him, Liana stirred but remained asleep. He felt for his wineskin and took a long, slow drink. There was no wind.

8. TO THE EDGE

The next day they climbed, as the stream alongside went from placid into a series of breaks and falls. They rode past stands of slender hazel, tall, the new shoots red with rising sap. Jettaret eyed them dubiously. Hazel was sacred to the old Druids; it was supposed to be magical, though what it did or how the Druids had used it he didn't know. He glanced sideways at Liana to see if it had any effect on her. No. She was pensive and wasn't watching the trail ahead, but showed no sign of being disturbed or affected by the hazels. No magic. Or maybe it took a different kind of tree.

A wind passed through the hazels, rustling their leaves. Then a branch cracked behind Liana, a small one, not enough to start the horses. Jettaret pulled up and checked their rear. Liana did not. She spoke looking straight ahead.

"There's nobody there."

"Not even a rabbit?"

"Don't make fun of me."

Jettaret rode back up beside her. "St. Michel defend me, I forgot. It's not a good idea to get on a witch's bad side; didn't they ever tell any jokes where you come from?"

"Jettaret."

"What?"

"Yes, we did."

Artless she was, Jettaret thought. No guile. Damn.

Liana looked to the west. Far off, the last ribbon of the high road wound northward. They passed around a low hill and it vanished.

"Jettaret."

"What?"

"How come you're traveling alone? Lords always go around in a procession, like Easter, with a lot of wagons and—" She stopped, unsure. "Don't they?"

He nodded. "Most of the time. I've already sent my household necessaries and servants to Lyon. I had some other business to take care of first." What it was he did not say. They rode on.

"Jettaret—"

"*What?*"

"I'm sorry."

"Never mind. Go on."

"How long before we get to Lyon?"

"Mm, the way we're going, off the roads, roundabout, the country the way it is, keep to the mountains a while, then turn east—a week, ten days."

"She'll find us before then. Why do you stay with me?"

"Respectfully, my dear young witch, what's made you so optimistic this morning?"

"Malaxia could come for me any time she wanted. Your sword wouldn't help. Why do you stay?"

"I took the scenic route and you were on it. Look, maybe I can't do anything about Malaxia, or dragons or demons or the Prince of Darkness, but I can stop a farmer with a scythe, or a knight with a lance, or anything normal that comes at you. If we met a band of Saracens you'd be safe." He paused. "Have you ever been more than a day's walk from Peranville?"

"No."

"I have. And believe me, there are things almost as bad as Malaxia out there. I may not be St. Michel, but I'm the only help you've got. No." He touched Fortuna Domini's hilt, slid it from the scabbard an inch. "There are two of us."

"What do the letters mean?"

"Fortuna Domini." He stroked the crosspiece gently. "Latin, 'Fortune of the Lord.' I carried it on the Crusade."

They stopped before Sext for a midday meal of sorts, where leafy branches overhung and shaded the stream. Jettaret cut carefully rationed slices of bread and dried sausage; he didn't want Liana to use her magic for catching food, throwing around a power she couldn't control to kill a rabbit. But he would have to stop at a town somewhere soon. The wine was almost gone. The bread, what was left of it, was turning moldy and the sausage was tough as dried hide. It would have to boil for a day if you really wanted to be able to chew it. He could set snares and get a rabbit for later tonight, or try to catch some fish.

The Witch's Hand

Jettaret walked over to the stream and studied the bottom. Shadows writhed and rippled back and forth, but they were from dappled sunlight on the stones beneath the water. It ran strong and fast here and there weren't eddies enough to spot fish. Further up, along the bank, Liana knelt and trailed her fingers in the water, her head bent.

"If you can catch fish like that we're out of provision trouble." Almost like having a trained bear on a chain to stand in the stream and flip the fish out to you, into the pan.

Liana paid no notice. She rose and started to walk away from the bank, toward the forest.

"Liana? Where are you going?"

She looked back. "I saw some watercress over there. It's good for colds. I'll be right back." She headed for a boggy area and disappeared behind a growth of brambles.

Puzzled, Jettaret inhaled deeply through his nose. "I don't have a cold." He looked where she had gone. "Liana?" There was no response. He growled, shook his head in disgust, threw a rock at the trees and was about to follow, then changed his mind. They were in an area too remote for Watch riders, or even bandits for that matter, and Liana was probably right about Malaxia. If the witch wanted to attack them and seize or spirit the girl away, she could do so at will, any time. He looked at the stream again, fixed on the current running past him, studied it. Then it hit him.

"The water's going this way—she's going that way—Mother of God!" He sprang to Pasquale, seized the reins and slapped the horse forward. "Come on, Pasquale!" Pasquale broke into a run as he swung up. He headed through the trees in the direction Liana had gone, searching right and left. Finally he spotted her, far ahead, and urged Pasquale on still faster.

Liana looked up through the trees, a clump of still wet watercress in her hand. It was past Sext; the sunrays were beginning to slant, and leftover mist from the morning rose in shadows through them. She fingered the cress, gently shook drops of water from it. No one had ever told her if the stuff's virtue lay in its irregular leaves, large and soft, in its minuscule white flowers or stringy roots; but brewed into tea or added to boiled squash, it kept head rheum away, got rid of any colds you already had, and kept you from getting another, usually.

One spring she'd been continually down to the stream and back, pulling handfuls of cress for her mother, downed for nearly two weeks with the malaise that went from her head to her throat into her chest, and made her breathe like a dying sheep. But she'd recovered. Liana tucked the watercress under her belt.

The forest drew her on. Sunlight filtered through boughs, blending multitudinous shades of blue and green amongst each other. For the first time since the cottage fire Liana began to feel better, sorcery forgotten, the bonds of apprehension loosened. The surrounding trees, her feet on the ground growth, and the soft air were all that existed. She skipped along for a step, another, twirled round on one foot. Sunlight sliced across her upturned face. She leaped for a low branch and managed to hit it with her fingertips, spun on her toes again and danced round an imaginary circle. She kicked to the leaves above her head, kicked again sideways with her hands thrown out, coming off the ground this time. Air filled her lungs and her ribs surged out with force.

A fallen tree lay before Jettaret. He sent Pasquale over it, upright branches poised to take his knees off on either side. He closed on Liana, who remained unaware of his approach despite the running drum of Pasquale's hooves. The trees grew more dense and thick, with brush beneath; he pulled Pasquale to a halt, leaped off before she'd come to a complete stop and charged after Liana.

Liana slipped between the trees and through waist high bushes, with leaves the size of water lily pads. Before her the crown of a birch tree rose, but at eye level. She hopped a fallen log and parted branches to get close enough for a better look, reached out toward the birch and abruptly started to slip, down—straight down into a glacier-cut gorge.

Jettaret reached the cliff and made a flying leap over the log and through the last bushes, diving after her. Liana flew half around into the cliff as she fell, splayed fingers skidding down, searching, grabbing for a solid hold and Jettaret was there, an outstretched hand reaching for hers. He seized it and dug his boots in.

Liana scrabbled for a foothold while Jettaret fought to keep from going over himself, pulling her up by the one hand he held. The birch, which grew from a rooty knob in the nearly sheer face, was no help; a sapling, its branches were too weak for even Liana's weight, and

The Witch's Hand

provided no upward spring for leverage, either. She kicked and struggled and clawed to get back up, the stream five hundred feet below.

Halfway over the edge, gripping her left hand, Jettaret fought to haul her up. Her right hand scratched fruitlessly at gravel and dirt, then she tried to shove herself up with the heel of her palm, which proved equally futile and she let it hang. In a reflex, her fingers tightened, released and blasted a chunk of the cliff away, big enough for a toe hold. Banging her knee she found it, pushed, scrambled; Jettaret strained up with all he had, and finally she breached the rim and they both tumbled backward to safety. They lay there catching their breaths, Jettaret on his back looking up through a crossed maze of leaves at the sky, Liana face down. He drew himself up and leaned against the fallen log, his legs sprawled out on the ground before him. Flopped like a chamois skin, Liana did not move.

"Turn over. You'll breathe better." Liana started to push herself over with an elbow, toward the cliff. "Other way, witch. I'm not going after you again." She turned away from the cliff onto her side, her knees drawn up, her eyes shutting out trees, cliff, everything. At length she sat up. Jettaret reached out and pulled a briar from her hair, oddly gentle.

"Liana. Listen. I know this country; you don't. Stick close. Next time you want to pick flowers, I'll go with you. And we don't know where this witch friend of yours is."

Liana's eyes went wide. Malaxia. She had been gone, absent from apprehension for a while. Jettaret got to his feet. "Are you all right?" She nodded. "Come on." He extended his hand to her, for once without any wariness or caution, and helped her to her feet. Half the cliff face was still stuck to her; she looked like a wood grub.

"We'll get you a change of clothes someplace. Before you wear those bare. Can't dress like that around the chateau, in front of my lady. Wouldn't do." He stepped over the log and started back toward Pasquale. Liana followed. "Can you tend pigs?"

"I don't know. I never did. We didn't have any pigs. Sheep, a goat—"
"Forget about the goat."

They reached Pasquale, who was tearing at the grass, foam still around her mouth and on her neck under the reins. Jettaret took her head, annoyed, and worked the grass and slobber free from the bit and out of her mouth.

"Never let Bluestone do this."

"Do what? Eat?"

"Eat while she's saddled." He slid his hand under the girth. "Makes her swell up and chafe under here; can give her sores if you don't loosen it. And if you do loosen it and forget to draw it tight again later, you can take a quick trip underneath. I've seen it happen." He mounted and leaned down to help Liana up, but as she reached her hand out, he drew his up in warning. "Careful with that." He bent again, took her arm and pulled her up behind him. They started back toward the pool where Bluestone was.

"Jettaret. I used magic back there."

"No you didn't. That gorge was there before you were born."

"No. To get back up the cliff. I blasted a foothold, a little one, I didn't want to—"

"Want to or not, you got us both back up."

"I couldn't help it."

Jettaret reached down and made sure both her hands were joined round his waist. He put his own hand over them. "Don't do anything to Pasquale." He paused. "Or me." They rode back through the trees in silence.

That night they camped in a field where the rocks were darker and stuck straight up out of the ground, in joined columns. Light from the fire jumped from one edge to the other, setting them in stark outline. Liana leaned against one of them and tried to get comfortable. Jettaret watched her efforts.

"It gets worse."

She looked at him, warding off discouragement. "Why do you stay—"

"Quiet, girl. The day after tomorrow we should be far enough away from people who know about you to find an inn and stay there. The country gets strange from here."

Liana watched the firelight play over the stones, making them rise and shrink, demon-like. Beyond the fire they were intermingled with the surrounding gray tree trunks and it was hard to tell wood from stone.

The Witch's Hand

"Liana. This fire and ... these things you do. Could you always do them?

"No. Only after Malaxia came. I never did them before; I never thought I could."

"You never tried?"

"No. Not like that."

"Just little rhymes and stuff?"

"Yes."

"No Turkish fire?"

Liana shook her head.

"But you thought others could?"

"Well, some maybe. There was a wise woman down the stream a ways who knew all about herbs and potions and she chanted things and—" Liana stopped, confused. "But she wasn't a witch. Not like Malaxia. I never saw anyone like her before. I thought a real witch would be different."

"How?"

"Well, different. I don't know. Uglier. Older, scarier—well she is scary—but not the way I thought. She's soft, sort of; but grand, beautiful." Liana's eyes were large. "She doesn't attack or snarl like a boar. She just stood there, listened, and sounded like—" She'd sounded like Maman but Liana didn't say that. "She isn't the way I thought a witch would be. She's like a great lady and—" Maman again, "but she's stern. I think if she got angry she could pull mountains down."

"She almost did."

"I don't know what she came for, why she wants me," then her fading hope rushed out, "maybe she doesn't anymore; how do you know, how can you tell about witches?"

"You can't. If there are witches."

"She is. I'm a witch and I know. She does things—"

"Hold it, hold it. I don't want you getting any more upset over her. She's a strange lady, I'll grant you that. But I've seen a lot of strange things and heard of worse. Sometimes they're not so bad if you can figure them out. There are mountains that shoot fire. Sometimes the sun goes dark and day turns into night—"

"The Death Shadow! I saw it once. Everyone thought the world was going to end. When it didn't, the Bishop said it was only a warning. There weren't any poachers for a long time after that."

"Poachers?" He eyed her little shoulders. "Is that what you do, catch poachers?"

"I ... sort of. I helped. My father was a game watcher for the Bishop. We could have rabbits and small things, for keeping track of the deer and boar and making sure nobody else hunted them. My father was a chaser and beater on the Bishop's hunts. I went sometimes. They weren't supposed to see me so I had to hide."

"Ever take a deer for yourself?"

Liana looked away for a moment, then back at Jettaret. "You've never been hungry, have you?"

"I have. And worse. You've never butchered people."

"Why would you want to eat *them*? Dead people stink."

"I didn't say eat. They were between us and Jerusalem."

"Oh ... they were Infidels."

Jettaret shook his head. "No. They were Christians. The different kind, the ones from the East. And they were in the way."

"How could they get in the way? Why didn't you join together and go to Jerusalem?" Cautiously she added, "How different were they?"

Jettaret shrugged. "One dead body looks pretty much like another after a few days."

"You were on the same side. Why were you fighting? It's not right for Christians to kill each other."

Jettaret looked at her. "No."

"It's complicated then."

"Yes." He sighed. "There's a lot of things I can't explain, little lady. The Crusade is one of them. There was a guy from Picardy in the next camp, Robert de Clari, who went around taking notes on the bloody thing the whole time. Maybe he can make some sense of it. There was a lot of stuff going on we didn't know about, rumors mostly. Nobody even knew who was running things for a while—Venice or the Eastern Church or the Pope or Philip of Swabia or maybe the Devil. The policy guys in the big tents don't discuss strategy with the guys in the little ones."

"I guess not. Philip of Swabia ... who's he?"

"Good question. He wasn't even there. He's one of the guys trying to be Emperor."

"Emperor of what? Does the Church know about it?"

"Oh—never mind." Jettaret tried again. "You see, there's the Church and the Empire, the Pope and Philip or whoever it's going to be, and they don't get along. They're both Christian but they fight all the time and yes, you're right, it's complicated, go to sleep." He poked at the fire with a stick, turning embers. "Do this, do that; *Deus vult*. Yes sir, yes, my liege, yes, your Eminence; *Deus vult*."

"What?"

Jettaret glanced at her. "*Deus vult; Dieu lo volt,*" he added in her Auvergne langue d'oc, though the Latin was close, "'God wills it.' They were saying that on the First Crusade."

"How come everything went wrong?"

"Why does anything go wrong? If God willed it then He knows, I don't. We swore to deliver the Holy Land;" a twinge of pain shot through his features, "the only thing it needed to be delivered from was us."

Bluestone snorted and Liana jumped, alert.

"It's only your horse." He watched her. "Isn't it?" Her head was up, listening. He looked around and leaned closer. "Anybody there?"

Liana was still a moment, then released her breath. "No." Firelight silhouetted the angle of her nose but her eyes were in shadow.

In the morning, before they rode on, Jettaret checked the ground around their camp for footprints. There were none.

9. RECONNAISSANCE, OR SPYING, IN HOLY PLACES

The country became curious. From the midst of a softly greened slope, a curved rock crag rose, like a huge wave about to crash down. Just beyond reach of its shadow stood a sheer slab of stone, rectangular, and tilted. They were like the claws of a pincer, one rounded, one straight. Both were twice the height of Peranville's cathedral.

"Jettaret. Did Druids do that?"

"Even Druids would have had a hard time shoving those things around. If God did it He had His reasons, but whatever they were, *Deus vult*."

They followed a broken trail and saw no one. The country rose, became close with ridges and opened up again. Then the way bent left along the crest of a high escarpment, which fell away abruptly. Jettaret reined in.

Before them stood a dark enormity crowned with vicious serrations. The mountain was an embodied threat. Jagged pinnacle rose from jagged pinnacle, demon's teeth daring the sky to fall on them. Impale a giant boar on top and he would be cut to ribbons.

It was alien, and for the first time Liana felt how far from home she was.

"Think you could get us over that? Witch?"

"I can't fly."

"Neither can I, but there's got to be a spell for it. Take us right through." He swung a leg up and hooked it lightly over the pommel. "Come on, say the right words. *Vobiscum-iscum*, prayer at Prime, things aren't always what they seem—"

Liana smacked Pasquale's shoulder hard with the ends of her reins and the startled horse broke sideways. Sitting as he was, Jettaret didn't have a chance. He was in the dirt before Pasquale stopped moving. Liana was looking straight between Bluestone's ears.

"Don't make fun of me."

"I forgot." Jettaret sat there a moment longer. He rose slowly, dusted off his leggings, reached for Pasquale and his ribs and left shoulder spoke. "Ow." He stood a second, then swept Liana out of her saddle with one arm and seated her flat against a rock. She stared back up at him, neither defiant nor cowed. *Damned enigma.*

"Look. If you want a guide out of here, and somebody to keep you away from witch hunters, *and* a blade and maybe some protection against Malaxia, hmm . . .? You take a little care to see that guide stays in one piece, all right?"

"Then don't make fun of me." She got up and went around Pasquale to get to Bluestone. As she passed Fortuna Domini's saddle scabbard, Jettaret stepped quickly between the sword and her, his hand on its hilt, staring *don't even think about it* to her.

Her look told him she wasn't.

Astride Bluestone again, Liana studied the mountain. The trail ahead led away from it, along lower ridges, and lost itself after a few turns.

"You know, if we went up the middle of that scooped out place, and skirted the ridge that sticks out there, above that it's not so bad—"

"Forget it." Jettaret drew up beside her.

She pointed to the terrain below. "We can go right down here, and over that way a little, it's mostly flat—"

"The hell we will."

"Then how are we going to get over the mountain?"

His smile was blissful. "My dear young witch—and I mean that in all sincerity, with all respect—we are not going to go over the mountain. I never planned to do that. We are going to go around it, and only part way. This way." He continued along the trail, now bearing to the right, northeast.

The day warmed on Jettaret's back. If the weather held and they kept this pace, they could reach Orcival by sunset. He debated going into the village for supplies, with an ear open for any muttering about witches in the area. Orcival was not large, with no Watch garrisoning it, and they could escape through the woods and be away from any threat quickly, if necessary. They were four days out from Peranville now, two from the Watch attack. Keeping to the high country, they'd seen no one since. News of Liana might not have traveled to Orcival yet, and then again maybe it had. He would have to leave the girl hidden outside the church and sparse cluster of shops and houses around it, get what they needed, and hope Malaxia didn't show up in the interim. There wasn't much he could do about that. Another cold night lay ahead, and there wasn't much he could do about that either. He couldn't risk taking Liana into town, and he couldn't chance a fire nearby. Nothing more delightful than being surprised by a bunch of suspicious villagers in the middle of the night.

The next day they would turn northeast more, through strange country that few traveled. The forage there for the horses would be rough, but by the time they descended into leveler ways he hoped to have left the witch-suspicious and Malaxia behind. Whoever she was.

What made witches witches; why did they join with the diabolical and become so? But then why did God—*Cur Deus Homo*—why did God join with us and become man? St. Anselm of Canterbury's argument came back. God was greatness beyond thought, His existence proven even by the idea of His existence, a greatness "than which a greater cannot be thought." It was in reality and beyond reality, this greatness, in one's being, mind, actions; in fear, in pain, in hope, happiness, joy, despair. It, the greatness of God, could not be held or contained. It was in the mind and went past the mind, past thought; it staggered the faculty of understanding, though it begged to be understood.

Anselm, his first reading.

And why did God *want* to become man, why did He want to throw in with, take on the guise of a thief, liar, cheat; the worst of creatures, those who fought and hated each other—men, full of misery and deceit, false in more matters than Eve, than the Serpent, than Judas. Why indeed. Was there no other way to save us?

I understand nothing.

"Jettaret. Jettaret?"

"What, girl?"

"Where does this road take us?"

He nodded his head north. "Up there. We get to a little town, bear right from it, and head east, more or less, toward Lyon. There are shorter ways, but no one's likely to find us on this one." Jettaret lifted his reins. "Pasquale." He rode on ahead, fast. He was pushing it, he knew, but he wanted to get within striking distance of Orcival before sunset so he could scout the town from the trees. Twilight strangers were not welcome, and he wanted all abed before he entered.

Early afternoon brought them to a series of rolling descents, each rise and dip lower and more stretched out than the last. The brush, never cleared, ran wild. Atop the last low mound they stopped.

The country kept getting stranger. Before them a valley opened up, the entrance flanked by two imposing sentinels, natural keeps of solid rock that faced off in a mutual challenge. The crest of the left hand one rose at a gentle angle and dropped sharply away; the one on the right was a cragged contortion, its peak like a castle of jagged battlements. Dense undergrowth filled the scooped valley between them and clawed its way up their sides.

"They're looking at each other."

"What?" Jettaret turned toward her.

"Waiting. They're guardians. They could close on us."

"No they won't," Jettaret growled.

Liana was gazing straight ahead through the guard gate into the valley. "Jettaret. Why do we have to take this way? It ... no. It isn't the right one."

"It's the best one for now. And you are an ignorant, superstitious peasant." Jettaret moved Pasquale forward and yelled back, "I didn't call you a witch!"

They headed down into the valley. Above the treetops Liana watched the dual rock guardians grow larger. They looked closer together now. The nightmare fortress on the right lacked nothing in intimidation to the left one, a vertical pile of what looked like broken firewood, stacked end up and bleached ash gray from the sun. They could slam inward at any time.

Away, away. Get away. There was a bond, a link between the two cliffs, and Liana shuddered, reined to the right and struck Bluestone into a fast lope.

"Liana! Where are you going—hold up! We can't take this pace, it's a long way to go still—ahh!" He spurred after her, caught up in three strides and, seizing Bluestone's bridle, brought them both down to a walk.

The Witch's Hand

"I thought you knew how to keep your head. What's this about? Hm? She did not answer. "All right." He let go of Bluestone's headstall. "Play falcon and break like that again and I put you on a lead." He rode ahead coldly. "We've too much ground to cover for acts of idiocy."

Vespers found them slowly crossing a wide field that had known sheep but not a plow. Sunset's rose gold was interrupted by a brownish haze hovering over a thick bank of trees ahead of them, town dust. Orcival. Jettaret rode on with his head bent, scanning the ground. No hoof prints. Orcival still didn't have a Watch.

Bluestone was lagging behind. Jettaret reined around, trotted back, and saw Liana was half asleep in the saddle, her head unsteady and eyes nearly closed.

"Not much further, girl. Hold on." He reached over to brace her sagging shoulders and she almost fell off against his arm—God, she was thin. Only a kid but her stamina—no. He didn't want to think where that came from. "Almost there."

They approached the edge of the field. In front of them the bank of trees fell away down a slope, and through the dust beyond rose the spired hexagonal tower of a church. Jettaret pulled up.

"Is Malaxia around?"

Liana shook her head.

"Think you can stay out of trouble for half an hour?"

Liana nodded.

"Wait here." He rode forward a few steps, peering through the deepening shadows into the trees. Then he swung down and led Pasquale back. "Here." He handed Liana the reins. "Better if they don't know I'm mounted." He eyed her and added, "And don't make me regret this." He unsheathed Fortuna Domini, drew the folds of his cloak around it and vanished into the woods.

All was quiet below. Jettaret waited till darkness was complete and the stars icy lanterns, then made his way down the slope and came out facing the lengthwise nave of the church, near the entrance. He paused there.

Not yet. Check the square first. He moved alongside the church's cold stone wall, past the cross wing of the transept. The apse, the portion around and behind the altar, jutted out in a peculiar formation. Its one circular wall had four smaller abutments above, like round towers halved and joined onto it. The roof tiles of the large tower flowed out onto the smaller roofs, making them look as though they'd grown from the main one.

The town square lay behind, not in front of this church. The moon had not yet risen; the stones of the square were blue and silent. Jettaret cast his hood over his face and stole forward.

In the middle of the square was a well. Jettaret crossed to it and stood there, alone in the starlight. There was no sound. A haphazard collection of shops and houses lay ranged around him and he couldn't see the hanging shop signs well, half starlit, half in shadow as they were. He went to one side of the square and started around it.

A long wooden sign banged him in the head. *Prime merde—!* Sunrise shite; he held the oath in his teeth, and grabbed for the swinging sign. It was carved into a long loaf of bread, a baguette, but a sniff found no scent of a banked fire behind the door, not yesterday's bread, nor yeast for tomorrow's. It smelled more like a leather shop, one that had been dyeing ox hides, from oxen that had been dead for a while. He tried the door. It was closed and locked. He hesitated, looked around back at the square, the church, the line of darkened casements. He would break in here only if necessary.

Oh. There was the reason for the oxhide smell; the shop next door was a tannery, a large one. He moved past it, looking for the bed and barrel sign that said inn and tavern. Or at least a barrel. His wineskin had more of goat innards about it than vintage, and that was sour and mostly water now. He continued down the square.

A cat yowled, a long screech; he froze. There was another short yowl, then something clattered. Then silence.

He passed into a dark enclave. It was an entryway; he felt for the sign overhead but found none. The Guild Hall? He made out a plank-shuttered window, a door beyond, and stepped close, concluding from the smell it was a tavern. The door did not give, and there were no sounds within. He gripped the ends of the shutters and tried them, but they were barred from the inside. Tavern definitely closed. He would hear no whispers tonight.

The Witch's Hand

Jettaret headed back toward the church, a lone figure crossing the square. He kept his eyes open for whichever building might be the priory but couldn't distinguish it. He turned toward the church again; it was the Eve of St. Julius, and someone might be keeping vigil by the altar inside.

St. Julius. Pope in 337, over eight hundred years ago, when the Arian heretics were still disputing Christ's divinity. The First Council of Nicea had spelled it all out in precise detail back in 325, but some people were slow to learn, and then reluctant to adhere to it. Some people were slow about everything. Like figuring out what heresy was. The first Christians were heretics to the orthodox Jews and the Romans, Abelard had been a heretic to Bernard and his followers less than a hundred years ago, the Church itself was split between Rome and the Constantinople heretics. And now there was a new heresy in the South; Albigensians, they were called, from their being gathered around the town of Albi. They held the Arian-derived teaching that all physical, material things were evil—the entire world in other words, including people. They might have something there.

We're all heretics.

He approached the side door of the church—the main door was too noticeable—and knocked. He waited, knocked again. Footsteps shuffled on the stones within.

"*Sanctum Sepulchrum,*" Holy Sepulchre, "who's there?" The voice within was weary.

"A pilgrim."

The door opened and a rotund monk stood illuminated within the frame. He carried not a candle but a cresset, a bowl of oil with a floating wick, which could be slung from a ceiling chain or suspended, as it was now, from a U-shaped holder atop a short staff and used as a torch. In the light Jettaret could see lice crawling in his cowl. Must be a very holy man; no thought for his own person, only God.

"What do you want?"

"Bread, if you have any. For the Virgin's sake."

The monk shook his head. "We've little enough—"

Fortuna Domini glittered cold in the starlight. "And the blessings of Christ and all the saints be on you," Jettaret added.

"Come in."

Jettaret stepped through the door. "You are alone, and late," observed the monk. "Are you stopping here for the night?"

"Thank you, no." He felt the monk's relief. "I am on my way to St. Martin de la Tours and cannot stop."

"You won't get there till after Matins."

"The moon will guide me, and I don't wish to stay." He turned toward the monk. "I've heard there are witches in this area."

"No, not since last fall, St. Michel be praised." He led the way up the nave toward the altar, his cresset throwing an amber circle of light around them as they moved through the darkness. The monk's station was on the bare floor, some yards short of the transept; beyond, black iron grillwork closed off the altar.

"Here." The monk undid the cresset from the staff and set it on the floor. Besides an open prayer book, Jettaret could see a lumpy sack lying half in darkness. The end nearest the book was open, and just inside was a half-eaten loaf of bread. This was not a fasting vigil.

The monk groped through the little hoard in his sack and gave Jettaret a small bundle wrapped in cloth. It was hard, and crackled when he pressed it. Twice baked bread then, with little or no yeast, monastery and siege fare, pilgrim crackers, stuff for nuns in Lent. The loaf the monk had been working on was full with leaven, plump, rich and dark. The others in the sack were smaller, varlet's loaves the size of a fist. With less hurry the monk handed him a small wineskin, barely large enough to fill one flagon. His own monastic issue wineskin was considerably larger, and he stood strategically placed between it and Jettaret. *Son of a sow,* Jettaret thought.

Now the monk looked nervously around at nonexistent things on the walls. "I am expecting other vigilants soon—"

I'll bet you are. "Thank you, you've been most kind. Do remember me to St. Julius in your prayers, won't you?"

"Assuredly."

Jettaret turned to go. "St. Julius—the Arian prophet, wasn't he?"

"Yes, monsieur."

"You're a good and learned man." *Heretic.*

"I'll light you out, monsieur."

Wants to make sure I go.

The Witch's Hand

Jettaret outpaced him down the aisle and went out the side door. He re-climbed the hill, turning once to look back down. The church was so quiet. He wished he could go back. *No. To Lyon. With Liana. I am going to Lyon.* Fatigue hit him; he trudged on up, dragging the rest of the way. He reached the top and saw Bluestone, riderless.

"Liana? Liana!" She was at first nowhere in sight. Then he spied her, a tiny heap in the bushes. Life shot through him again; he sprinted over to where she lay. She was asleep, but in an awkward position, and he realized she must have slipped from the saddle and remained where she'd hit, too spent to move. He reached for her shoulder and stopped. *Careful.* Her neck was twisted.

"Liana." She did not stir. "Liana, wake up. It's Jettaret, wake up. Wiggle your toes."

"What?" She opened her eyes, barely.

"Wiggle your toes, don't ask why, wiggle your toes!" Her toes wiggled slowly. "Good. Now move your hands—careful—just a little." Her right hand moved; her left was hidden somewhere beneath her.

"I'm stuck."

"You fell off."

"What?" She pushed herself unsteadily up. "Where's Bluestone—ow."

"Right here. You're lucky you landed in this stuff. Rocks wouldn't have been as kind." He helped her sit up. "Careful. Where do you hurt?"

She didn't answer for a moment, then in a small voice said, "Everywhere."

He reached out and steadied her shoulder. "You're doing all right. You rode further today than we did most days on the Crusade."

Her eyes got bright. "I did? As good as a Crusader?"

"As good as a Crusader." He looked away, silent.

Later in the night a soft thump close by woke him. Hand on Fortuna Domini, he listened. Another thump and a rustle, like an animal snuffling around, in Liana's direction. The noise continued erratically. He rose on one elbow, shoving hair out of his eyes—he had to get to a barber soon—and looked. The horses were quiet, and there was no sign of Malaxia.

It was Liana. Still asleep, she was kicking and twisting under her blanket. He moved toward her slowly; whatever she was brewing, he didn't want it coming in his direction. When he reached her, he stayed away from her feet, cautiously found her arms through the blankets and took hold of them. Immediately awake, she tried to turn away.

"Liana. Girl. What's the matter?" He held her still and his tone softened. "What is it? Thinking about home?"

"I'm afraid." It came out like a puppy's whimper. Jettaret drew her up and began to rock her like a child.

"Of what? Malaxia?" He felt her shudder.

"All those people down there—they want to kill me—and I'm all alone."

"You've got me." The only sound for a few moments was the wind in the grass.

"No. I'm alone anyway."

"That Greek fire of yours trying to get out again?"

She moved her head 'No' and pulled away, sinking down. *He didn't understand about the apartness of being a witch*

"Think you can keep it under wraps?"

"Yes."

Jettaret did not rest well that night. Sometime in the early hours between Matins and Lauds he dreamed that one of the magic spheres was bearing down on him from behind; he turned aside as it went past him with a vicious sound, slicing the air. The shock of it sat him upright.

Liana was asleep.

10. BANDITS!

Dawn found them working their way slowly along a ridge. Ahead lay barren hills ringed with fog at the top. Jettaret pushed on relentlessly, knowing they had to get over this chain and down to better country soon. The grass was sparse and too new, too short; it was worse up here than he'd thought.

At mid-morning he stopped to assess the horses. His staunch, strong-winded Pasquale was getting a haggard look, and Bluestone was positively bony. Liana sat silent. Since daybreak she had not said a word. Fatigue lay on her like a leaden robe; she'd ceased to see the surroundings, then Bluestone's black-tipped ears before her disappeared. But her eyes were still not vacant.

When the sun reached its height and the monk back in Orcival would be chanting Sext if he was keeping his hours, Liana felt a sudden *snap* through the reins, though Bluestone hadn't jerked her head. Jettaret saw; he pulled up and dismounted quickly, taking hold of Bluestone's headstall.

"It's almost ready to go . . . hold still." Still holding onto the headstall, he reached into one of Pasquale's saddle bags, scrabbled around and pulled out a long leather line. "Whoa . . . whoa . . ." He ran it beneath and around the parted leather by Bluestone's ears, up and back, figure-eighting it snugly together.

"Jettaret. Someone's coming."

He stood alert and looked about. "No. You're going trail blind, girl. There's nobody there."

"There is."

He checked again. They were alone. She had the desert blindness, seeing water and towns where there were none. This wasn't a desert, but the girl was weird.

> *Is there no one at this well of mercy*
> *To draw a cup of cold water for me?*
> *Does no one hear? Is it nothing to you?*
> *I have desert fever; will no one do*

The smallest act to save a cruciato's life?

A dark horseman, an Arab horse
From far away he comes to us
Hola, hola!
Rider, halt!
He sees; thank God, he sees
On his way to somewhere else
He stops here

I give you water as a friend
Tomorrow, an enemy
I will kill you

The sword and scimitar sing far off
He rides to them
The desert stays
A watchman till the rider returns

"It sounded better in Latin." Jettaret handed his wineskin to Liana. "The Arabs taught me about courtesy. The desert was not a very courteous place."

"What were they like?"

He didn't answer right away. "Like us, in some ways. Different in others. They dressed differently. They prayed different." Jettaret took the wineskin back when Liana had finished and drank slowly, his eyes watching from instinct rather than Liana's trail-blind warning.

They continued up the ridge. At the crest the ground fell away into bare, uneven folds, descending into a shallow valley, and Liana stared at what lay on the other side.

They were level with the hills of the morning, which were conical, with wide spreading slopes. But some were only half hills. The fog on top had cleared and revealed that their summits were gone, sliced off and scooped into flattened bowls. Streams of fog stretched between them and floated in the hollows on top.

"What happened to them?"

Jettaret glanced back at her, waited a stride and replied, "Some say a giant came along and took his sword to them," the mischief in his eyes averted from Liana. She twisted around in her saddle, looking for signs of the giant. Jettaret smiled.

"It happened a long time ago."

They crossed the valley and skirted the chain of hills, their path curving continuously but still bearing north. The hills—giant lopped or created by divine conceit—remained on their right. Liana kept watching them.

"Jettaret. Lyon's on the other side. You said it was toward the east."

"Good girl. A little more Euclid and you could draw maps. There's a pass a little further up."

He began to veer right and soon the hills were on both sides of them. The highest one rose in grand self acknowledgment to the north. Its crown was broad but not scooped; it still rounded upward the way a mountain usually did. From the ridgeline, silhouetted against the sky, was what looked like a giant torch head, broken in pieces, atop a short column. Jettaret nodded toward it.

"The Romans used to worship Mercury there—pagan, like a druid, sort of; messenger of the gods, protector of travelers. We're in good company, if you believe in that." Pagan country. Witch country.

"Who were the Romans—never mind. Lyon. I can wait."

Good. She was learning when to shut up. There was no whining in her question, no underlying attempt to annoy him. She'd asked who the Romans were because she wanted to know, with the same straightforwardness she would have had if she'd asked what the name of a strange town was. There was no deception in her. She rode along, slightly ahead of him, a small girl on a tired horse, unpretentious.

And she had destroyed a forest.

Enough. Don't think, too much. Keep moving, keep going. Get the horses out of here. Stick to your plan.

What plan? Situation, untenable; solution, unknown. He doubted he could hold Liana back if her powers broke loose again.

Jettaret glanced at Liana—there was something like a puppy just out of water about her—and deliberated their course. The Temple of Mercury marked the last turning point. Due east now, toward Clermont-Ferrand, but cut south to avoid the city, and head for Lyon via Issoire. He didn't think any post riders would have brought news of Liana to either city yet, but better to avoid them all the same.

They had begun to descend into flatter, rolling country, leaving the scooped domes behind, when Pasquale took a sudden misstep.

"Uh-oh." Jettaret was off and examining Pasquale's near foreleg, lifting the hoof with care. Liana would have run into him if Bluestone hadn't had the equine aversion to stepping on things that went squish.

"What is it?" she asked.

"Stone bruise."

"I didn't do it."

He looked at her and set Pasquale's hoof down. "No. But we'll have to find an inn now. With a decent stable. Nothing here to make a poultice."

"Yes there is, I can find stuff—"

"No you don't. Wander off again and God knows what you'll bring back, a demon this time, the Devil himself maybe, I'm not taking chances—" Once more Jettaret looked at her. *Not with you.*

"I shouldn't expect you to trust me."

"No." That grave insight again. This girl was no dumb peasant—all right, even if she wasn't a witch—*I'll be skewered if I know what she is.*

Jettaret led Pasquale down the path at a slower pace, the sun at their backs now; it was somewhere around Nones. He unslung his wineskin for a drink but didn't stop to pray the hour.

Their shadows were growing longer before them when a faint, muffled thump of hoofbeats reached them, from ahead. Liana's head and the horses' ears sprang alert at the same time. Jettaret reined Pasquale to a halt and listened.

"Come on." He made for a sparse cover of brush and rocks, and they concealed the horses as well as they could. Jettaret crouched and drew Liana down behind him. "Down."

She listened as the hoofbeats neared and stopped.

"It's not her."

"No, bandits." Jettaret drew his sword. He'd been wrong about the area's remoteness. Three, four horses—he couldn't be sure.

The Witch's Hand

Dismounted. Aware we're here. Heard us as we heard them. Could be coming around us—below or above? The trail they followed was on a steep hill; it bent around a shelf of boulders and vanished.

Looking about, he saw an undecided Liana eye his sword—and extend her hands. Preparation for only one thing.

"No!" He struck her hands down with the flat of his blade.

"Ow!"

"Don't you see? The more you use your power, the more hold it has over you. Now stay down."

Two figures emerged on the trail from behind the boulders. They moved in a half crouch, furtive, but they hadn't seen Liana and Jettaret yet.

Weasels. Fortuna Domini lay drawn in his hand, low to the ground and turned away from the sun to avoid throwing a reflection. Its point rested on a rotted, half buried branch. The bandit in the lead paused, tilted his head toward Jettaret and Liana, continued on; the other followed, bent like a hound on a scent. *Cautious bastards, I'll grant you that.*

Then Pasquale snorted. *St. Michel, not now—* Jettaret was up and out of the bushes before the bandits saw him coming; he smashed a branch aside, leaped a rock and fell upon them. The leader managed a mangled parry as Jettaret drove Fortuna Domini's hilt to the midblade of his sword and ripped it away to the right, rebounding back with his dagger to slash the man across the throat. Gurgling blood, he fell, dust and vermin puffing from his rags as he hit the ground. Jettaret kicked him savagely down the hill.

Broadsword and dagger ready, he went for the second one out of a crouch. The rogue didn't flinch but his courage, or catatonia, was wasted; Crusader steel and fighting speed whipped his short sword away, and Fortuna Domini drew blood this time as Jettaret coldly sliced his sword arm at the shoulder—the man was *à bras sinistre*, a lefty—nearly taking it off. He would lose the arm if he didn't bleed to death outright. The bandit wavered toward the edge of the trail and went down, but held his footing enough to keep from going over.

"Uhh!" Liana gasped as an arm snaked around her from behind and a third bandit yanked her backward. She flailed and twisted, straining; her arms were free but she fought the dynamo that drew them upward, force surging through her hands—*don't use them, hold them down, don't use your magic—*

Jettaret turned and saw the bandit with Liana. Her eyes grew ferocious in her fighting, as she warped and writhed like a trapped squirrel, then shoved back hard and forced the bandit half-way around, off balance. But there were no explosions. She was keeping her magic under control. Jettaret leaped forward.

The bandit put a rusty knife to Liana's stomach. Bad; it looked ready to break at the hilt but at gut level it could do a Pandora's box of damage. Jettaret halted, hesitant. He let his dagger fall, then Fortuna Domini's point lowered and clanged to the ground. He turned back and away in defeat. The bandit's eyes went bright with disbelief but he had no time to celebrate, for in dropping the great sword Jettaret had moved toward the second bandit's forgotten sword; it was in his hand and he'd flung it backward *without even looking*—Liana couldn't believe that—and the bandit holding her went down, struck in the leg. She wriggled out of his grasp before he could fall on her; he wasn't very big but dead weight turned a small man into an ox. His knife clattered to the ground. She grabbed it as he started to rise and stabbed him in the front, low of center where there wasn't any bone. Blood arced across her hands as he fell forward. Liana looked at Jettaret.

"I can do it the old fashioned way. Can't I?"

A scratching on the rocks above sent their attention up. A fourth bandit stood there, his sword brandished high, ready to jump, while the second bandit plunged forward, bleeding profusely from the shoulder, the first bandit's hiltless blade in his other hand. Jettaret dove for Fortuna Domini but was still defenseless as the bandit above leaped. Liana was without a choice. She flung both hands out, one low, one high; the bleeding bandit went down, and the one from above slammed back up to the crest of the rocks, toppled, and fell down the other side. A long way down. His scream rose to a hideous pitch and they could follow the length of his fall as it faded, and was gone. His goat hide spoils sack dropped almost on top of them; Jettaret had Fortuna Domini now, and spitted it from the ground before it hit. It was empty. The leather, he noted, was dry and cracked nearly through in places. Business must be bad. He flipped it away.

The Witch's Hand

The irrepressible second bandit refused to bleed to death and forced the attack again. He made it to within two feet of Jettaret's boots before Fortuna Domini cut him down, and he slipped over the edge without a sound.

Jettaret retrieved his dagger. He stooped and wiped the blood and gunk off both blades onto the sprawled third bandit's clothes—he wasn't going to soil his own with it—sheathed his dagger and strode toward Liana. His knuckles were white around Fortuna Domini's hilt. He took no pleasure, no gratification in his work; he was a master at killing and it revolted him.

Liana sat shamefaced, her head down, both hands knotted on her knees. Jettaret walked up to her deliberately, stopped and planted his sword, point down, in front of her. Slowly she looked up the blade to his face. She spoke first, Jettaret overlapping her.

"I'm sorry."

"Thank you."

Jettaret let out a short breath and settled Fortuna Domini in its sheath. "This once it's all right. Unless we meet other bandits." He pulled her to her feet. She looked at the dead third bandit, then out past the cliff.

"May the angels lead them—"

"This bunch?" Jettaret snorted. "Well, where there're bandits there's an inn. I'll go up there," he indicated a nearby summit, "and look for it." He glanced at the sky, which was clouded over and threatening. "Maybe we can get there before it rains."

"It'll rain but it will be over soon."

Jettaret stared at her. "How do you—no. No." He looked at the sky again. "Witch or saint," he pointed skyward "nobody can do that. Stay here and watch the horses." He continued along the path.

Liana went over to Bluestone and stroked her head. "But I can tell when it will rain. And when it will stop." Then she heard footsteps behind her and drew back between the horses.

A pair of dusty old shoes vied with a walking stick for dominion of the narrow path. Peering from under Bluestone's neck, Liana saw an old, shabbily dressed woman picking her way slowly along, but coming unerringly toward her. The woman stopped a short distance away, and Liana stepped forward to see her better.

The old woman looked at Liana without eye contact. "Ah. I have found you." Her voice was as withered as her face.

Liana was unsure. "Malaxia?"

"No, no. Just an old woman who felt like going for a walk. To find someone."

Liana cautiously waved a hand in front of the woman's face and realized she was blind. Not the egg white kind, though. She smelled not as a weary, dusty traveler would but clean, like fresh soda soap, and her weathered, wrinkled skin had an odd translucent glow from beneath, as if the sunset behind shone right through her.

"Malaxia. I know her, child." Liana was apprehensive. "Oh no, I am not of her ... origins. Or practices. She chose me once, when I was your age, and you see what I have become." Liana drew back. "No, not evil, child; I was unequal to any power. But you—you are in danger. You will become as her, unless you can control your power, your will toward what she would have you be. You may come to love it, and then there is no hope, for you must destroy all to return, every thing and everyone you cherish."

"But I have nothing, no one—" Liana spotted Jettaret coming back up the path and realized there was still one left with value to her, who her powers endangered. "No ..."

"A monk well versed in witches told me this."

Jettaret had increased his pace when he saw the old woman and now stepped between them quickly.

"Liana, are you all right? Has this crone done anything to you? She isn't—"

Liana shook her head, whispering, "No."

The old woman held Jettaret's suspicious gaze, strength for strength. "I have done nothing but tell her the truth."

"Yes, well, I know the sort of truth mad old women know. Come on, Liana." Jettaret started to pull her away by the arm but she resisted.

"No, wait." Liana went up to the old woman and placed a hand over the gnarled hand on the stick. "If I were you I would thank God for not being what she wanted."

"I do, child. Every day." The old woman placed her other hand over Liana's. "You are not all hers yet. I will pray for you."

"I wish I could for you."

The old woman's nod held the understanding that prayer was impossible for a witch. "I do not need your prayers. I have made my peace and will die soon. You," she hesitated, "may not die for hundreds of years."

Liana drew back in horror.

"Liana—" Jettaret hauled her away. "Stay away from women older than you are. Just to be safe."

Liana said, "I don't know what safe is anymore," but in her own ears and by Jettaret's staring reaction realized the words had come out in a strange language, full of fluid vowels and soft consonants, one she did not know. *"N'ar mahth a cuinna sheeya."* Her horror increased so much that Jettaret had to pick her up and place her in the saddle; she could barely move, much less mount by herself.

"How did you know that?"

"I didn't." Liana was white-faced. "It came out on its own, by itself; I didn't even think about it. Am I making sense now?" Jettaret nodded. "What was it?"

"I don't know. An old Druid tongue, I think. Try not to do it again." They had to get out of here. Weird women showing up out of nowhere, Liana speaking a language she did not know—this was dangerous ground. He spurred Pasquale ahead.

The old woman listened to them ride away, her head cocked up in their direction. She raised a hand in benediction, then bent again, turned about and continued back the opposite way.

One league away, Malaxia moved down a path through the woods, her raiment flowing about her without once getting caught in the needles and leaves hedging inward as she swept by. Her brow was set, brooding; she looked like an eagle whose eggs had not yet become hatchlings. Normally, the thought of the responsibilities regarding her craft was not a burden. Now it was.

Acolytes were rare in her art, each one with a host of possibilities. Liana was a jewel whose cutting and polish would reveal unequaled illumination; she was priceless. Malaxia had not been absolutely sure at first about when to commence the work, but since the testing of the magic storm, she was certain. The girl must be guided with great care and discipline along the path, and it was time to begin. Malaxia sensed correctly that Liana could not be bullied or coerced, that she had something of a badger's ferocity about doing anything against her will, and that her powers of comprehension were *la puissance*, strong, but volatile as quicksilver. She would not learn the needed skills if she didn't want to. Training her could well be like putting silver through a crucible for both teacher and student, but this one would be a masterwork, one who could draw the ignorant into enlightenment. And they would follow. She smiled. Oh yes. This one they would follow.

Malaxia caught a faint whiff of burnt pork and knew she was close to her destination. The tall witch hurried.

11. *ALBERGE*

Jettaret checked the sky behind. Dark clouds loomed up out of the west and moved eastwards above the trail ahead, but there was still no rain. He reined in and spotted what he sought in the wooded vale below—a small, ramshackle inn, with a stable and what looked like a storage outbuilding. Four horses stood in the yard, probably the bandits' and therefore probably stolen. He headed down the hill toward the inn, Liana following slowly. Then she caught up with him.

"Jettaret."

"Hm?"

"You studied, in Paris?"

Jettaret nodded.

"You know things from the doctors there, you learned about witches, maybe?"

Jettaret shrugged assent.

"Can you make me ... not a witch?"

Jettaret looked at her, regretful.

"No, Liana. I can watch you, try to keep you from using—whatever it is, but I can't get rid of it for you. I'm sorry."

"I thought not, but thank you."

"For what?"

"For doing what you can."

The sun had not yet set behind them but the dark clouds hid it completely, and as they descended the last low slope to the inn the first drops fell. They quickly got the horses into the stable, and Jettaret made a poultice for Pasquale's hoof out of mud and straw, Liana helping him pack it in around the v-shaped frog inside the hoof's bottom. As they crossed to the inn, the rain hit hard. They dashed the rest of the way to the door.

Jettaret paused in the entryway. Lit by smoky torchlight, the room was filled with travelers and their retinues, some at rough tables, others by the serving counter at the rear. A continual commotion circled about the room, loudest over at the right from the Servants' side. A wooden sign designated this area; hanging from the rafters, it had a rather cheerily favored goat's head painted on it. On the left side of the room hung another sign, this one of a richly antlered stag. The nobility of some of the patrons beneath was questionable, but if their deniers were good and their blades sharp, the innkeeper left them alone. Over an open fire on this side, a pig roasted on a spit.

Liana stepped up alongside Jettaret, then halted as she came eye to eye with an upright torch on the wall. Though she could control fire this size, still she feared it. Jettaret pushed her past the torch and directed her to the right.

"That side. Servant."

Liana looked at the low lifes there and didn't feel very comfortable. "Jettaret, I'm not going over there alone—"

"Yes you are."

"No I'm not." Her soft *sotto voce* still carried weight.

Behind them the door opened again, and Liana rounded with a start, expecting to meet Malaxia. But it was not she. A bent figure brushed past them, and the room went silent.

For the man wore a yellow hat that looked like a pointed mushroom top, with a yellow patch on the front of his cloak, and on his way to the serving counter people moved back and crossed themselves; some spat at him.

"Christ killer!" one hissed.

"Jettaret. Who's that?" Liana whispered.

"A Jew," he answered, and saw her trepidation. "Don't worry," he cast an eye around, "there are worse Christians. He won't hurt you. Now over to the Servants' side."

"Jetta—"

"I'll be right here." Jettaret was impatient. "Now I'm thirsty. Scoot. And act like a servant." Liana went, unwillingly. "And no ..." he waved his hand in a magic gesture. Liana nodded, and continued into the Servants' side as Jettaret muttered to himself, "Or they'll burn us both."

Liana made her way through the Servants' tables to a quiet corner. She stopped by a large, slovenly man seated at a table, finishing off what looked like hog slops.

"Excuse me, may I sit here?"

The Witch's Hand

He sat slobbering and made no sign that he had heard her, and after a moment she sat down.

Jettaret headed to the serving counter, of darkened oak, which curved outwards and had an opening on the Servants' side. There the Jew was speaking in a deferential voice to the innkeeper, who shook his head.

"There's no rooms here, or wine, for you," the innkeeper said.

"I know," replied the Jew, tired and patient. "May I have some water, please?"

The innkeeper didn't move. Jettaret stepped up to the counter and ordered two stoops of wine, signaling to a server that one go to Liana. When they were brought, he handed his to the Jew, and met the innkeeper's aghast look.

"I'll have another," he said. With one hand on Fortuna Domini's hilt, he dropped several deniers on the counter, and the innkeeper grudgingly brought him a new tankard. The Jew drained his, and turned to go. The innkeeper threw the empty cup into the corner slop barrel.

"Thank you," murmured the Jew to Jettaret.

Jettaret nodded and watched the man leave. Then he noticed a pair of eyes set upon him.

Across the room to his left, a cloaked figure sat hunched over a trestle table. His hood was up, and as he bent to his drink his features disappeared into shadow. A tall, pike-sized staff leaned against the wall behind him. Jettaret kept one eye on him as he watched the server take Liana's wine past.

A cretinous old man near her, with a small goat's stomach bagpipe, launched into an estampie, the melody strange. The nasal piping rose above the din and picked up speed. Two peasants started to dance, then another joined them, and suddenly there was a circle of dancers, blocking the winebearer's way. The bagpipe's incessant whine grew faster; the tune the piper played was from *Outremer*, the Holy Land Oversea, God's tree-forsaken desert, where the Crusaders had fought and died. Jettaret watched to make sure Liana finally got her wine. She'd earned it.

"What I'd give for a wench like that to follow me around."

Jettaret turned and saw an ox of a man with an arrogant bearing, one eye on Liana. His reply was cool. "She's not for sale."

"Aye, but maybe her services are?"

A flicker of amusement lit Jettaret's eyes. "You'd find her services far beyond you. I don't use them myself."

The ox man eyed Jettaret and laughed. "I never met one of you before. Well, if you can't teach her, I can." To the Servants' side he called, "Franz! Bring the little wench over here!"

The big peasant sitting next to Liana reached out and grabbed the girl dancing in front of him.

"No, the other one!"

Franz picked Liana up and started over to the Gentles' side.

"No!" Liana fought to not use her hands. "Jettaret!"

In two strides Jettaret was across the floor with drawn sword at Franz's throat. The bagpipe and dancing stopped.

"Put her down. Drop her!" Franz did. "Touch her again and I will gullet you." The ox man loomed behind; Jettaret wheeled and put Fortuna Domini to his crotch. "Deride my manhood again and you will be picking yours off the floor." He sliced the money bag from the man's belt; he bent to get it, but Jettaret held his chin up with the flat of his blade.

"A fine, sir, if you please. For insulting the young lady, and dishonoring me, four deniers." The man stooped to get them, but Jettaret held his chin up again. "Wait. What is your rank?"

"Knight. Monsieur Vincent de Chille, chevalier d'Anjou."

"Eight deniers." For the first time in two years Jettaret the Vicomte felt wickedly pleased to pull rank. He smiled. De Chille picked up his purse, got out some silver coins and handed them over, then slunk back to his place and nursed his drink. Liana and Franz returned to the Servants' side, Franz keeping a good distance from her; she sat at the furthest table, trying to be inconspicuous. Jettaret went back to the counter to get his drink, when the stranger who'd been watching him spoke.

"The Vicomte de Solignac. Defending a lady's honor." The basso growl from the hood seemed to find the idea enormously amusing. His curiosity and memory piqued, Jettaret still had the courtesy for an automatic, "At your service and the king's—" when the stranger put his hood back.

"Alberge!"

The Witch's Hand

"The same. But not the same." True enough. The craggy face, black eyes lost in deep creases, and coiled black hair were unmistakable. But the eyes had less focus, the devilish gleam was more cynical, and the hair, though thick where it was left, had receded more, and now was streaked with gray.

"I thought you were dead."

The voice he'd heard beside him for three years growled again. "I was. I came back." Alberge nodded toward a tarnished crucifix on the wall, a tarnished twinkle in his eye. "Men have been known to do that."

"I don't believe this."

"Then I am the most solid ghost you ever saw." Alberge took a long quaff from his tankard, still watching Jettaret, and shoved a half eaten loaf toward him.

"But here, in this quarter, miles from anywhere? At Antioch I thought you were through. I was going to run you through then, end your suffering. But I couldn't."

"Oh?" Alberge nursed the irony of the word. "You seemed to enjoy it enough in Constantinople. Killing, taking, wenches, money; one was like the other. Putting a whore on the altar of Hagia Sophia."

"I was mad then."

"We all were. Twenty thousand mad men, running around in a burning city, taking whatever we could get. Christians. I wonder what God thinks of us. Or our glorious Crusade. Save the Holy Land! Fight for Jerusalem!—city of peace. I meant to ask you, if I lived to see you again. Did you make it there?

Jettaret gave a slow nod. "Yes, I did."

"Was it worth it?"

"No."

"I didn't think so, but I wanted to be sure." An odd sad smile played around Alberge's mouth. "Thank you."

"What are you doing now?" Jettaret queried. "And how did you get back? I looked for you on the way home but couldn't find you."

"You didn't look in the right part of town." Alberge bent to his drink again. Over on the Servants' side, the bagpiper picked up a wooden reed pipe and began to play a slow, plaintive air, once more from *Outremer*.

Wendy Joseph

"Are there any Christians here?" There was an odd looking piece of wood on the door jamb, and Alberge wondered if it were some sort of amulet. He knocked again, the movement making the burning in his left ankle shriek. The door opened, and a forty-ish woman in the dress of the East came out and knelt by him. A bearded man her age and a younger man he supposed was their son came out and helped take him inside, his teeth clenched so hard he felt one break.

"In Antioch a family of Jews took me in. I found they're not the monsters these people think they are, as we were taught, Antoine. I was lying near dead at their doorstep, and it was their Passover. There's a part in the ceremony that says anyone who is hungry or wanting, can come in."

Inside, an elderly man sat before an assortment of food—flat crackers, hard-boiled eggs, some sort of sweet meats, a sheep shank and a bowl of greens. He held a small book open before him. The woman tended to Alberge's foot, trying to be gentle, as the other two resumed their seats. In the shadows, he spied a girl not yet twenty. The old man read aloud as he held up one of the crackers.

"This is the bread of affliction, which our ancestors ate in the land of Egypt. Let all those who are hungry, enter and eat thereof, and all who are in distress, come and celebrate the Passover. At present we celebrate it here, but next year we hope to celebrate it in the land of Israel. This year we are servants here, but next year we hope to be free men in the land of Israel; next year, in Jerusalem."

Through the crowded room, Jettaret watched Liana, who looked small and alone against the wall.

Alberge continued, "Christian though I was, they took me inside and gave me food and care till I was well. A stranger, and a Crusader. Well, I stayed there some time; even took a fancy to one of the daughters. I couldn't pronounce her name, so I called her Morianno, like the song." His raspy bass rumbled forth, drowning out the nasal reed pipe.

Lo bouolé lo Morianno!
Lo bouolé maï l'ourraï!
L'onoraï you, quéré!
l'inménoraï!
Molgré soun païré
l'espousoraï!
I want Marianne!
I want her, I will have her!

*I will go look for her
and lead her here!
In spite of her papa,
I will marry her!*

"But to marry her, and," he then noticed Jettaret wasn't paying attention, and waved a hand in front of his face, "and she wouldn't have me on any other terms, I would have had to turn Jew. The beliefs didn't matter too much; they do nothing on Saturdays, there are rules for eating—"

Jettaret watched a man at the next table slobbering over a haunch of roasted pig in his hand. *Should be some rules here.*

"—but there is the matter of circumcision." Alberge shifted uncomfortably and settled himself again on the bench. "And what is marriage? The first year, nose to nose; the second year, arm in arm; the third year, break camp. So, I bid my sweetheart farewell, thanked her and her family for saving my life and all their other kindnesses, and made my way back to Provence."

Alberge saw Jettaret's attention was again distracted; he seemed to be watching the far wall on the Servants' side, but there were too many people in between to see what he was looking at. The piper there ended his piece, and the uneven cadences of conversation resumed.

"Despite the Pope's injunction against it, I discovered my brother-in-law's family, supposing me dead, had seized all my land. It would have meant a long battle, legal or otherwise, to get it back, and I am tired of fighting."

"Where was Aurore?"

Alberge stared into his tankard. "Plague took her. Before I got back. And the two boys." He ran his fingers along the tankard's handle. "I thought of turning monk, but the Church disgusts me, Antoine. I cannot stand incense now; holy water, chanting appalls me. The ranks of candles—they remind me of ourselves, so bright, so naïve—so soon out." Slowly and deliberately, Alberge put the table candle out with his finger. Then he straightened up.

"Well, 'tis getting late. Suppose we go up to my chamber and talk about old times—" He reached behind him for his six foot staff and lurched up, but sank back down in pain.

"Alberge?"

"Oh, a little memento from our days of glorious conquest." Alberge leaned his staff against the bench. "Remember the Turk who put his spear in my boot?"

"Yes, and I remember the sound of his head as it hit the ground." Jettaret patted his sword. "Like a bad melon."

A gleam escaped the narrow slits of Alberge's eyes. "I see you haven't lost the touch. Still ready at the blade at the first opportunity."

Jettaret glanced over at De Chille. "In the old days I would have spitted him."

"Yes, I know," Alberge replied dryly. "Antoine the Mad! The Bloody Vicomte! I think you wanted to rack up more Infidel kills than anyone else."

"I did."

Alberge stared levelly at him. "Had any women yet?" Jettaret's eyes said it was pointless to answer. "Still can't, huh?" Alberge slammed his tankard on the table. "More ale!"

Over at the next table, a relic seller held up a tiny piece of wood to a prospective buyer. "And here—a splinter of the True Cross." Jettaret snorted.

Alberge looked on with benign detachment. "Yes. Of course he has a piece of the True Cross." He pointed to a nearby pilgrim, designated so by a rough cross sewn to his tunic. "So does he. There are forests of them." A plump and buxom serving maid came and refilled his tankard. Alberge eyed her, but she moved away.

"Alberge." Jettaret spoke softly. "How stupid we were."

"Were, and are." Alberge drank. "They are calling for another Crusade."

"No."

Alberge set his tankard down. "I heard it last Sunday. You'd think after four tries they'd have learned. Same appeal, same tax—ten per cent for the Church, twenty per cent for us—even the same songs."

Arise, arise ye faithful;
Arise, arise!
Gird on the sword and buckler;
Arise, arise!

Hasten to the help of Christ;
He leads on to victory.
Arise, arise ye faithful;
Arise, arise!

Jettaret heard himself joining in to sing the old battle cry but the words were bitter in his mouth.

Alberge continued, "You asked what I am doing now. I am going about the country as a revered, battle-scarred Crusader, telling people to stay home. Forget the Crusades. They are a way for popes and kings to make money at our expense. I am, of course, in danger of being branded a heretic. So I spend my time in out of the way places like this, one night here, two nights there; they haven't caught me yet." He drained his tankard. "*Vive la vin!*" long live wine. Then he glanced out the window. "I think it's stopped raining." It had.

Jettaret's eyes shot to the window, then to Liana and her proven prediction. She was sitting sideways against the wall and didn't see his look.

Alberge was busy fumbling with the ties to his purse. "Ehh, let's see if I have enough to cover the charges—" The worn purse was nearly empty. "Hmm . . ." He scanned a practiced eye round for the nearest mark. Jettaret recognized that look.

"Alberge—"

"Vicomte, you can avert your priestly eyes." Alberge shoved his bench sideways and back into a knight standing close by. "Oh! My dear sir, a thousand pardons." He turned solicitously toward the knight and straightened his rumpled tunic. "I didn't see you standing there. Are you all right?" The knight's purse fell into Alberge's hand after a deft sweep with his knife, and vanished under his ratty cloak. "I'm so sorry," Alberge indicated his staff and bad foot, "I've gotten rather clumsy of late, since returning from the Holy Land. Do forgive me, there's a good man." The knight nodded to Alberge in a courtly and respectful manner, befitting the cutpurse's Crusader status, and turned back to his companions.

Alberge settled back on the bench. "Well. Will you help an old cripple upstairs, comrade at arms? And you can tell me what you have been up to."

Jettaret rose and helped Alberge up. "I have been consorting with witches—"

"Ehh?"

"I will tell you about it upstairs." They turned toward the stairs at the back, and Jettaret put a steadying hand around his friend's shoulder as Alberge stumbled. He received a growl for thanks. As they passed the serving counter, Alberge slapped two coins on it, and Jettaret indicated the stairs and called to the host, "Let my servant girl know I'm up there if she asks," getting a preoccupied nod in return.

"Servant girl?" Alberge chewed over this piece of information.

"Part of a—an arrangement. At the moment I am on my way to a rather belated wedding—"

"With the lady you told me about on the ship to Venice?"

"Same one." Behind them, the bagpiper started up again in a rousing rhythm and the Servants' side commenced to dance.

"She must be twice mad," Alberge growled. "First to wait and then to have you. Well, hang up one sword and take out another. There is no hope for you, Vicomte. None at all."

They disappeared up the stairs, Alberge clumping awkwardly with his staff. Below, the swirl of dancers and projecting serving counter masked their exit to Liana.

Liana looked into her empty mug. She did not know if Jettaret had ordered any food yet, but as she watched a servant across from her sop up the last of a bowl of soup with a crust, her stomach said he should have. She had no idea if she were allowed to order herself. Vainly, she peered through the dancers to see where Jettaret was, then got up and went to the host at the serving counter.

He was busy near the open side of the counter with an abacus, the counting machine the Crusaders had brought back from the East. Liana waited politely, then coughed to try and get his attention. She turned to the Gentles' side and managed a brave, "Jettaret?" Finally she stepped into the counter opening and tugged at the host's apron.

"My ... my master, Jettaret. He was over there; where is he?"

"I don't know, girl." He sounded mildly annoyed, but checked a pegboard behind him which had big keys on some pegs, signet rings on others. "He hasn't taken a room." The host turned back to the abacus.

The Witch's Hand

Liana stood, slowly searching the Gentles' side, but Jettaret was nowhere in sight. Suddenly she became aware of a large presence behind her. De Chille had seen his chance.

Outside, Malaxia emerged from the woods, stood in the shadows of the trees and watched the inn a moment, her face a study in the lights from the inn and shade. Then she approached. Slowly she extended her left hand.

"Master's not around now, is he?" De Chille leered, and stepped closer. Liana felt her bony backbone press into the hard curve of the counter as she tried to avoid him, but there was no escape. De Chille's wine breath was in her face.

PFOOF! Every torch flared up in a sudden burst of light, followed by a thunderous boom that reverberated through the room. Servant and gentle alike dove for the floor, under tables and benches. The torches all nearly went out, flickered back weakly and died. De Chille ducked behind the counter. Liana saw an opening through the scramble and dashed for the door.

Upstairs, in Alberge's cramped little room, the flash of light burst from below as Jettaret was helping Alberge toward a chair, already halfway through relating the magic storm. Knowing and not knowing what was happening, Jettaret let go of his friend and dashed back out.

"Bloody hell, Vicomte!" Alberge struggled with his staff to stay upright.

Darkness met Liana outside after the glare of the torches. She ran blindly across the inn yard till a sudden cushioned *thump* stopped her. She fell forward, flinging her arms around a soft billowing over a solid something, and looked up.

Malaxia stood there with her luminous eyes, calm. "You should have called, my darling. You are lucky I was near." Her tone held sincere concern, but Liana disentangled herself from the witch's skirts, stood up and backed off, frightened.

"Jettaret?" Her eyes growing accustomed to the dark, Liana looked about the deserted inn yard. "He's gone."

"So do they all, child. The ones who loved you are gone." There was grave sympathy in her voice. "The one you trusted is gone." Malaxia took a small step forward, and offered, "I have always been here." Liana stood still.

"He said he wouldn't leave. On the word of a nobleman." In her confusion, Liana did not notice Malaxia hold back a smile. "He must be coming back; but I ..." She looked back at the inn, now full of probable witch hunters, all out for her, and De Chille there, too. "I can't stay here."

"I have a dwelling not far away. You may come, and leave whenever you like." It sounded like an invitation to a castle. Resolutely, Malaxia added, "I am not of the Devil, whatever you may think," and then a shade of urgency crept in. "A greater darkness is coming. Quickly, decide." Liana could not find an answer. "You can return tomorrow," Malaxia reassured her. "Nothing will prevent you." She half turned away, one hand still out beckoning to Liana, who threw one more look back at the inn.

Then De Chille's bulk filled the inn door and he stepped into the yard. "Looking for your master? He's gone. He left you to me!"

Liana's cry was that of a wounded lynx; torn between De Chille and the witch, she raced past Malaxia into the woods. De Chille halted when faced with Malaxia, who stared back at him. He flinched first, ducked back into the inn and slammed the door. Malaxia disappeared into the woods after Liana.

Tree and branch caught at and closed in on Liana as she ran, but she could not hear Malaxia behind her. Then her foot snagged on a root and she catapulted forward, hit hard and lay sprawled, trying to catch her breath. Immediately a hand lay on her shoulder, and she scrambled to sit up.

Malaxia was kneeling beside her, unwinded. Gently she brushed some dirt from Liana's face. "If you wish to sleep on the ground I cannot stop you. But I mean you no harm." Liana looked at her, unsure.

Jettaret clattered down the narrow stairs two at a time, taking the last three in one stride. He burst into the common room as the host was relighting the torches, amidst a subdued babble from both gentle and servant, and halted for a quick scan around.

"Liana?" She was nowhere to be seen, and, spying De Chille, he stepped up and seized his tunic. "Where have you put her? What have you done?"

The Witch's Hand

"Nothing. Nowhere!" De Chille was completely minus his sneering bluster. "She got up, and there was thunder and dark, and she was gone." He sounded scared. "What have you got there, a witch?"

Jettaret let go of him. "Malaxia. Oh Christ, Malaxia!" He ran to the inn door and threw it open. "Liana!" He ran out across the inn yard and into the woods. "Liana!"

Inside, Alberge finally made it down the stairs. Charging ahead as fast as he could with his staff, he hurled De Chille out of the way with his free arm and hurried out the inn door. In the yard, he paused, searching in one direction and another, not sure where Jettaret had gone.

"Antoine!" He stumped to the left. "Antoine, come back!" He looked to his right. "You can't find her in the dark!" Pain from his foot jabbed him and he clutched his staff.

Jettaret emerged from the woods, rushed up to Alberge and helped him sit.

"Thank you." Alberge settled himself back, holding his staff upright. "You're finally showing some sense. Now think, man; where might she have gone?"

"She could be in Flanders by now," Jettaret sighed, sinking down beside his friend. "That thing she's with could have taken her anywhere."

"Do you know if this ... this thing—"

"Malaxia."

"If this Malaxia can travel that fast?"

Jettaret thought a second. "No."

"Does she seem to have been heading in any one direction?"

"Northeast, toward Lyon, but that's the way we were going. She was after Liana, God knows why."

"Then it's likely she would head in some other direction now. Say ... south?" Alberge's level logic was irrefutable.

"South ..." Then Jettaret knew. "Languedoc."

"Full of heretics, possibly witches; they would fit right in. So? Tomorrow you head south."

Jettaret rose and took a torch from the inn entrance. "Tonight, Alberge." His friend grumbled a sigh. "Tomorrow you get a wagon and take the St. Martine road. Ask at every town, every farm, of whatever they've seen."

"And the St. Martine road hits the main road south, I know; I'll meet you there." Alberge slowly re-gripped his staff.

Jettaret paced back and forth. "Take Pasquale and her horse, the dapple gray, with you. Hers won't pull a wagon—"

"Why not sell it for traveling expenses?"

Jettaret faced him. "Alberge. She's a witch. If we sell her horse the devil knows what she'd do to us." He clasped his friend forearm to forearm, and helped him up. *"Bonne chance, mon ami,"* good luck, my friend. Jettaret headed off into the woods.

Alberge watched Jettaret's flickering torch bob through the woods until it disappeared. *"Bonne chance."* He sighed. Whether he knew it or not, his friend was still throwing himself full-heartedly into causes he didn't wholly understand. Alberge rose and returned to the inn.

He tried the door and, finding it locked, thumped on the heavy oak with his staff. "Service!" He waited; no one came to open it and the burly ex-Crusader sat, resigned. He looked up at the stars. "Life only opens its doors for the beautiful."

Thirsty, Alberge got up and went to the nearby horse trough. He sniffed it with some repugnance, then dipped his hand into it and proclaimed, "Water turns to wine for the blessèd." He drank and spat it out. "Water." Alberge eyed Heaven.

12. A LEAP IN THE DARK

Liana stumbled over a stone and felt Malaxia's reassuring hand support her. "Not much further, child. Look."

Through the branches and leaves ahead, Liana made out the high narrow tower against the sky. They rounded a turn in the path and came into a clearing, where she beheld Malaxia's formidable dwelling and stopped.

"No one will bother us here. We are well protected. Come."

Malaxia led the way up to the entrance and extended her hand. Inside there was a deep sound of wood sliding against wood, and the great door opened of its own accord. Malaxia went in, and cautiously Liana followed. Her view was blocked momentarily by Malaxia's height, then the witch moved aside, and it seemed that jewels spoke out of the darkness.

"Here, child. A place to get out of the damp." Malaxia's left index finger flicked casually to the side; an elaborate silver lamp there flared into light, and a dazzling array spread itself before them.

From the back, a concave wall of crushed amethyst glowed and sparkled faintly. Much of the surrounding walls were filled with floor to ceiling shelves, holding an immense library of scrolls and books, some with bejeweled covers; their titles stood forth in alphabets and languages from Latin and Greek to Egyptian hieroglyphics and Hebrew, none of which Liana could fathom. Other shelves held a mélange of strange items, the ordinary mixed with the exotic; corked glass jars held dried flowers and herbs, while open bottles with spiral twisted necks fostered living plants and blooms, several of which Liana had never seen before. Gnarled pieces of oak branches were sculpted into grotesque forms, and straight lengths of reddish hazel cut with what looked like animal tracks lay amongst them; again, many of these were set with glimmering jewels. Feathers of birds tied together and carefully strung from hooks under one shelf shared space between large gray stones, inscribed with strange letters, on the shelf below.

Malaxia moved to the lamp and from its base took a glowing blue jewel. Liana recognized it.

"Ah, you remember this? It was a gift from Attil—from a former admirer." Malaxia was certain Liana had not heard of the Scourge of God, or that he'd died in 454, nearly six hundred years earlier, but it paid, emphatically with this one, to be circumspect. She put the jewel back in its lamp base holder, approached Liana and examined her clothes.

"Your clothes are stained, and filthy." She took some folded clothes of rich fabric out of a nook in the shelves and gave them to Liana. "Here are some clean ones."

Liana stood and fingered the clothing. The glowing blue jewel had raised the flicker of a glowing fire and crashing timbers, a week ago this night.

Malaxia touched a nightgown on top. "This for tonight," and indicated the other gown beneath, "That for tomorrow." Liana was still fingering the fabric slowly, looking as though she didn't know what to do with it. Malaxia smiled. "I trust you've never heard of a seamstress witch, one who works with her hands?" Liana shook her head. "I hope then it will lay some of your fears to rest. Put it on." Liana stood embarrassed, looking for a place to change. "Oh—" Malaxia pointed to a tapestry hung before the amethyst back wall. "You may change behind there."

Liana went behind the tapestry and stopped. Before her stretched the witch's inner sanctum, a large, domed cave made entirely of amethyst, and filled with a magisterial array of apparati, books and scrolls. To the right, elixirs of unknown formulae bubbled and steamed, blue and green and violet. From a glass alembic over an open flame, one tincture of ruby red changed to pale amber as it wound through a spiraling glass tube into another glass below; in another, something liquid lay in blue translucence at the bottom and transformed through dawn purples to red at the top. Whatever the solutions were, they were a long way from Maman's greens steaming in crockery pots.

She set the clothes down on a counter next to a small wooden box, triangular, with gut strings across a sound hole, caught a nail on one of the strings and jumped at the sound, a shimmering chime that stayed in the air as though it wished to last forever. On the nearest of several tables across from her lay a magnificent assortment of gems, sparkling and glowing with their own light, as if in response to the string. She didn't touch them. Some were joined together; a ruby burned from one

The Witch's Hand

sapphire, two diamonds flashed from another, and an emerald glistened out of a chunk of amethyst.

Next to the jewels a lengthy piece of parchment lay covered with writing, in different scripts. There were also diagrams of circles, triangles and other shapes, with numbers inside and alongside them. Of the writing, which looked to be in at least three distinct alphabets, one sign looked like a pitchfork, and another like a rooster. Alphabets. How much she wished she knew letters.

She looked further round the room. Toward the back the walls were filled with shelves containing more jars of stuffs unknown to her, and beyond that, darkness. On table and shelf, pestles stuck out of mortar bowls large and small. Powders and various kinds of rocks were arranged carefully on one table, and on another a sturdy stalk in a pot held blooms of no less than three different kinds of flowers—lily, smooth and white, a wine red rose and a floppy petaled burst of lavender-blue hydrangea.

Beyond the tables, from a deep recess, stared a human skull.

It was all both real and unreal, and though the room filled Liana with a fascination that tingled, a cold apprehension kept her from asking Malaxia what the things in it were for.

Beside the parchment lay an exquisite piece of lace; when she touched it, it immediately rose into the air and floated gently back down. Liana stepped back, watching it. She shivered.

She turned to the nightgown and changed into it; it was long, white, and warm, though the fabric felt light. Turning back toward the front room, she came head-on with a glimmering ghost and started. So did the ghost. She stood still and the ghost did not move. Then she reached out cautiously to touch it, and met her doppelgänger's own fingers as hers touched something cold.

It was a coffin-sized length of a hard glassy substance, polished to a reflective brilliance Liana had never seen before, and half covered by a lace curtain. She moved the curtain aside and ran her hand over the smooth cold surface, murmuring, "Frozen water? But not ice."

Malaxia suddenly materialized in the mirror and Liana jumped back, bumped into the witch and started again. She stepped away and looked about the room.

"I never saw things like this. Where did you get them?"

"There are better and stranger items and manifestations beyond your little part of the world." Malaxia turned toward a wall with a huge parchment hung on it, covered with odd-shaped line drawings. "A map of the known world, child. See how it extends." She traced her hand over it. "Here is Rome, there is Carthage, Athens, Constantinople."

"Where is Jerusalem?"

"Here." Malaxia flicked a finger toward a small dot. "Beyond it, the East, the land of the great wall, and silk."

"Where is Paris?"

Malaxia's hand went in the other direction. "Here," her hand moved south, "and here is where we are."

Liana's eyes went to the line dividing land and water. "And there?"

"The Great Sea, which stretches as far as the eye can see."

"Does it ever end?"

"Perhaps. No one knows. Some claim there is an edge, and those who venture too close will fall into a great abyss. Others, as this map maker, show dragons that live in the deep, to prey upon those who explore beyond the charts, past all that is known." Malaxia's eyes gleamed. "And the enlightened teach the world is not flat at all, but round, and the same ocean that reaches west also washes the shores of the East."

"No!"

"Yes. If you wish I can show you the work that describes this."

"I can't read." The confession hurt.

"You may learn. I could teach you, if you wished it."

"Not right now. I'm tired."

Malaxia smiled. "Of course." She took the psaltery and led the way out. Liana picked up the folded dress and followed.

In the front room, next to the wall, Malaxia pointed her toward a large Persian carpet of a cushion with furs piled on it; it had come from a Turkish harem but she didn't tell Liana that, though she doubted if the girl knew what a harem was.

Liana lay on the couch and pulled the furs up around her. The place was beautiful, but cold. She touched the folded up dress, of a rich fabric she could not identify; it shone softly, and the thread work was very fine.

The Witch's Hand

Malaxia moved close and gently tried to smooth her tangled hair, but Liana flinched back into the wall.

"You are still afraid." There was sadness in her voice. Liana, only her head showing above the fur, nodded. "You believe I am what some say I am; you need not answer. Witch is the mark people put on other people whose learning and accomplishments, and therefore whose powers, are greater than theirs. Believe what you will; I cannot change it." Malaxia sat. "Morning is but a few hours away, and then you may go. I shall be alone then. And I have been alone for many years ..." Slowly a tear left her eye and worked its way down her face.

Liana sat up, confused. "Witches don't cry ... real ones..." She left the warmth of the couch and went to Malaxia, tentatively reaching out a hand to soothe her. "Thank you for the dress. It looks beautiful."

"I am glad you like it." Malaxia took a deep breath and let it out. "I am all right now." She indicated the couch. "Go and rest; sleep if you can. I must compose myself." She rose and got a book from a shelf, while Liana returned to the couch and furs, and, making herself comfortable, watched as Malaxia sat and turned the pages.

"You can read." Her voice was wistful. "I never knew a lady who could read."

"Some of us have mastered the art, in many tongues. You too, perhaps ..." Malaxia rapidly became absorbed in her book.

"What does it say?"

"This? A most intriguing essay on measuring time, by Abu'l-Fath Umar Khayyami ibn Ibrahim, a Persian mathematician and astronomer. His calendar is far more accurate than ours—" Malaxia saw Liana's lost look and sighed. "It is late. Go to sleep."

Liana sank into the furs and worked at her stuck ring. Turned toward the wall, she did not see Malaxia cast a sleep spell over her, gently gliding one hand over the other repeatedly. Malaxia then took up the psaltery, plucking out a fluid melody of glass chimes that opened a door to soft winds and darkness, but not before Liana, unnoticed by the witch, finally worked the ring off and held it in her left hand, the one that made fire.

***

Deep in the night, long after Matins, Malaxia entered her sanctum with a candle and went all the way to the rear, the candle dancing splinters of light over and amidst the amethyst. Setting it down, she regarded the skull in its niche.

"Are you there, you charlatan?"

There was no answer. Malaxia waited briefly, and was about to close the sliding door over it, when a noise like sparks snapping in a fire came from the dark hollows of the eyes. Slowly the skull grew possessed with life, though it made no discernible motion.

"'Charlatan?' To what do I owe this unmannerly summons?" The *faux* insulted voice from within held the sound of dry leaves in the wind.

"It is one that you have earned."

"Ah, but would you keep me around if I told the truth all the time? How dull." Smugly the head continued, "Want to know about your new apprentice, hmm?"

"I do not. I already know she has the gift, more than anyone else. She will be my masterpiece."

"So?"

"So what I wish from you, you regrettable excuse of a miserable son of an abscessed mother, is what she may accomplish. That I cannot see." Malaxia was tight-lipped.

"Cost you a lot to say that, didn't it? Ho-ho, ho-ho, what would you have done without me?"

"I don't want to hear."

"Wish you had my cognitive powers, hm? The Sight. The one indispensable tool in a witch's bag of tricks, and yours is sadly lacking."

"I taught you what cognition meant. I taught you how to use the Sight—"

"Think so?" the skull cackled. "Do you know who else is on this side with me?

"I happen to know you have very few companions, where you are—"

"Because I said so? You should know better than that."

"Few companions that have impressed you at all with the importance of proper communication," Malaxia snapped.

"Oh, too bad," the head mocked.

"I could put you back where I found you—"

The Witch's Hand

"But you won't."

"Draw your brains out through your ears—" Malaxia's fury was unfurling like an oriflamme.

"How? I haven't any. Ears or brains. Anymore."

"I'll plaster your mouth shut."

"But I don't need it to speak. Isn't that enervating?" The skull's death grin was positively smirking, and Malaxia whirled away. "Want to know what I see?" it called.

Malaxia turned back. "I can see further than you in this case."

"Think so?"

"This time I see further." Malaxia was now deathly calm.

"But not everything."

"I'll boil you in hog fat and get another skull.

"Ho-ho."

"Enough! You are here at my discretion."

The head sing-songed, "I can see what you can't, I can see what you can't—"

Malaxia slammed the sliding door shut.

From within, the skull continued, "Somebody's coming, somebody's coming …"

13. TORCHES IN THE NIGHT

Clouds moved across the waning half moon, sometimes obscuring it completely. A squirrel perched on a branch paused in its work on an acorn and sat upright. Silhouetted against the moon, it cocked its head, listening; then it abandoned the acorn and scurried away.

A torch glimmered through the trees. Footfalls firm and sure approached; a shadow in the dark, the Vicomte de Solignac came tracking his prey.

Jettaret moved quietly, with drawn sword. His torch flickered feebly and sputtered, its fueling pine tar nearly spent. Through the leaves shifting in the moonlight, he saw a tall round wall and headed toward it, into a clearing, and stopped.

Neither the wall nor the rest of Malaxia's house was there to present its grim visage toward him. No light shown from narrow windows; all was now a barren ascent of sharpened bluffs, and only moonlight ghosted over them as the clouds above moved past. Jettaret looked about and saw no one. He stepped forward.

"Liana? It's Jettaret. Malaxia? Liana?"

A voice from above struck like cold thunder. "Up here, my poor Crusading fool!"

Jettaret felt an electric arc jolt him upright, toward a craggy ledge high above. Malaxia stood there in arch triumph, her long skirts aswirl over something on the ground. Jettaret recognized it and his cry burst out on its own.

"*No!*"

For Liana lay crumpled at Malaxia's feet, her little form twisted grotesquely, motionless. Her new white shift fluttered over her in the ghost of a breeze. And Jettaret's hope was gone.

Clouds covered the moon again and the two witches faded into darkness. Jettaret looked for a way up, then sank to the ground. His torch flickered and finally went out, but he noticed neither that nor, far away, another torch approaching through the woods.

Alberge kept a grim hold onto Pasquale's reins with one hand and his torch with the other, his horse at a lope that was mad through these woods in the dark but he didn't care. He saw the last spurt of Jettaret's torch and headed toward it.

Near the edge of the clearing, he pulled Pasquale to a halt, dismounted with pain and, taking his pike from behind the saddle, stumped along past the trees. Pasquale followed him. As he entered the clearing, the horse halted; Alberge went straight to Jettaret, who was kneeling before Malaxia's disguised keep.

"Antoine. Antoine!"

Jettaret beheld him through tired eyes. "I'm all right."

Alberge squatted beside his friend and handed him his wineskin. Jettaret drank, then sniffed; it was strong stuff but he couldn't place it.

"Bad news, my friend. A courier just came to the inn. They told him ..." Alberge hesitated, "they told him there was a witch loose in the woods. By daybreak half the countryside will be looking for her."

Jettaret handed the wineskin back. "They won't have to." He pointed toward the crag above and Alberge held his torch up. "She's up there—"

The space in the crag was empty.

Jettaret jumped to his feet. "She was right there ..." He finally spied a winding stone stairway on the left, dashed up and scrambled atop the rocks to the crag, searching.

"Nothing ..." Something glinted at his feet. "Wait." Liana's gold ring shone in the faint torchlight from below, in the apex of an angled piece of white thread. It looked haphazardly arranged but seemed to point toward one end of the clearing. He stooped and picked the ring up.

"What?" Alberge called.

"Her ring—she must have dropped it—then she's not dead!"

"Maybe it just fell off—or Malaxia put it there—"

"No." Jettaret remembered. "Malaxia never touched it. It's safe from her magic. It was stuck on Liana's finger—she must have pulled it off to show us the way, she's not dead!" He scrambled down and dashed in the direction Liana's ring had been set. South.

Too disgruntled to point out the lapses in Jettaret's logic, Alberge whistled, the battle shriek: two double blasts, each rising consecutively higher at the end. Jettaret halted and looked back; Alberge indicated Pasquale, still standing by the edge of the clearing. Jettaret ran back, mounted, grabbed the torch from him and galloped off southwards.

The Witch's Hand

Alberge started after him. "The St. Martine road! Tomorrow!" he shouted. He winced to a stop and watched. "Takes the only light ..." The moon came out from behind the clouds again. Alberge looked up. "Thank you." He stumped back into the woods toward the inn. There would be more intelligence there, and he sure as Satan wasn't going to chase anyone mounted, even Jettaret, on foot. Or maybe he should call it a foot and a half. There wasn't much left of the left ankle anymore. Alberge pulled at his wineskin.

Across the clearing behind him, Malaxia's house slowly reappeared. Its windows were dark.

***

A league beyond the other side of the inn lay a village, and residents were beginning to fill its square. Some held torches, and their glow showed others holding pikes, pitchforks, shovels and spades.

"How many witches?" Paul's sleep hooded eyes struggled to become round. Behind him, his wife Marie answered.

"Two, maybe three."

Their neighbor Maxine hurried up alongside them. "Why us? Why now?"

"I don't know." Paul normally couldn't stand Maxine's persistent questioning but tonight—or maybe it was morning already—he was asking the same thing.

A clump of people entered the other side of the square, with doughty dark-haired Claire leading them, indignant. "This morning my cow's milk was turned." Behind her, her husband Alain nodded assent.

"Someone took my gate down," Henri chimed in. His younger sister Danielle, whose fiancé had never returned from the Crusade, followed him; their field was the first beyond the town.

"My horse is off his feed," Alain grumbled.

"My sow won't eat," added Danielle, she of the low hunting horn voice.

"My hens won't lay," Maxine chirped.

"My roof is leaking," Marie remembered.

"My bread is sour."

"Your bread is always sour," Alain retorted to Claire, who promptly hit him.

"Who here knows anything about witches?" The eldest *gran-mère*, Gabrielle's still commanding voice rang through the crowd. There was a silence.

"They drink mare's milk," Paul was the first to put in.

"And dead infant's blood," Marie offered.

"And conjure the Devil." All but Gabrielle gasped at Maxine's statement. As if to exorcise the mention of the Evil One, everyone hurriedly clamored on.

"They make wine go bad."

"They eat raven's eggs."

"They take gates off hinges."

"They have horns."

"They steal plows."

"And chickens."

"And seed."

A slower voice spoke. "They have red hair."

All turned and stared at Robert the dull-witted, then at Henri, whose hair looked aflame in the torchlight.

"Has anyone here seen one?" Gabrielle burst out impatiently. Again there was silence.

"I would know a witch anywhere!" cried Alain. "Are we going to let them ruin our farms, our families, our lives?"

"Steal our cows!"

"Rob our cradles!"

"Blight our corn!"

Danielle leaped up onto a barrel. "No! Now, for God's sake, strike down all witches!" The peasants charged out of the square, not all of them in the same direction, and their cries rose in fury.

"Death to the witches!"

"Burn every witch!"

"Not one alive!"

"Burn them!"

Henri paused as he saw Gabrielle wasn't budging, and halted. "You're not going?"

The Witch's Hand

Gabrielle shook her head. "I'll hunt witches on my own doorstep. These people wouldn't know a witch if they stepped on one." She shuffled back toward her home, and Henri dashed after Danielle. Through the darkness a chant began, from whispers into a shout.

"Witch. Witch. Witch. Witch! *Witch!*"

The torches threaded their way through the night.

14. IN MALAXIA'S HANDS

In the early pre-dawn light, Bluestone was barely visible against the weathered boards of the inn's storehouse. She stood tied to the back of a wagon, her head low; only an occasional swish of her tail showed she was not asleep. The sorry looking cart horse gave no sign that it was even alive. Alberge crouched by the door to the storehouse, his knife working through a narrow knothole.

Inside, the door latch slowly moved till it was off its catch, and Alberge's pike pushed the door open enough for him to sidle in, with a covered lantern. He pulled the covering up enough to see and set it atop a barrel. Before him, the remains of the winter's stores stood stacked and laid about on shelves; he eyed them, figuring what would fit where in the wagon, and set to work with flinty eyed satisfaction, grabbing rounds of cheese and bread, eyeing the mold and crunching a mounded loaf with his hand, not that hard yet, though not very recollective of Rosinella's fine breast either, or maybe it was Lucinda, sniffing the cheese and good, not too rancid, and stuffing it all into an empty barley sack, with a snap shake to knock off the dust first. A string of onions vanished next, followed by one of sausages, minus the end link his teeth caught for breakfast.

A bird chirped outside and Alberge listened; only the bird, no one up yet. The bung on a wine barrel went with a *thump* under his fist, and two wineskins grew plump with the vintage. Sideways onto his pike he rammed them, hanging by their drawstrings, to be jolted and joined by another train of sausages and a lumpy set of excellent squashes strung together. Alberge shouldered his pike and gimped out, slid the fare off the pike into the wagon, and on returning spotted a cooking cauldron just inside the door. Garlic up above it and more onions, ah, there's a fine taste for you, warm up your insides till something more substantial comes along. Full into the cauldron they went.

He dumped another hard loaf of bread in and took it all out to the wagon, where Bluestone snorted at him.

"Haven't forgotten you, my lady." Alberge went back in and returned with an opened sack of oats. Feeding her a handful, he muttered, "Don't pull any witch stuff on me, mare." Then he took some oats to the cart horse.

Returning to the near-emptied shed, he surveyed it, saw an abacus for counting stores and eyed its account of the inventory. He started pushing more beads to the side to make it accurate, then grabbed the last turnip, shoved all the beads over and went to the door. A little St. Jaques de Compostelle shrine glared down at him. He gave it a cherubic "Thank you," and a courteous wave.

Alberge gimped out and closed the door. A second later the door reopened, his hand reached in, took the lantern, and the door shut again.

Wineskins safely beside him in the cart, Alberge shook the reins. "*Ave Maria!*" Hail Mary! The horse jerked in his traces and started forward.

***

The east told of sunrise but the stars were still out, as Malaxia led Liana quietly through the woods. The girl's new dress made her look like a smaller version of Malaxia, in different hues. Malaxia cast a glance back at her.

"We came some way in the dark last night. I will guide you back toward the inn, as you wished." They continued on, then Malaxia said, "You look quite becoming. Did you sleep well?"

"No. I had a strange dream—"

"Dreams can be meaningful. What was yours?" It was imperative that the girl be honest with her. She should have some recollection of the scene Jettaret had beheld.

Liana tried to describe the sense of almost catching something you wanted and reached out for. "I—nothing. I don't remember it very well." She went to turn her ring and shock hit her when it wasn't there. Leaving it somewhere had been part of the dream. "It had to do with losing something—"

A sudden rustle stopped her words, and a deer flashed fleetingly in the woods beyond. Liana smiled. "Deer. You can tell them by the sound they make when they first jump, and then there is no sound at all." *What had she done with her ring?*

The Witch's Hand

"Ah. You are observant." There was no sense coaxing an errant memory. "Deer, bird, rabbit; all survive by their speed, their instinct to quickness. They act without thinking, as many people do. Still, it is good to learn the ways of others. It is the first step to accomplishment in all the areas where they are lacking—such as thought."

Filled with respect and a bit of awe, Liana looked at the witch. "You talk as if you'd been here for hundreds of years."

Malaxia held in her sudden start—*did the girl suspect? —no, there was no subtlety of disguise in her, but it would do no good as yet, would frighten her if she knew the witch's full years and tutelage*—and smiled. "I have hundreds of years of study at my disposal. My desire is, and has been, for knowledge, for learning, and the fruits thereby obtained. You may share in them if you wish—"

Liana was scared again and didn't wish.

"—but only at your own bidding." Malaxia's eyes held the barest glimmer of eagerness. "With applied study, it is possible to reveal and control your own particular abilities. When with your errant knight, for example. How easy it was for you to handle his sword." She dismissed it with a gesture. "That is a small talent." She saw Liana was about to speak. "You have discovered others?"

"I can make fire, and—was it you?" Malaxia as the source of her new-found powers struck with force.

But the witch shook her head. "Everyone has the potential, daughter. My wish is to teach you how to use it, for your own service, and for others."

Liana stopped suddenly. "What about the storm?" In front of her, Malaxia halted. "The storm you made and nearly killed me."

Malaxia turned and faced her. "It seems to me you played a part in making it too." It was time to call the girl's bluff, if she was bluffing; had Liana developed her powers previously with someone unknown? "Is there something you are not telling me?" Liana was silent. She was holding nothing back. "As for killing you, your traveling companion came closer to doing that than I did."

"What was it then?" Liana persisted. "What caused the storm? I didn't want to." She sat, disconsolate. "I destroyed trees and birds and—how do you control power like that?"

153

Malaxia moved quickly toward her. "Through study and practice. I did not know it was so strong in you, and I am sorry that things got out of hand. Had you stayed within the circle, as I asked, you would have been in far less danger, and caused less destruction."

"But why—?" *Why had Malaxia started the storm in the first place?*

"It was both initiation and release. Forgive me for not telling you sooner. But I had to know if your gift was truly something I could assist, and that was the only way. I would have preferred it otherwise. Doubtless you have found your powers have grown since?" *How much stronger had the girl's skills gotten?*

"I haven't used them that much."

Malaxia masked her relief. "Caution, the true course of wisdom. Would you like to learn how to use them?"

"Yes!" Liana jumped up, and just as quickly got her comportment back. "Yes."

"Good." Malaxia was business like. "Then we begin with concentration; concentration and control, the two C's."

"Two seas—oceans?"

"Letters."

Liana went sad again. "Oh. You know I cannot read. Letters to me are like the stars." She looked up to the fading points of light. "I can see them—" she stretched her right hand out, "but I can't reach them."

"*Astra, castra.*"

"What?"

"The stars, *astra*, like letters, are a *castra*, a fortress to you now. But you can learn to read them both."

"Oh." Liana was pensive a moment. "Con—concen ... what is it?"

"Concentration. It is when you think hard, and focused." Malaxia snapped her fingers and a ball of light the size of a firefly appeared, skittering about the leaves at their feet.

"Whoo—!" Liana jumped. "What's that?"

"It is harmless. A toy to train you. Sit, so." Malaxia crossed her arms; Liana sat cross-legged. "Concentrate. Make it stop moving." Liana raised her hands. "Do not use your hands. Think."

Liana fixed her eyes on the firefly, following it about its haphazard track. *Um, stop. Stop.* The firefly did not respond. *Slow down, stop.* She

The Witch's Hand

concentrated. *Slow down.* Finally it began to slow, then more, and stopped just to her left.

"Bring it center."

Liana tried. The firefly refused to budge. Malaxia was standing ahead of her and to one side, and when Liana thought the witch couldn't see, she motioned slightly with her hand and head, and brought the firefly just past, then back to center.

"Good. Make it larger." Malaxia's eyes now held on her, and Liana knew she'd seen. The girl took a deep breath. *Big. Get bigger.*

Slowly the firefly expanded into a sphere. *Bigger. Come on.* She struggled to keep it going. It grew till it was larger than she, then Malaxia spoke again.

"Smaller."

Releasing her focus did not make the sphere shrink. It was harder to reverse the sizing; the more she tried, the hotter a sharpness in her head burned. Slowly the sphere shrank back down to a pinpoint. Liana was working hard and was struggling to breathe when her concentration suddenly snapped, and the firefly skittered about again.

"It is enough." Malaxia snapped her fingers; the firefly vanished, and Liana was left looking for it. Her eyes met the other witch's.

"Magic. They say magic is the work of the Devil."

Malaxia spoke with authority. "What is called magic is nothing more than energy directed, a focusing of power. That is all. The sword smith wields magic. The master falconer deals with winged magic. Those who create and direct power work with magic. Some call it evil; it is not." She looked at the girl carefully. "Can you do more?"

"Yes, I—" Liana realized the one she was with deserved respect and scrambled to her feet.

"This time you need only watch. Observe." Malaxia held out her left arm. "The mind imagines fire—" she put her fingers in the fire spell position, left thumb and index finger out, "and a circle, thus." Malaxia made a clockwise circle, horizontally, in the air. A ring of light like the one from the magic storm appeared before them, revolving like a dropped hoop in front of Liana. When it stopped, Malaxia made a discreet gesture across her own eyes, then one toward Liana, who did not notice.

Flames began to fill the ring. They grew and grew, flickering over them, until Liana shrieked in terror and fell at Malaxia's side.

"What do you see?"

"They're burning me! They're burning me!"

"The power of prediction is also a result of applied study. However," Malaxia made a counter-clockwise circle with her left arm, her hand in the fire spell position; the flames vanished and the ring of light faded, "predictions need not always come to pass." She turned to Liana. "Develop your own power, and you will not burn. You will punish those who would try to annihilate you, and like the rabbit who escapes the trap, you will find freedom."

Liana looked up at her. "I can do that?"

"Only you know your limits." Malaxia waited for the girl's response, but Liana remained sitting with her hands around her knees, her head bent, lips moving, and began to rock back and forth.

I don't want to burn, I don't want to burn, I don't want to burn— Slowly her words became audible.

The sun was partly past the horizon, and lit Malaxia's face as she bent close. "Fire can be controlled. You know that already. It is one of the four elemental powers." She put a hand gently on Liana's shoulder, and Liana shuddered and was silent. "The others are air, water, and earth. They are but the first steps. Learn of them, and of further matters I can teach you, and you will know the paths that lead beyond this world."

Liana looked, not believing, at the witch kneeling beside her.

"Knowledge, craft, and skill, beyond that of any book. And an indescribable sweetness. It is part of the gift I still hold for you." Malaxia hid her frustration at Liana's silence and rose. "It is late. You will want to go back to the inn—" She turned away.

"No!" Liana jumped up and looked in the direction of the inn as if listening. "Jettaret isn't there—he's not here—he deserted me."

"As he has previously deserted others. Yes, you have it."

"What?"

"Something called the Sight."

"Tell me more. About the Sight, and air, and fire—"

"And water, and earth. Come." Malaxia turned and went back the way they had come. Liana hesitated, then followed her.

The Witch's Hand

The sun, completely up, burned brightly.

15. CRUSADERS AGAIN

Forenoon found the woebegone cart horse and its creaking cargo on the St. Martine road, Alberge soured already on the paths of possibilities ahead. Find Jettaret and you'd find a witch, maybe two; find either witch and you'd find trouble, maybe death, but the sticker with that was that if you found Jettaret you'd find trouble, witch or no witch. Antoine couldn't stay away from it, and if the bloody fool didn't have someone like him, Alberge, to pull him out of the fire when he needed it, he'd have been in hell long ago. The poor vicomte had one foot in Lucifer's lair already, though he didn't know it, bloody bastard, with that infernal rotten idealism, hadn't done him or any of the other Crusaders any good, only made things worse after the Crusade went astray; couldn't have just been satisfied with booty and plunder, like any ordinary marauder, he had to add a purpose, a bloody pristine purpose to it, and when it was all over who cared?

"Rot." Alberge spat.

A league beyond, Jettaret sat by the main road and watched for his friend, Pasquale's reins in his hand. Ranging through the woods at night hadn't been such a great idea. The sun was almost to Sext, and he'd brought nothing but his wineskin with him, nothing for a midday meal. But the roil within was more than his stomach. The witch girl was pulling at him, and he wished rather that he were back in Paris with his Boethius, before the Crusade, before his brother had died leaving him to inherit the title and estates of Solignac, before all this turmoil. Oh, and his promised marriage too. Before all that.

Something was bothering him, something deep, and not pleasant. He wanted to cry with Boethius, "*Ah me! how dim grows the mind when sunk below the o'erwhelming flood! Its own true light no longer burns within, and it would break forth to outer darknesses.*" But unlike his sixth century Roman, there was no strong and rational goddess of Philosophy to bring him comfort. And no help from Heaven, either.

There was a coil of pain twisting about inside, of conscience, of his wrongs, of Malaxia's icy stare, and Liana's sad level gaze. And more; Jettaret felt something he hadn't known since Constantinople, the surge within to do something not because it was necessary or enticing, but because it was right.

Saving a girl from witchcraft—this was legally the Church's business, but their way of handling the problem was to destroy the victim, not the Perpetrator, not the evil cause itself. And now he, malefactor, defiler of virgins, who since Constantinople had not been able to manage a pretense of passion for anything, whose interest in women had waned to the point of vanishing, who wondered if he were in effect if not fact a eunuch, now he burned again, but not with desire, not the way he'd known before. He yearned to be there for Liana, to protect her from Malaxia, to hold her. He wanted very much to hold her.

He had to find her.

"Vicomte!"

Jettaret turned and saw his dusty comrade driving up. Alberge tossed him a wineskin.

"It's a matter of debate, Vicomte, whether the horse or the wagon will fall apart first, but life is too short to drink bad wine. And we will eat well. Come and dine before it all goes bad." Alberge one-hopped clumsily into the wagon bed. "Oh, and since your wet nurse no doubt has more interesting things to do these days, if she's still alive, here's your equipage you forgot and left at the inn. Never know when toilet articles and another shirt might come in handy." All Jettaret's traveling gear was roughly stowed in the wagon, and he smiled.

"Let's dine up there." Jettaret pointed to a rocky plateau above them. "We could see most of the countryside."

"Good luck climbing it, Vicomte."

"Come on, Alberge. I'll carry the food."

Half an hour later, they reached the top of the plateau, Jettaret helping Alberge, whose face was set in a permanent grimace. They stopped and sat to catch their breaths.

"*Sanctum Sepulchrum adjuva,*" Jettaret breathed.

Alberge glowered at him. "Help us, Holy Sepulchre? I never thought I'd hear that from you again."

"I never thought I'd say it again. But we—" Jettaret turned to him, "we were Crusaders, you and I; we believed in that once. It destroyed a lot of people, ourselves maybe. This one is not going to die."

The Witch's Hand

"I'm curious, Vicomte." Alberge tugged at his wineskin. "Why all this trouble for a peasant girl?"

Jettaret looked around before he answered; far below was the wagon, with Pasquale and Bluestone tied behind it. There was no sign of anyone on the road. "She ... despite all she's been through, she remains ... untouched. If she had seen ten times what you and I have, I think she would still be the same."

Alberge eyed his friend. "Didn't see much of her when you came in. She is, ah, pretty, a beauty?"

"Not beautiful, yet. But virtue—more than I've seen in a long time."

"Ha. T'was never a virtue that had beauty and never a beauty that was virtuous." He looked askance at Jettaret. "Why am I telling *you* this?"

"She's not a common peasant. And now that this witch has gotten hold of her—"

"You think she will become a demon."

"Don't laugh, Alberge."

"I'm not laughing. Demons may exist. One may have hold of you, driving you after this girl—" Alberge's pike emerged from between his legs at the crotch, "in fact, one does have hold of you, and I think I know its name—ehh?" Alberge, half a-chuckle, found Jettaret's drawn sword pointed at him.

"Don't taunt me on an empty stomach!" Jettaret glared, then laughed.

Alberge pushed the tip of Fortuna Domini aside with his finger. "Point taken. I shall set a snare or two and see if I can't catch us something fresh." He prepared a snare with Liana's dexterity. Jettaret watched, then looked away. As he got out the bread, cheese and sausage; he scanned the area below again; there was still no discernible movement.

Alberge seemed more than usually intent on his knot work. "Remember the Witch of the Mountains that cutpurse of a fishmonger told us about in Zara?"

Jettaret put his round of cheese down. "Don't remind me of Zara."

"So we destroyed the place. Nobody ever heard of it before; now it's famous."

Jettaret looked at his friend, stern. "And the Pope excommunicated us for sacking a Christian town."

"Antoine. A pilgrimage to the Holy Land reverses excommunication, you know that."

"And a pilgrimage to Spain."

"To the shrine of St. Jacques de Compostelle?" Even Alberge sounded a trifle respectful.

Jettaret nodded. That had been his business before heading toward Lyons.

"Did it help?"

Jettaret looked at Alberge, then away.

"The fishmonger," Alberge resumed. "He told us of this witch, the Dark Lady, he called her; dark eyes, dark skin, dark hair—wonder if she was some kind of Queen of Sheba?—impossible age, but still a beauty. And she had more powers than any witch. She could control the weather, do things like this magic storm you told me about, turn into anything, fish, fowl; wasn't much she couldn't do. Had more learning than the scholars in Paris; they say she knew things the spirits taught her. There was more than one king who listened to her. Nobody knew where she came from, or where she went; she hadn't been seen in that part of the world for some time. What do you think?"

Jettaret was dubious. "That witch was dark. Arab, African maybe—"

"Witches can change their color. Or maybe she faded."

"I don't believe in witches and neither do you."

"Why all the dragonfly flap about them if they don't exist?" Alberge asked reasonably. "And as for magic—when he knighted you, the Bishop blessed your sword, right?"

Jettaret assented; Alberge indicated Fortuna Domini.

"One edge to serve God, one to serve man. Considering how you've used it, I'd call that blessing a potent and strongly operative magic spell." He shrugged and tore at a loaf. "Magician, priest; what's the difference?"

"Alberge?"

"Hm?"

"In Venice. While we were waiting for the ships. How many died of the fever that summer?"

"I don't know," Alberge shrugged. "There weren't enough of us left alive who were well enough to bury them. Good thing too. I might have buried you by mistake."

The Witch's Hand

Jettaret eyed him. "Thanks for the oversight."

Alberge rose with his snare and gimped away some distance toward a clump of rocks and brush, a good place to find rabbits but not to be one. Unheralded by their night torches, Paul, Henri, Alain and Robert burst from the cover and held him at bay with their farm tools.

"Stop there!" barked Paul.

Henri leveled his three-pronged wooden pitchfork at Alberge. "Name yourself!" His courage was bluster; they'd seen the two coming from far off, and had thought their position, well above, to be safe till Jettaret and Alberge came up to the plateau as though they were hounds on a scent. It was really unnerving.

"We haven't seen you in these parts," Alain threatened.

Alberge was unperturbed. "Quite understandable. I am a stranger here. A former Crusader—" He pulled back his cloak to reveal a cross stitched on the left of his tunic, as Jettaret charged up, sword at the ready. The four farmers fell back; Alain and Robert crossed themselves. Jettaret looked at Alberge in surprise. "—escorting my friend—oh put it away Antoine, these are but farmers—to Lyon. Will you let us pass, and perhaps tell us the way to the nearest inn? What is the trouble here, why do you go armed? More heresy?—oh dear God, when will it end?" he cried.

"Not heresy," Paul corrected. "Witches."

"Have you caught any?" Jettaret asked quickly.

"No, but they are said to be in the area," from Henri.

"No witches in this township," declared Alain. "If we find them, they burn."

Paul indicated the edge of the plateau with his pike. "You came through the woods down there? Did you see anything?"

"If we had you would be the first to know," Alberge assured them. "Gentlemen, at the last place we stopped, I believe someone said they had sighted a witch—" he turned to Jettaret,"where was it now?"

"On the St. Martine road. Some miles north of here."

"Quite right. That area would be the place to look."

"The St. Martine road." Paul was decisive. "Come on."

Robert hesitated. "I have work in my field—"

"I'll go." Alain stepped forward. "Witches, ahh. We want to make our country safe!"

The peasants left, heading north along the edge of the plateau. Alberge watched them go and put his head against his pike.

"I'm not sure how long I can do this."

"You weren't our negotiator for nothing, I thought you did very well," Jettaret complimented, then his mood darkened. "How long we can keep misdirecting them and find Liana ourselves, that's another matter. And I don't like it that a bunch of clods managed to stalk us." He rubbed the dull burnish on Fortuna Domini's hilt with his sleeve. "I start out on my way to a bride and end up looking for a witch."

"What's the difference?"

Jettaret feigned an attack with the flat of his blade, and Alberge fell as he stepped back.

"An unarmed cripple! You would attack an unarmed cripple?" Then he deftly disarmed Jettaret from the ground with his pike.

"Alberge, you astound me." Jettaret helped Alberge up, then retrieved his sword. "By the way, I didn't know you still wore your cross."

"It *does* help in a tight situation!" Alberge stomped off. Jettaret, grinning, followed.

No sooner had they gotten underway again when the wagon axle snapped, cracking like a log in a hot fire. Alberge spent a good ten minutes railing at it, then, with Jettaret's help, packed what he could onto the cart horse, kicked the wagon and mounted Bluestone.

"Get up, mare. Witch horse."

"I don't think Liana did anything to her." Jettaret reined over to make room as his friend rode up alongside, leading the now pack horse.

"Right."

16. NOVITIATE

"Up there, the bright star, brightest one in the sky. Sirius. Were there none in your village who studied the stars?"

Liana looked past where Malaxia pointed, at bright Sirius. "I don't know. They all hated me. In Peranville, they saw what I could do. They were scared, and I was scared, and they are still chasing me, to try to kill me."

"They would destroy us both, child."

"Jettaret didn't."

"He tried, did he not?"

"Not exactly." Liana was hesitant. "He could have, but—"

"He abandoned you."

Liana was silent. He had disappeared.

They were standing atop a rise where the path met the night sky, after a supper Liana thought must be the kind kings feasted on: venison and chicken in a pie; cheese so tart it bit your tongue; chunks of glazed boiled apples and raisins; and bread rolls baked with cinnamon and honey.

"There are other beings, some which can be commanded, some which attack one's own will, and some which can become companions," Malaxia went on. "These may be of more comfort, and more use. I will guide you in the ways to call, confront, converse, exchange, and deal with them."

"Who are they?"

"You will see. It is not time for their company yet. Or perhaps I am merely jealous, and wish to have you all to myself for a while."

It had been three weeks since Malaxia had taken Liana in, and in that time Liana had begun learning what she had cherished most—letters. Regarding the multitude of alphabets on Malaxia's soaring shelves of books, "I want to learn them all!" she had cried, but Malaxia had smiled and said that one at a time would have to do. Now Liana had her name down, was building her vocabulary in Latin—"Only one of several scholars' tongues," Malaxia had informed her—and was beginning to put together simple sentences. She had also read off triumphantly the titles *De Anima, Of the Soul*, by an Aristotle, and *De Bellum Gallico, Of the Gallic*

War, by a Caesar. "A bit of the history of your region," Malaxia had said of the latter.

Malaxia had also demonstrated that a tincture from one vial mixed with a solution from another caused the resulting mixture to heat till it steamed, and that the potions her mother had brewed for cough and rheum of the head were only the beginning.

There was but one discord. Despite diligent searching, she had not found her ring. She remembered taking it off and then putting it down, but hadn't mentioned the loss to Malaxia yet; it didn't seem of value in her world.

Liana listened to the crickets' quiet chatter. A nightingale warbled and she looked in its direction.

"Sometimes I think I know what they say."

"Keep listening."

"There is so much I want to learn; how this works—" Liana spread her fingers briefly, "why I can do what I do, how not to destroy things—"

"You will, child," Malaxia reassured her.

"How?"

Malaxia extended her left hand, upraised with the fingers arched, toward a large stone. The stone began to glow, shimmering till it became a globe of bluish light. She moved her hand around and the globe slowly left the ground.

"How do you make it do that?"

"How do ideas travel, how are worlds made?" she asked. "The mind." A flip of her hand and the globe vanished in a blitz of showering light, which landed in shivers on the ground. Liana stepped back. Spear-sharp pieces of glowing rock surrounded her.

"That looks like the way the world is destroyed."

"Destruction is father and mother to creation. Impurities must be purged before the new and better can arrive, and then reach and thrive to their furthest extent."

"I don't understand."

"You are not required to understand." Malaxia's tone was sharp. "What is, is, and whether or not you comprehend it now is immaterial." Malaxia knelt and seized a shard of the glistening rock. She held it up. "You see the power that the mind can unleash?"

The Witch's Hand

"Yes, and I'm scared of it."

"Child! You have it within yourself to control and direct far greater forces than this! These are toys; truly, these are toys." Malaxia cast the rock down and turned away, exasperated but sad.

"Can you see that our studies, our efforts, lead down paths few have taken?"

"Yes."

"It is a long road." For the first time Malaxia sounded weary. "Long, and yes, there are dangers." She turned to the girl. "But I would not lead you on it if I feared for your safety. You are stronger than you know." She smiled. "Our attempts now are like the apple tree. Barren in winter, blossoming now, but the blossom is not the fruit. That takes a summer of time, and care, and enough rain, enough sun, the right amounts of each. Then the fruit will flourish, become perfect, and made into a cider that will last through the winter. That is what we do; the fruits of your study will repay you, and abundantly, but that time is not yet."

"Oh. I get it, sort of."

"You see that you *will* see?"

"Yes." Liana was sure.

"To lift the blindness, even momentarily, is an accomplishment. And that is what our art does."

They stood together, mistress and novice, and beheld the stars in the vast deep of night.

"You speak of understanding, of why it is so hard to determine why people are as they are, why destruction and not hope and enlightenment are the cornerstones and guiders of our destiny," Malaxia said at last. "It is because we must go beyond hope and despair and blind faith, and deeper than appearance, to the essence of what *is*. Only then may we master it. The charts of the Kaldean astronomers were misguided attempts to solve these dilemmas, their divining by star signs, by the influence of earth-like planets, wrong. No, someday we will talk directly with the powers that move the stars themselves."

"We?"

"You certainly. Myself, I fear not. But you, yes."

"What if I don't want to?"

"You need never do anything before your time, before you are ready for it, and wish to. None but the few may do this in any case, and then only those who dare may succeed. But for the few who dare—ah, there is a select enthronement for them, a place unique in all time, in all history, for their reach exceeds the grasp of all save another select few, and it is for that small gathering, which has been refined as in a crucible, to lead and guide the entirety of the human race on its proper course, to the highest limits of thought and reason, and then beyond where even those faculties reach."

"What if I don't know where to go? How do you find a path where there aren't any?" Liana was trying very hard not to be lost, but Malaxia wasn't making a lot of sense. Learning was a joy when you understood it, but this stuff—even Jettaret explained things better.

"You will know. When you are astride the mountaintops, you will see, much more, much further and with a grander vision than when the peak was still before you, still blocking your sight, still hampering your senses. You will know." Malaxia picked up the still glowing shard of rock and turned away, back down the path. Liana followed, a little forlornly.

"What's a crucible?"

"You have seen the silversmiths at work?"

Liana nodded.

"The urn they melt the silver in, to purify other matter out of it, is the crucible."

"Am I in one now?" Liana already knew the answer.

"Yes."

"I don't like it very much." But Liana knew that, incomprehensible as much of Malaxia's teaching appeared, she did like being, if not where one understood all the mysteries and saw with complete vision, at least an initiate on the road that led there.

***

Two and a half weeks of hard industry later, Malaxia watched her novice in the woods, by a quiet pool of water. Liana sat within a circle of bluish-white light, which was itself surrounded by a shimmering blue glow, like the sun's corona in an eclipse. It was protection from disturbances, both of this world and the other. Liana worked laboriously over a parchment with a quill and ink, a pile of books beside her.

"*Quis, qui?* What?"

"Who. 'What' is *quid*."

"*Quis, quid*—" Exasperated with her efforts, Liana cast a right-handed spell and the parchment disintegrated. Malaxia moved silently beside her and handed her another piece of parchment. Liana sighed and went back to work. She wondered if Jettaret had been through this kind of frustration with his studies. She wondered too if she would have liked being a lady-in-waiting at his court. She didn't think life there would be the same as it was at other courts, whatever it was at those. Jettaret was different.

She missed him.

Malaxia stood aside. With her magic, she toyed with a squirrel, guiding it this way and that with tiny concussive spurts in the ground around it.

What will this child be? With her inborn gifts, with my guidance and the help of that beyond, what will this child of my choice become? Heiress . . . apprentice . . . herald . . . and then? There is always one, a teacher, a leader, one whose talents exceed those of others. With the proper training, her powers will have no boundaries.

Yet I fear for her. The child still believes in her useless, treacherous, outworn God. But she thinks, and those who think will bring faith to its knees. I have no faith, and for that I am called accursed. But the weak, the slavish believers will be made strong and freed only by those of no faith, by those who think, and question. The Church's faith destroys thought, and thought is the leaven of life. Without it we are beasts. The believers are lost children, who cannot or refuse to see the unimaginable varieties of truth. I teach her the means of discovering those truths, and of controlling the powers the world is afraid to recognize.

Malaxia took the glowing blue jewel and the shattered, now cold rock shard from a hidden pocket, and put them atop a volume of Pliny the Elder's *Naturalis Historiae* on a flat boulder. His skill at observing the details and phenomena of the natural world was admirable, but among the numerous pronouncements he'd gotten wrong, he'd been mistaken about the power of the mere presence of a naked menstruating woman to kill insects in a cornfield; it still took a stomp of the foot to accomplish that.

The squirrel came too close, and with a right-handed magic bolt, she laid it out flat and lifeless. Liana was in a near trance-like state within her circle, and did not notice.

With both hands Malaxia covered the jewel and rock, brought them together and murmured, "Join, fuse, become perfect." Blue-white light shot through her fingers, and when she lifted them the single stone beneath was smaller, harder, and seemed to burn from a fire within. There were no scorch marks on the book under it.

The jewel was now made perfect, as she would perfect Liana. She fingered the book.

I have begun to teach her letters, and she picks them up faster than I did. All my life I have worshiped the difficult studies, but they can be one's own destroyer, without the proper guidance. I have made mistakes, from time to time. Malaxia pocketed the jewel. *I shall, I think, pay for them, but I do not know the price.* She seized the Pliny and threw it on the ground. *How? With all my strength I cannot see*—she regarded Liana intensely—*perhaps you can.*

Malaxia clapped her hands sharply once, then twice. Liana didn't react. Malaxia smiled, gestured, and Liana came out of her trance. The magic circle of light and its corona faded.

"Excellent. Your concentration grows daily. What did you see?"

Liana tried to speak but couldn't. Malaxia motioned her to a clearing, where a tree stump was covered with an elegant cloth and set with bread, cheese, olives, and wine.

"You need not answer now. Someday you will be able to, and soon your training will lead you to the next step."

"When?"

"Patience." They sat, and Malaxia cut the round of cheese into chunks. She showed Liana how to dine properly, wiping her mouth with a napkin, not licking her fingers like a peasant. She also showed her how to use a small metal prong to spear food with and then put it in one's mouth, instead of using the fingers.

"It's called a fork," Malaxia explained. "Very useful. Regarding your progress in the art," she resumed, "I did not attain my abilities in one night, or a year, or many years."

The Witch's Hand

"How long did it take you—how old are you, anyway?"

Hiding her start, Malaxia replied, "Older than you. There is a means of prolonging life past its normal course. I will show you, when you are ready. You have time; I do not."

"What?"

"I will not always be here. For a long while, yes. But one day you will be alone. I remind you there are other worlds; this is but the first. And there are many forms, many essences besides this, the physical one; I shall continue to be, but as what is yet to be determined."

Liana lowered her fork. "When are you going?"

"I do not know. Enough of this!" Then Malaxia gentled. "Not for a long time. But, thus the necessity for someone to carry on with my work here."

"I can't do that."

"Do not worry about it now. Your talents are such that it is more a matter of holding you back. For one can progress too fast, and that is dangerous. You run the risk of losing your powers that way, as water is lost when dashed too quickly into a glass. Beware of overstepping yourself. Too much, too quickly past the boundaries of light, and all we have worked for would be gone—all save the Sight."

"The Sight?"

"Yes, you were born with it. I merely awakened you to its presence. Peasant or queen of this world, or the one beyond, whatever may come, the Sight will always be with you."

"Why—" Liana finally asked the question that she needed answered, "why did you choose me?"

"You think you are too young, too low born. No. Youth is no barrier to the highest learning. As for position—rank, birthright—they mean nothing. There are but four requirements. Your mind must have the freedom of the air without its capriciousness, fire's intensity without its destruction, feelings strong and mobile as water, without going mad, and you must be rooted in the earth without being buried. You have these, but they must be further developed in order to achieve a degree of knowledge of the highest order, which will then come of its own. But the potential from these must not be forced. Otherwise it is false; it will fade, and have no power."

Liana was confused. "I thought the power was mine, natural."

"Correct. But one may focus the natural gift and enhance it through—"

"Concentration," they said together.

Liana sighed. "How long do I have to concentrate before I can do anything?"

"You must have control first. Without it, chaos." Malaxia looked at her reprovingly. "As you well know."

Liana hung her head, remembering the magic storm.

***

Half a league beyond them, in a field bordering the woods, three figures poked their pitchforks into hummocks as they crossed, searching for anything amiss that told of witchcraft. Henri fervently hoped he wouldn't stab any witches hiding inside. Make a mess of him, they would.

After the first night's witch scare, they'd divided up; Gabrielle had determined a better system, and most now stayed to watch their farms and get the planting in, while smaller groups forayed out to hunt the witch.

"Henri! Not so fast!" Paul cried. Alain, behind him, was wheezing, and he didn't know where Robert had gone. Paul kicked at a hump of turf as he passed. Hot and sweaty business, this witch hunting. He wished he were home with Marie, but she, Claire and Danielle had taken a cart on down the southern road to Aurillac, to warn the people there; Danielle's mother was a server at the Aurillac inn, where they were to meet in three more days.

They caught up with Henri, and Paul handed his wineskin around. "We should wait for Robert."

"Gone home, I'll lay odds," Alain muttered.

"If he can find the way," added Henri.

"Maybe the witches got him." Alain's riposte was sour.

"Wait." Paul held up his hand. "I think I hear something." They fell silent, listening; then Paul picked a path and led the way through the

The Witch's Hand

trees. Alain looked back for Robert but didn't see him. Had the witches really taken him?

***

Their dining finished, Malaxia picked up a book and opened it. "Enough of the highest orders. Some of the lower ones, now, though these works are hardly mundane. The Arab physician Averroës, who we shall read next, has much more to say about the paths to perception than this writer, whose work is easier to read. Now, the line from yesterday?"

"'Learn your art slowly, step by step; only thus will you bring it to perfection.'"

"Good." Malaxia handed Liana the book and pointed to the right place. "Here. Go on."

Slowly Liana read, "'And be not like my friend Angelo, who won his ba—b—'" She held the book out to Malaxia. "What's that?"

"Battle. A fight, war."

"'... battle with the others ...' Others?"

"The invisible ones."

"'... at the ex—ex—'" She held out the book again.

"Expense. Price, cost."

"'... who won his battle with the others at the expense of his hu-man-ity.' Human—humid. Dampness? Rain? Fog?" She saw Malaxia's cold stare. "No. Hu-*man*—himself."

Malaxia took the book from her. "Let me see that. Correct." She closed the book. "You are doing quite well in your letters.

"Do I memorize that one?"

"No." Malaxia put the book down.

"The others ... the invisible ones," Liana spoke up. "It is true, isn't it?"

"Yes. As Flavius Josephus has written, they are there, to help or hinder, as you are able to control them. That will come, later."

"Always later. I'll be in a grave before I can do anything."

"Possibly—" Startled, Liana looked at her, "but I do not think so," Malaxia continued. "Your powers may blossom sooner than you expect, and there are certain rites to help achieve this. But we have done enough for now. Time for relaxation. A little fun, I think. Yes, witches may amuse themselves, like anyone else." Malaxia produced a shimmering red ball and tossed it to Liana. "Catch!"

Liana bobbled the ball; it fell, and abashed, she chased it. Red lights that seemed to come from within flashed as it rolled.

"Drop it too much and the rubies will fall out."

Embarrassed at her lack of skill, Liana got the ball and handed it back to Malaxia, who pocketed it.

"I need more practice, I guess. More concentration."

"There is another exercise, simple, even fun."

Liana didn't think it was going to be much fun.

"You will need to know how to use your hands. It is of utmost importance. Now," Malaxia extended her arms, "let my actions be your actions."

Liana held out her arms, mimicking Malaxia.

"That's it. Don't worry; neither of us will do any harm." Malaxia arced her arms gracefully; Liana repeated her movements.

"Good; good. Now, follow me."

They began to dance, two sylphs in flowing gowns, reflected in the pool. At first they moved side by side, the sorceress and her shadow, Liana watching Malaxia closely. Then, as Liana's confidence grew, they separated and their fluid movements spiraled in complimentary opposition. Lastly, without a word spoken, they faced each other and drew together around a shrinking circle, made of antiphons in motion: Malaxia made a gesture; Liana did a slightly different one; Malaxia's next movement followed out of the first two, to which Liana would respond. Their *pas-de-deux* was its own music. Malaxia watched her novice closely, without it seeming to appear so. It was also with an affection that was startlingly new.

This is how a mother loves a daughter, not a master a student. I never trained one I could love like this. Strange, it is the first time. When have I last had a first time? She is growing to magnificence, so honest, so pure, and I will purify her more. My creation, and she will be greater than I. Now, for the first time too, I am afraid. I was always a master, never a mother, and now I am becoming one.

The Witch's Hand

They finished with their hands entwined, Liana not realizing it was the same way as Malaxia had done it in their first meeting. Unsettled and very unsure about her new role, Malaxia released Liana's hands.

"Oh—oh—let's—oh—let's do it again." Liana was breathless.

"Enough. You've done far too much for today. But I am proud of you." Malaxia turned away. "You do have a gift." *She masters the dance faster than I did.* "You may find now that it is easier to focus your power."

Liana looked at her mentor, then at a maple leaf at her feet. With only the first finger of her left hand, she traced the outline of the leaf in the air above it, and a corresponding etching of fire ran along the outside of the leaf. When the entire leaf was outlined in fire, Liana raised her finger; the fire brightened, then she dropped it and the fire went out, leaving only the leaf with singed edges.

She could control fire.

They picked up Liana's books and prepared to leave. Then Liana's head went up, and Malaxia too was suddenly wary.

"Wait. Stand still," Malaxia cautioned, then put her armful down and motioned to Liana to do the same. With a quick gesture, Malaxia turned the books into a pile of dead sticks. She pulled Liana close, closed her eyes and murmured, "*Arboris sylvanus, arboris sylvanus.*" Standing immobile, Liana watched Malaxia's arm turn into a scaly black branch with twigs and leaves, then realized the same thing was happening to her and her feet were growing into the ground, entangled and merging with Malaxia's and now they stood joined, rigid as a tree, Liana's eyes stuck open staring in one direction, she could see leaves in front of her face and *she was a tree.*

Henri approached them through the woods, came up and leaned wearily against the tree.

"Never knew witch hunting was this hard."

Henri went on. From opposite sides, Paul and Alain backed into the area Liana could see, neither one aware of the other's presence, then bumped into each other and jumped and cried out in unison.

"Ahh!"

Paul was the first to get his wits back. "Have you seen anything? Have you found Robert?"

"No." Alain indicated Malaxia and Liana. "Just a lot of dried up old trees. If we don't find something soon I'm going home."

Paul and Alain left, and the clearing was silent for a few moments; then, with a *whissh* like a windstorm, the tree morphed back into Malaxia and Liana. Malaxia raged out of her stance; Liana stepped back.

"'Dried up old tree!'" Malaxia fumed. "I have not made that mistake in years!"

"But they didn't see us."

Malaxia sighed. "No, daughter, they didn't."

"I'm a little stiff, but it was fun being a tree." Liana gathered up her books and the lunch remnants.

"It was not meant to be fun. It was meant for protection. I thought we might have had an easier time of it here. I was wrong. There is another place. Come." Malaxia swept out of the clearing. "When we get there I will teach you the craft of summoning the powers of the sky itself, and of the earth."

17. BROTHER DOMINGO

The barley planting had gone well this day, and Brother Philippe was satisfied they would have enough at harvest not only to last through the winter, but to sell at a profit too. He was not that sure about the rye and oats, however. Rats had been at the storehouse holdings of these, despite the prowling vigilance of Magdalene the cat. He gave the earth a last tamp with his foot, and glanced up at the monastery of St. Jude, a buffed ochre ramble of buildings. A flash of white at the church caught his eye; there was movement between the arches of the outer corridor.

The Bishop of Peranville, ornately dressed, walked along the corridor, up a couple of steps, and past an open door with a view into the transept of the church, where monks were gathering. Long sunrays of blue and red fell over them from the stained glass windows; peasants stood further back. The monastery bell rang twelve times. The Bishop continued on.

"Vespers! Inside for Vespers!" Brother Philippe sang out. Peasants and monks shouldered their tools and headed toward the church. Two workers, Emile and Louis, lagged behind. Not in a charitable mood, Emile watched the Bishop's progress.

"Chausable climber. His brother married a Cardinal's niece."

"Daughter, you mean," Louis retorted. He too looked at the Bishop. "They say he skips over parts of Mass."

Brother Philippe called out, "You there! Hurry up!"

"It's in Latin, how can you tell?"

The Bishop went up a spiral staircase; through a small window, the planted field was visible far below, aglow with russet from the setting sun. He stopped before a chamber door and knocked.

"Father Domingo?"

From inside a soft voice answered, "The blessing of Mary upon you, come in."

The Bishop entered the small chamber, lit through one narrow window, where Father Domingo De Guzman, a Castilian, sat at a table piled with books and parchments. At thirty-six, his appearance belied his accomplishments; he wore a shabby off-white habit, with a hair shirt visible beneath. He was barefoot. A simple wooden cross hung from his neck. His reddish blond hair and fair skin showed the effects of many days in the sun.

Domingo's walking staff leaned in a corner, with a worn, dusty black cloak hung on a peg next to the staff. A crucifix with a twisted, tortured Christ was nailed to one wall. Domingo rose.

"Your Excellency?"

"Sit down, please, Father Domingo." The Bishop's tone was only a little unctuous.

Domingo sat. From the choir of the church below, strains of the *Magnificat* rose, and he paused to listen a moment before speaking. The singers halted abruptly, broken by an impatient "No! Late again on the second entrance!" then resumed at the beginning. Still practicing, then. The *Magnificat* didn't come till later in the service.

"Your Excellency," Domingo resumed, "though I am an ordained priest and therefore called 'Father' by the flock, I would be grateful if you and the other clergy called me 'Brother' instead. I am truly far beneath the title of 'Father,' which we use to address our own Lord in Heaven."

"As you wish, Brother Domingo. I merely wanted to see if you wished to join me for supper after Vespers?"

"No, thank you. If you would send up some bread and cheese later, that would be most kind."

The Bishop sat down. "I will see to it."

"I shall only be here a few more days, at this rate," Domingo indicated the array upon his table, "and I appreciate the hospitality you have shown me. I will certainly mention it in my letters to Rome."

The Bishop leaned forward eagerly. "The deputy of the Pope is deserving of all kindnesses we can render."

"Thank you." Domingo smiled, then became serious. "In these times, and especially in this place, heresy has become a most difficult matter with which to deal. The Count of Toulouse has been, and continues to be, our most serious obstacle in eradicating the Albigensian heresy—those whose leaders, known as the—" he consulted a parchment, "ah, here, the 'Perfect,' deny the sanctity of life, and the dual nature of our mortal bodies, part God's, part the Devil's."

Domingo warmed to his argument. "These heretics would have it that the earth is the Devil's, not God's creation, and that we are all undeniably

The Witch's Hand

evil from birth; nay, from conception. Some, I understand, wish for nothing more than death, and to this end they starve themselves, earning the praise and sanctification of the people, while in reality they are but committing suicide."

He rose and paced.

"It is an abomination, both to the teachings and the commandments of our Lord, who has said, '*Non occides*,' you shall not kill, and has clearly indicated in the Scriptures that we are to live a holy life, and preferably a long one, in order to carry out and exemplify His Word through doing His will."

The Bishop had never been a good listener, and now tried to keep from falling asleep. Absorbed in his passionate reasoning, Domingo continued.

"You cannot obey the greatest commandment, you cannot love God or your neighbor if by your own hand you are dead. They reject the Sacraments, they allow women the same duties and privileges as men in their church, if church it may be called; and the songs made about women and love by these ... these itinerant musicians, if musicians *they* can be called, reek with lechery under the guise of worship. Still, there are some men of learning among them. They call themselves, for example, *Cathari*—Greek, pure."

At the mention of purity, the Bishop was suddenly fully awake.

"And they do have some claims to decency in their tenets, Domingo continued. "They refuse to shed blood, they take care of the sick, feed the hungry, and refuse all earthly ostentation, as did our Lord." He looked at Bishop's finery. "However, they also refuse to attend Mass, scoff at the Trinity, do not venerate the saints, and worst of all, they deny the virginity of Our Lady." He sat. "I would like to dispute with these presumptuous believers their disciples call, the 'Perfect.'"

"And I would like to hear these disputes," the Bishop put in. It would be hard for the Perfect to get a word in against this one, he thought.

"Yes, unfortunately the Devil has been hard at work in these times, but in this area we have, I think, kept most of his evil away." Domingo paused. "Until now."

"The reports here are most interesting," he went on, "not only from the point of view of the investigation of heresy, but also from the fascinating conjectures given by many of your parishioners on the nature and conditions of witches; you have read them of course."

"No, I have not." The Bishop shifted in his chair.

"Indeed. Read them after I am done, then. A most remarkable variety. Witches causing ills, witches curing ills, turning themselves and others into all manner of bird and beast—here is a beast with seven heads; interesting …"

Domingo reached into his hair shirt and withdrew a louse, depositing it on the floor. The Bishop tried to keep from flinching as it scurried past his feet. Why did holiness have to depend on things like how many vermin you carried on your person? He wondered which preferred to infest the Pope, lice or fleas.

"… various invocations of the Devil, taken of course from our prayers," Domingo continued. "The problem is, these reports are all at least at second or third hand: 'My grandmother told me; I heard it from someone in the next town; it is said'—really! These people believe anything they're told, by anyone who claims it comes from either demonic or divine inspiration."

"Including the teachings of our Church?"

"I meant no disrespect, your Excellency, and God keep me from heresy. But the earthly routes to belief are the same, whatever the belief may be; in Church, Islam, or witchcraft. They all teach by story, history, and example. With the grace of divine reasoning, and with faith, we choose the right way, through the blood of our Lamb; without God's aid, we are lost."

"Interesting," the Bishop managed.

"Yes, his Holiness thinks so."

Again the Bishop was all helpfulness. "Please inform the Holy Father that the Albigensian heresy will be crushed here. The Bishop of Le Puy and I feel that a procession of the relics in this area would be a way to inspire awe and worship of the true Church, and thus win heretics back. The relics would be carried in a wagon covered with the gold-embroidered linen we use only on holy days, and accompanied by an entourage of bishops and other clergy—"

"Including yourself, your Excellency?"

The Witch's Hand

"As a guardian and overseer of the Church, naturally I would participate."

Now Domingo was the helpful one. "In the vestments usually reserved for holy days? Riding your finest horse?"

The Bishop nodded vigorously. "We do well to honor heavenly glory with worldly art and glory."

"Your Excellency," Domingo began deliberately. "It is not by the display of power and pomp, nor by cavalcades of retainers and fine palfreys, nor by gorgeous apparel, that the heretics win proselytes; it is by zealous preaching, by apostolic humility, by austerity, by holiness! They have outdone the Church in these matters, and now we must outdo them."

"You forget yourself, Brother Domingo!"

Immediately Domingo knelt before the Bishop.

"Your pardon and forgiveness. A display of relics may have some effect."

The Bishop passed his hand through the air in a blessing, and Domingo rose and looked out the window, where shadows were beginning to fill the fields.

"But there is still planting to be done. A lengthy procession would only disrupt this vital work and possibly lead to famine later on this winter. And the winters are harsh here, as you know." Domingo seated himself again. "I've no doubt the Albigensian heresy will be purged, as you say, with God's help. Witches are another matter."

"They are?"

"Yes. Unlike heretics, who hold to another canon of beliefs as a group, each witch is an individual case, and must be judged accordingly. They can sometimes be identified by certain talismans or amulets they wear—"

"I have seen these things," broke in the Bishop eagerly. "Some of them are figures of men and women in the most ghastly, distorted positions—"

"Your Excellency?" Domingo indicated the macabre crucifix on the wall. "What is that?"

"That is our Lord!"

"Yes," replied Domingo dryly. "I know. There is talk in Rome of a new council to deal with witches, heretics, and other matters harmful to our mother Church." Domingo sat back, and controlling his amusement said,

"I shall, with your permission, put your name among those who may be called to this council. We seek men of learning, with a sound theological background and training, some legal knowledge and experience, common sense, and of course, impugnable of heresy in any way. May I?"

"Thank you, yes." Surging with achievement and pride, the Bishop rose. "Please, go on with your work, Brother Domingo. I wish you all success."

"Thank you, your Excellency. But we are late for Vespers."

The Bishop quickly left the chamber, his mind churning over which vestments he would wear to his first audience with the Pope. Domingo put his head on the table.

"*Madre de Dios*, Mother of God, have I my work cut out for me!"

He rose and reached for his staff.

18. THE CRUSADE FALTERS

Lord, if you are not here, where shall I seek you? Surely you dwell in light inaccessible. And where is light inaccessible? I have never seen you, oh Lord; I do not know your face.
— *St. Anselm of Canterbury*

They had made camp in a sheltered grove after a fruitless day of searching. Jettaret was sitting by the fire, as Alberge threw blankets down over a pile of fern and grass to make the night ahead less miserable.

"You've been silent too long, Vicomte. What are you thinking?"

"Isaiah. 'Watchman, what of the night?' It's been a long night, a long dark night since ..." Jettaret looked Constantinople at his friend. "And the night is full of demons. We are chasing something terrible, like a dragonhound through hell, and I don't know how it will end."

"The night'll end, Vicomte. Always has."

"Mine has not. But there will be an end, finally. *Omnia finit veritas, et veritas finit omnia*. All things end in truth, and truth puts an end to all things. If Christ is the Truth, He it is who at the Last Judgment will put an end to all the things, all the terrible things, of this world." Jettaret sounded more dispirited than encouraged. "*Omnia finit veritas*."

Alberge came over and sat. "That isn't verbatim Isaiah. Or your Boethius."

"No. I heard it when I was reading for the priesthood, in Paris."

"Who told you?"

"An Irish monk. His Latin was better than mine."

"Hm. Did you slit his throat?"

Jettaret sighed. "I wish we had some of the Comte de St. Pol's knights with us," he said wearily. "Two field lines, twenty armed horsemen, would do well right now."

"So would a side of venison and a steady line of ripe and ready camp followers. These villagers out looking for your witch girl and her Mother Superior. Commandeer them, Vicomte; make them into an army, a little band of knights with their very own Crusade, conveniently right near home, and we'll go make war on the witches. I'll take the big one and you can have the little one."

"I have put war behind me, tried to forget it; I use the sword with a cry of the soul now, mindful of my sins. I do not do this battle willingly. And all the time I listen for the sound of peace, but I do not hear it."

"What do you think it sounds like, Vicomte?" Alberge poked up the fire, then went to his makeshift bed and got under the blankets. "You don't really want to do this? You don't like chasing witches; reasonable. So why—"

"Because I have to."

Alberge sighed and settled back. "Jesus had Gethsemane. I've got you." He stared up at heaven.

***

Late afternoon the next day found Jettaret and Alberge afoot through a wooded rise, path finding. Behind them, the horses fed. Alberge, in pain that would have been obvious had Jettaret turned an eye, lagged behind.

"Antoine. Wait."

"*Mea culpa,*" my fault, "God forgive me." Jettaret quickly went back to help Alberge sit down. "I'm sorry. Is it bad?"

Alberge dismissed it. "Ahh. Death will have us all crowned; king, queen, Vicomte . . . Alberge. I'll likely end up burning with the heretics down here, the Albigensians. I'll be at the stake with people who try to live a pure life." He chortled, then winced.

"Albigensians. They say the Devil made the world."

"They've got something there." Alberge tried to get his wineskin, slung over his back. "*Vive le vin; vive la morte!*" Long live wine; long live death.

"Shut up, you Provence fool. I'll get your—what is this vintage anyway?" Jettaret handed Alberge the wineskin. "It tastes like distilled bull water."

Alberge didn't blink. "Goat, actually." He drank. "With one or two physics to stave off pain."

The Witch's Hand

Jettaret's revelation came hard. "Rosemary and wormwood. The odor is unmistakable. You've been going slower and slower; we haven't made six miles today. If you wish to die that's your affair, but I've an affair of my own to settle."

"I am not trying to die, Vicomte. Not yet. Maybe you are the one who should slow down. You took off with a virgin on the way to your wedding. The Church can fine you."

"After Constantinople? What does a fine mean?" Jettaret sounded suddenly old. Alberge assented to his logic.

"Antoine. July 17th, three years ago. Outside the walls of Constantinople, double walls. You and I and three thousand other Crusaders—knights, archers, crossbowmen, sergeants on foot. With Pierre d'Amiens and the Comte de St. Pol; the Comte de Flandre in the vanguard, Henri d'Hainault behind us. Against that phony Emperor, with his thirty thousand. The odds were ten to one. Then Flandre and Hainault turned back, with two thirds of the men, and it was thirty to one. With only a rise of ground between us. But Amiens and St. Pol kept going, up the rise. And Amiens—remember what he said? 'Forward now!' With one thousand men. Against the Eastern Empire. You remember what day of the week it was?"

Jettaret didn't know and didn't care.

"Thursday. And when the ones who'd turned rabbit saw we'd kept going, they came back, spread out all abreast, and we went up that hill and broke the crest in one line, straight across. Three thousand men. Three battalions, on a lonely hill. Three to one against us. And they turned tail and ran! What are we up against now? One lousy witch."

Jettaret turned to his friend. "Two, Alberge. And we don't know what Liana can do yet. *She* doesn't know."

"What is this girl to you? And if this Malaxia witch is what you say, it is better to keep a good distance. By my honor lost, I have seen love work in many ways, but—"

"I don't love her, Alberge. I want to save her life; that is different."

"So you say."

Anger roiled within Jettaret's breast. "You didn't have to come with me; you could have stayed at the inn, preaching against the new Crusade, drinking whatever you could find; several women there would have even had a lame man, I—"

Alberge silenced the Vicomte with narrowed eyes. Jettaret turned away, and Alberge knew how worn out he was.

"Antoine …"

Jettaret indicated he was all right.

Alberge's raspy voice became gentle. "We have been on the road for days, my friend. It is not wormwood that slows us down. You asked why I came. This witch, one or the other, may have hexed you, therefore you are mad; madmen need a keeper."

Jettaret's eyes went skyward. "Your reasoning is not of the university—"

"A man of parts needs no university!" Alberge drank, and saw Jettaret take out Liana's ring. "Doesn't that ring of hers show you the way?"

"It's not a magic ring," Jettaret said, wistful. "It's only hers."

"I would it were magic. We'd be a lot better off. Could it show us the way to an inn?"

"*No*, Alberge. The further magic from this ring, the better."

"Put a little curse on those villeins following us?"

"I don't believe in curses." Jettaret put Liana's ring away and rose.

"You don't believe in anything. You're worse than I am." Alberge pulled at his wineskin. "That woman on the wall in Constantinople, the one that cursed you, looking right at you? She meant all of us. Can't blame her. We ruined her city, burned her own house no doubt, probably killed her husband, her kids; it wasn't just for you, that curse. We all got it."

Jettaret strode away several paces.

"We are making no progress." He turned back to Alberge. "We should divide, take two ways. Here," he knelt and drew on the ground, "we are heading, more or less, toward Toulouse. If you were to go north, here, then circle around while I made a circle south, we could cover twice as much ground."

Alberge studied the lines in the dirt. "Hmm …"

Jettaret kept drawing. "We meet here, then make another set of circles …"

"And?"

The Witch's Hand

"And keep going." Fire was growing in Jettaret's eyes. "To the end of Gascogne, over the Pyrenees, across Castile, Portugal—"

"And beyond, where there be dragons? I'm not following you there, Vicomte," Alberge rumbled.

"No, you're going to steal another wagon—"

"Mary's ass I will!"

"Blasphemer."

"Idiot."

Jettaret hoisted Alberge up by his shoulders and moved him along. "You're going to steal another wagon and meet me three days from now outside Aurillac, here. Keep your eyes open—" Alberge, unnoticed by Jettaret, mouthed Liana's description.

"Liana, you know, is a small girl with long dark hair, and Malaxia— you feel she's there before you see her, if you see her at all. She's dangerous; your pike won't help you. Look in any places where there's been a fire, or a lot of trees down. She could probably divert rivers too. Check anything out of the ordinary—"

Alberge ground his staff and good heel in. "Antoine. You're acting like a goat girl."

"Alberge. See those trees on the hill over there? All she has to do is—" Jettaret flicked his fingers, "and they're gone."

"You talk too much. *Au revoir.*" Alberge started off toward the horses.

"Wait. What's that?"

"Huh?"

Jettaret pointed to a small group of people on the road in the distance. Alberge came up alongside and squinted. "Your eyes are better than mine. What are they doing?"

Jettaret watched the crowd accost a young woman in dark clothes; one man brandished a live chicken. "Four, five men—a lady in black— they're trying to give her a chicken but she won't take it."

Alberge recognized it. "It's a test. They want her to kill the chicken." He saw Jettaret's puzzlement. "The Albigensian heretics don't shed blood. Of any kind."

Jettaret drew his sword and started forward. Alberge went after him.

"Antoine!" he hissed. With his cloak and pike, Alberge brought Jettaret down, and struggled to hold him. "Defend her and they'll burn you too. It's Liana you want to save." Realization stopped Jettaret's resistance. Alberge let him up and pulled him away. "Come on. Three days, outside Aurillac. Uh—" With a raised hand he silenced Jettaret, who was about to speak, clapped him on the shoulder and moved him off.

"Oh, Liana's not pretty, not beautiful—"

"Shut up." Jettaret stalked over to Pasquale, mounted and spurred away. Alberge stood watching him; in his eyes and chest was an uncommon burning.

"I have wept for the living and the dead," he muttered. "What good did it do them?" Then he growled it off and turned to the business at hand. "One wagon—two horses." Alberge mounted Bluestone and rode off, leading the cart horse and singing.

Wagons, women and innkeepers
Can never be shaken too much.

Behind him, the crowd closed around the woman.

19. THE CAVE

Barely a mile off from the southern road, the path Malaxia took led through rolling terrain, punctured here and there by sharp boulders. She halted before a slab of rock that masked an opening, dark and narrow, in the rise behind. There was just enough room between the slab and the rise for them to squeeze through and into a passageway that led down, down, then opened into an underground cavern.

Within the cavern, stalagmites rose to meet or nearly meet stalactites hanging from above; fissures opened into dark abysses, and crystalline formations jutted in impossible shapes, seeming more brilliant than they were, as their blue and purple shades were reflected back from a pool of water. The colors wavered over the rocks and water, making them full of movement, almost alive. The light had no obvious source.

Malaxia's voice sounded hollow and disembodied, like a singer's in a cathedral. "Air is thought, fire is longing, water is blood, earth is death."

Liana's voice joined hers. "Air is thought, fire is longing, water is blood, earth is death."

Malaxia and Liana stopped in a recess, the waters glimmering at their feet.

"Earth is death, death is life, life is air, air is thought," Malaxia continued.

Liana did not understand, but repeated the words with her.

"Good. The meaning will become more apparent with time. Patience! If you have one fault it is your lack of it."

Liana stood apart, watching the waters. Life was water, she thought, and the light within it was the soul. Then, suddenly uneasy, she lifted her head, seeing. Malaxia listened and strained to sense and see other presences, but that insolent beggar of a talking skull had been right; Liana's gift in the Sight far outstripped her own.

Malaxia withdrew out of Liana's peripheral vision and quietly placed the glowing blue jewel in a nook underwater. The rocks about it quivered but she arrested them with a stern look. The jewel had come from them, but it was hers now, remade as she would remake Liana.

"Do you see anything above ground?"

"People—many people—looking for us!"

"We will be undisturbed here," Malaxia said. They were far south of Peranville now, deep in Albigensian territory wherein the Church itself feared to reach. Even without the Sight, she did not fear discovery by that contemptible wretch who'd been with her protégé. "I myself did much study here, deep in the earth." She spread her graceful arms toward the water reflections on the rocks. "It seems dead, yet it moves, it shimmers, it lives. The power of light in its true brilliance, and you are ready for it."

"Now?" Liana was eager.

"Yes."

Recognition filled Liana's voice. "Earth is death," the coldness and hardness of the stone, "death is life?" the lively motion of the light and water over it.

"Precisely." To herself Malaxia added, "And I hope it will ground some of your flightiness."

"What?"

"The ground under the waters holds what you seek. It is yours to find."

Liana searched. Seeing a flash of blue light beneath the water, she reached out to it.

"Not with your hands," Malaxia reprimanded. "Bring it to you."

Liana stared at the jewel, drawing it toward her. When it broke the surface, she looked at Malaxia, who nodded; Liana took the jewel into her hand. There was a rumbling and a cracking noise. Liana looked about, afraid.

"The cave gives up its treasure unwillingly. As always."

Malaxia silenced the noise with a flattening gesture, annoyed; the cave's spirits went back further than even she had studied, and had been difficult to control. But she had mastered them. Liana held the jewel up; its light dazzled, filling and overflowing the recess, and she spoke with understanding.

"Air is thought, fire is longing, water is blood, earth is death."

Liana lowered the jewel and the dazzle began to fade.

"Earth is death, death is life—"

"Life is air, air is thought," Malaxia finished.

The Witch's Hand

The light from the jewel slowly went out. Liana put it in her leather bag.

"And now for the sky spell. To control its powers, both arms up—"

"How do I reach the sky from here?"

"It is a precaution. In case the spell gets out of hand, our sky to work with is only the air in here. The powers of nature are not to be dallied with; they can, without magic at all, take a most destructive course. A rock from a hillside can be driven a mile away, a tree can be uprooted, if but the wind is strong enough. I have seen this." Malaxia moved to a wide area beside the pool. "One can draw power from both earth and sky, one arm down, one up, so," Malaxia stood with her arms diagonally spread. "I myself believe it is the more powerful of the two, though some disagree. But first now, the sky spell. Arms up—"

An hour and forty-five intense minutes later, Liana had only dislodged a few chips of stone from above, though the pool still rippled with a wind that had whistled through the rock formations and put a crack in one. Meager results but even so, she was weak and wringing with sweat. Malaxia, cool, waited for her fledgling to collect herself.

"And now the earth spell; later, we will combine them. Arms, thus—" Malaxia held her arms out at a forty-five degree angle toward the ground, then indicated a stalagmite in front of them. "Face that. Do not take your eyes off it.

Pulling strength from a source she did not know, Liana extended her arms, the left hand drooping toward the ground, the right raised despite an assault of tremors.

"Now, draw the power that made mountains and cleaved the valleys. Draw it up, into yourself, all of it; draw it up! Up!"

Liana's left hand was crushed from all sides with a terrible weight, and she could not keep her fingers apart but there it was, something was coming up through them, though her hand felt encased in a lead globe, and her right hand wanted to fuse with it like a magnet dancing in sparks; but she felt taller, weightier—

"To the rock! Now!"

A mighty surge from the Earth itself burst through her, and the stalagmite flattened into dust. The shock of its transformation dissolved all the power in her, and Liana found herself crumpled on the ground.

Wendy Joseph

"You have done well, my child. You have done well."

20. ALBERGE VERSUS THE WITCH HUNTERS

Alberge hoisted himself with difficulty to a rocky ledge over a shallow pool and growled, the kind of growl that would have frightened any small children in the vicinity. He scanned the area, got his wineskin and drank, long and slow. Bluestone—the witch mare hadn't pulled anything on him, at any rate—was tied further down the slope below the pool, which was really more of a gathered pause in the course of a thin stream, water enough for his wine if he needed it. Water it too much and you had infant's milk, and dying of thirst was the better option.

"Ahh... I should have stayed out of that inn." He drank again, then heard a commotion below. "Ehh?"

Fifty feet below, next to the pool, the determined hunters Paul, Maxine, Henri and Alain converged. They didn't see Alberge above them.

"Have you found anything?" Paul asked.

Henri shook his head. "They say the witches have been sighted near Toulouse."

"Toulouse? That's more than three days away," protested Alain. "Why can't we let them handle it?"

"The Count of Toulouse will probably give them refuge," Maxine pointed out.

"That's right, Henri agreed. "The sooner we burn them, the sooner we go home."

I'll see if I can't distract them. Alberge pulled his hair forward around his face, wrapped his cloak around himself, and stepped forward on the ledge.

"Ahh! Ha ha ha ha! Ha ha ha!" The searchers looked up as one, and saw an extremely ugly witch.

"Up there! Get her!" cried Alain.

"Sneak up on her," Paul hissed in a low voice. "This way!"

The peasants ran off. Alberge cackled, then heard them ascending the rocky trail behind him, and turned as they attacked with their farm tools, poking and jabbing and swinging with unexpected dexterity.

The greatest pikeman of the thirteenth century fought back.

They fell away like threshed wheat and retreated, but getting past them and back down to Bluestone was a fool's effort with his piece of crap leg. He went back out to the ledge.

Below was a near perpendicular cliff and the pool. He stepped over the edge, slid part way down the cliff, fell the rest of the way, caught his fall with his pike one foot above the water, and hung there between two rocks like a spitted boar, in plain view from above. Alberge considered his options, looked about, and decided.

"Vicomte! I'm doing this for you." He shoved off with his pike and splashed into icy water. Bubbles rose. Finally he resurfaced, gasping and shivering, and hid under an overhanging rock. The peasants reappeared above.

"Where'd she go?"

"She's vanished."

"Maybe the Devil took her."

"Holy Mary." Alain crossed himself.

Paul resumed command. "All right, we'll find her. The demon tree—"

"The dead one back there?"

"Right, dead trees draw witches; this way!"

The witch hunters vanished, and Alberge waited, listening. He reached behind him and threw out a croaking frog. When he was sure they weren't coming back, he left his hiding place and looked about. For all he knew the fools were already lost in this convoluted terrain, looking for the lightning blasted tree which he'd passed and knew was a good league off. Growling, he made his way out via the stream.

"Damn horse probably gone poof by now anyway, witch horse, back to her bloody magic maker, ow! Move—" he thrashed at a stone with the gall to be in his way, "can't find a trail, bloody witches probably don't leave trails, outta my way—" a growth of reeds this time, "how he's gonna get a witch to play nice, never gave that any thought, sorry bastard, end up taking us both to bloody hellfire—"

21. DOMINGO AND THE TROUBADOUR

The dust rose between his toes, and the callouses on Brother Domingo's feet weren't enough to ward off the sharpness of the stones here. *Gratia Deo*, God be thanked, Our Lord felt the stones of the road too. And much worse.

The road wound south, around gentle rises and copses of trees, and presently he heard the wind through their leaves joined by a voice, strong but far ahead, singing. After a few minutes, Domingo saw a troubadour with an Eastern looking lute coming toward him.

Ma maire, maridatz-me	My mother, let me marry
Ara que soi madura	Now that I am ripe.
Mon galant me b'a agachat	My sweetheart, looking at me
En viran la pastura, dal prat	While turning meadow hay,
M'a dit qu'eri madura	Told me I was ripe.

The troubadour stopped before Domingo with a flourish of his cap. "Jules de la Tour is most gratified to make your acquaintance, holy father."

"I am not the Pope, my son," Domingo smiled, then gently admonished, "Have you nothing better to do than sing about ripe maidens and lecherous lovers?"

Jules protested, "No indeed, holy father, for 'among all men on the earth, bards have a share of honor and reverence, because the muse has taught them songs and loves the race of bards.'" His smile was wickedly blissful. "Homer, a pagan. So I can sing you a sad song, or a blessed holy song, which is the same thing; or news of the north, or west, or south—"

"What is the news from the south?" Domingo asked quickly.

"Much, and bad."

"Of heresy?"

"Of witchery." The troubadour was arch. "Two witches, and the worst kind—young witches. Going about the country and raising the Devil's own. They'd all gone out to chase 'em—left their houses open to me," he concluded with glee.

Which might be the reason for his attire, and Domingo confronted him. "Is that where you got your fine shirt?"

"No, dear blessed holy father, 'twas given to me by a man who said he was trying to dispense himself of the finery and trappings of the world."

Urgency entered Domingo's demeanor. "Did he say why?"

"Aye, he said 'twas some new teaching, some holy teaching. If all were as holy as he, I'd be rich soon enough," the rascal chortled.

"Where did this man live?"

"Oh, up a ways, up the road a ways. I know not where he lived — maybe in the next county. But he was going to meet some other, someone he called 'pure.'" Jules suddenly sounded sincere as a child. "Are there pure beings in this world, father?"

"There have been some. Did he say where this man lived?"

The troubadour's eyes gleamed. "The shirt is fine, but the purse is empty."

Domingo searched his own purse and gave Jules a copper obol.

"Two coppers gets you twice the purchase," he offered brightly. Domingo looked but couldn't find another obol. The rogue sighed, then appeared to decide he'd gotten the best deal he could.

"Now, this other man lived somewhere between Albi, Aurillac, and Toulouse; but where exactly I know not. Still, the witches be there, and 'tis from there I am going," Jules declared.

"This 'pure' man. Did he have a name?"

"His name? Nay, I know not his name. But I have heard the ones called pure are called perfect also. They would go together, would they not, father?"

"Yes, they would. Do you know any more about them, these 'pure?'"

"Only that they kill no beast and eat no meat, and so to my mind live a most dreadful dull life. And some are called saints, and are thought to be as holy as yourself, dear father. Is it true?"

"I do not know. It is one of the things I wish to find out. Go along, now, and you do well to scurry from witches."

The troubadour looked at him, shrewd. "But that is where you are scurrying to, is it not, dear father?"

"It is. And I expect to have my hands full."

"That you will indeed, holy blessed father, that you will indeed." He went on his way with a new song.

Ome et femna	Man and woman
nos al luèit	go to bed
Farèm le mestier	To make the trade
de cada nuèit	of each night.

Domingo prayed for patience. Holding back his rebuke, he tried to consider Jules' manifest joy in life, a God-given gift, and prayed he would put it to more chaste ends. The troubadour disappeared around a bend to the north.

"Musical fool," Domingo finally vented. "I scarcely know which is worse, a heretic or a wastrel." He continued down the road south.

22. "CHARMING SITUATION"

Not far from Malaxia's cavern, and secreted away in a defile surrounded by cliffs, a wide brook raised mist and a foaming hiss as it fell forty feet to fill a pool below. A clearing of sorts, made of flat boulders and tangled growth surrounded by trees, opened the area about the pool to the sky. Steep streams rushed onward from it, divided by and tumbling over the jumbled rocks.

In the cliff just beneath the lip of the falls and to one side, a mossy recess offered refuge from both water and a horrific plunge. A tiny trail snaked up to it from the pool below, and by this way Malaxia and Liana entered the recess.

Liana fingered the blue jewel that hung from a chain round her neck. It felt loose in its mounting and she started to examine it. Then she noticed a flat topped, altar like stone at the rear of the recess, which seemed to be drawing the jewel toward itself. Malaxia ignored it.

"Earth you have. Power over air, the highest power, comes like the air, like the wind, which chooses its own time. But water and fire are specific. Water is blood, the fire of life, and you must bond yourself with both, physically, and with the spirits, the others. And then, the sacred circle of fire." Malaxia sounded exultant.

"Fire?" Liana's old fear was back.

"It will not harm you. Not if you are ready for it. Yes. You will pass through fire and not be burned. I will show you."

Malaxia circled with her left arm, her fingers making the fire spell, and a horizontal flaming disk hovered over the drop at their feet. Malaxia descended into it. Liana shrank away, then saw Malaxia reappear on a ledge below and dispatch the flames with a left armed counter-clockwise circle.

"Here, child. I am not harmed." Malaxia came back up beside her. "So will it be for you. There is something I have been aware of; doubtless your training has obscured it. Look toward Lyon." Malaxia made a small gesture over her own eyes, which Liana missed. "What do you see?"

Liana looked with the Sight, or so she thought; fuzzy edged, she saw the stones and stained glass of an unfamiliar cathedral. Lyon.

"The cathedral . . . people outside . . . inside, a ceremony . . . there, a lady . . . I don't know her . . . and walking toward her . . . no—"

"Who?"

Liana half whispered, "Jettaret."

"He has left you and gone to his bride. So much for the word of a nobleman. I am sorry, but you had to know. Are you willing now to renounce that world?"

"Yes."

"Go into the woods, then, to prepare. You must have time alone."

Liana descended the cliff, then looked a question at Malaxia.

"You will know when to return."

Liana crossed the stream quickly from rock to rock, a large leap to one, not noticing a flash as her jewel broke from its mounting into the water. She vanished into the woods. Malaxia went down and retrieved the jewel. *Her power. I will keep it for her.*

She needs this time, this last time with her thoughts, to consider, to resolve. If she still wants to leave, she must have the opportunity to do so. If she comes back, she is indeed mine. My own forever.

Liana went some ways, till she came to a cave-like grotto, scooped out from a rocky abutment and covered within and almost completely overhead by leafy growth. There she sat. She tried various spells, easily and with command now; their colors flickered over the leaves. With only thumb and forefinger, she made a fire. She played with it with small flicks and put it out.

Jettaret was a murderer. Yet he had protected her. He didn't seem to believe in anything, and he'd made fun of her. But he had fought the chaos of the magic storm to try and keep her safe. He was part of the world that would try to burn her, and not part of it; he had risked plunging to his own death to seize her from the cliff's edge, and she thought wistfully of the strength of his hand, the comfort in his presence when he was near. There had been pain and sadness in his eyes always, even when he was making lighthearted jokes. He was an enigma, a mystery, and exasperating, yet every time she looked past Malaxia, she wondered if he would be standing there.

The Witch's Hand

But if he had forsaken her altogether, he would never be back to look for her. She was abandoned. Sobs wrenched their way out and by their own force spilled her onto the ground.

Malaxia was waiting. Now. Liana sat up again.

I will go with her. The resolution came even as she shuddered with more tears. *Jettaret?* The sound of his sword still rang in her ears, and she wanted so much to go to him too. But he didn't want anything to do with her, and even if he did, that would mean Lyon, and the Church. *The Church has disowned me; can I disown the Church?* The only certainties were her studies with Malaxia, and Liana felt the chain for her jewel, the gift from the cave.

It was gone. Liana looked about frantically and searched the ground for it, then was oddly calm. *I'll find it later. Malaxia won't mind. Not now.* Liana wiped her eyes and left the grotto.

In a small clearing halfway between her and the waterfall, a voice broke the silence.

"Liana?"

There was no answer. Jettaret pulled Pasquale to a halt. True and trusted she was, nobler than most men who claimed a title, but even her animated pace had slowed to that of a drudge, a farm horse. It was no longer fair. He dismounted.

"That's all for you today, my sweet." The clearing lay amidst a heap of boulders, and he put his saddle and gear atop one, unbridled Pasquale and left her tied with a long line so she could forage. Then he sat down wearily upon a flat stone.

"I think we've covered half of Languedoc." Jettaret got out his wineskin and drank. "Water. Alberge . . ." It had been the Provence rascal's favorite prank on the Crusade. A translator, declared Alberge, needed more wine to fuel his tongue than those who spoke but one language. "He gets wine, I get water. Right now I'd even drink his god awful wine." The wormwood adulteration was a detriment to health and spirits, but Alberge was not much concerned with that. Jettaret sighed. "Charming situation. The Vicomte de Solignac, without wine, hunting prey without feathers or fur—" A squirrel chattered, sudden and sharp. Jettaret looked up.

"Liana?" There was silence. Jettaret kicked at the rocks at his feet. "Why am I looking for her? What is she? A witch—a virgin witch—there's no such thing. And what value is she to me? I've no alliances with—what was the name of that town of hers?—ah, Peranville. Mother of God, she doesn't come from Solignac, causes nothing but trouble, I should be glad to get rid of her . . . ahh . . . Antoine, you talk too much."

Behind him, Malaxia approached silently through the trees. Jettaret did not see her.

"Maybe she *has* vanished; maybe that witch turned them both into spirits," then the words exploded, "I don't believe in witches! I don't believe in magic, and I don't believe in you, Malaxia!" he shouted to the air. "What do you want with her? She's so small—"

"Small things may be stronger than they seem." Malaxia stepped into the clearing before him. Jettaret leaped to his feet.

"*Putain du Turque!*" he spat.

Malaxia smiled. "Neither a whore nor a Turk, as you shall see. I would not seek her anymore." She moved closer, her voice cold. "She is mine now."

Jettaret went for his sword. Malaxia cast a right-handed spell, knocking him down flat; a short swipe with her left hand sent a surge of sparks across Pasquale's line, and the mare took flight.

From the woods, Liana entered the clearing. She saw not Jettaret, but a pile of sword-like stones.

"Careful of the stones, child. They are sharp."

Liana stepped over Jettaret and stopped. Malaxia regarded her.

"You are not ready yet."

"I was—"

"You have bettered your skills faster than I had thought. But a few more steps, and the gift will be entirely yours, as I promised. Take a bit more time."

One last task, and the fool knight had provided it. What surer way to test her renunciation of his world and its attractions than by proximity to him?

"I too must prepare, for the ritual involves some degree of shared trial." Malaxia smiled. "Yes, I will be with you. Perhaps you would like some music while you wait?"

The Witch's Hand

Liana was at a loss. "We have no pipes, no flute; and I can't play them—"

"Music," Malaxia arced her right hand upward, "comes from the air." She left the clearing.

Liana stroked the air with her right hand. Tones that were a cross between a harp and cut glass filled the air. Liana began to sway, to turn, to dance, stepping lightly over the Jettaret rocks.

Jettaret had sworn to protect her, and he had vanished. The Church had held up redemption, and it was trying to destroy her. She had no one left in the world but Malaxia.

She would be a witch.

As she spun, a loose piece of lace drifted down from her shift without her noticing it. The lace fell by Jettaret; he sat up in a trance, not seeing Liana, nor she him. The music trailed off and Liana turned toward Jettaret, sensing a presence but seeing nothing, and scurried off after Malaxia. Some moments later Jettaret came out of his trance, picked up the lace, and they could have heard his cry in Jerusalem.

"LIANA!" He looked about and dashed out of the clearing.

23. FACE-OFF

Stand fast in your enchantments and your many sorceries, with which you have labored from your youth; perhaps you may be able to succeed, perhaps you may inspire terror.

—Isaiah 47:12

Malaxia entered the recess and readied the rock at the rear as an altar for Mass, with a linen cloth and a chalice; she moved like a pagan priestess on the way to a sacrifice. Using Liana's jewel, she cut herself, etching a deep gouge in her left arm. She put the jewel into the chalice and let the blood flow into it. Blood bubbled and steamed in the chalice. Malaxia added water from the stream, then bound the wound. Lastly, she took the amulet from her own chain and put it in the chalice. There was the barest sound behind her, as Liana entered the recess. Malaxia faced her.

"You are ready? Prepared to taste and then renounce the cup of mortality, of all things that pass?"

"Yes."

"And after, the circle of fire, to enter the world of the spirits, of that which does not fade?"

"Yes."

"It is done. The full gift of the others—power, everlasting youth, and the sweetness beyond thought, is yours."

Malaxia held the cup out to Liana, and they held it from both sides.

"Air," Malaxia began, and raised the chalice.

"Is thought, fire is longing, water is blood, earth is death," Liana completed.

"Taste, and you will be as one with every bird of the air and beast of the field, and more. The strength of the ox, the eye of an eagle."

Jettaret appeared at the crest of the cliff, on the other side of the waterfall. He freed a thick vine and swung out over the falls, toward the recess.

The two witches spoke together as they raised the cup. "Strength of the ox, eye of an eagle. Strength of the ox, eye of an eagle."

They lowered the cup and Malaxia gave it to Liana.

"Liana! Don't!" Jettaret burst into the recess, letting go of the vine as she was about to drink.

Malaxia seized the chalice before Liana dropped it. Liana ran down the rocky path beside the waterfall to the clearing, Jettaret in close pursuit. Malaxia followed them halfway down; her words overlapped Jettaret's.

"Liana! Liana, come back!"

"Submit yourself to your persecutor. He will pay for it."

Liana faced Jettaret warily. He stood his ground.

"Liana. Listen to me." Liana raised her hands toward him. "No. Liana, no! She's making you do this!"

"No, she isn't. It's my own power, and I've learned how to use it. And you deserted me." Liana was defiant. "I am a witch. But I will not burn."

Malaxia descended and approached Jettaret. "A man of learning such as yourself, a man who has seen what the world has to offer—why do you stay with her? Why just guard and watch her? Why not have her?"

"Non ars malificus!" None of your evil arts! "Away, witch!" Jettaret tightened his grasp on Fortuna Domini. "Seize her, very well; you face me."

"I applaud your courage. I spit at your stupidity." Malaxia smiled faintly. "Is it not just, that he who knows so well how to kill, should learn how to die?" She returned to Liana and moved behind her.

"Deal with him quickly, child. You must finish the ritual, and pass through the circle of fire. That is far more important."

Liana raised her hands higher.

"Do it. My daughter."

Jettaret eyed both witches, then stepped toward Liana, calm.

"Liana, it's Jettaret. Antoine. The vicomte. I found you outside Peranville. You saved us from the wild boar, remember?"

Liana drew back, her hands unsteady. She remembered.

"I was taking you to Lyon. We met bandits, and—do you still have any watercress?" Liana looked confused. "I did not desert you at the inn. I've been looking for you." With effort, he went on. "I deserted outside Constantinople, but I did not desert you. It's me, Jettaret. I talk too much, remember? Do you hear me? Liana, the thing behind you is a devil. She killed your family; she'll kill you!"

The Sight flung a vision into her head, of her home, all silent, on that night. Liana lowered her hands. "Jettaret . . .?"

Relief beyond all measure flowed through him. "Yes."

Malaxia came forward. "He lies. Life for life, my daughter!"

She saw Malaxia raise her hands, and a conjured destruction sped through the air, targeted in on the fireplace inside. Malaxia, not she, had done it.

Malaxia sent forth a cascade of force, and this one spelled murder; it was a death enchantment that went right through Liana like an electric current before it hit Jettaret, and he and Liana both fell like sheared grain. Jettaret didn't get up. Liana rose, shaky.

"Come, my heiress. We will continue."

Liana took a step toward her, halted and looked back at Jettaret. He had come for her at last, and had spoken the truth. And now he was dead.

She saw the timbers of her home crack once more.

"NO!" Liana spun toward Malaxia with both hands out. Uncontrolled, a blast Malaxia did not need to sidestep veered past her.

"Your jewel?"

"I don't have it." Liana didn't care about it anymore.

"A pity. It is no ordinary adamant; it would have made you stronger. If you knew how to use it." *But I have it now.* She regarded her discalced protégé. *So it was not to be. Her great work had been an illusion. Now it must be destroyed.* Malaxia was saddened, but almost relieved.

Liana side-stepped in a circle, Malaxia mirroring her, like two felines feinting and casting spells. Malaxia knocked Liana down again, hard into the dirt. She raised her head.

"You *are* the evil one!"

"No. Two hundred years ago I would have done to death evil in all its forms, but I saw that it was impossible. Had you more years, you would see it too. Now it is too late." Malaxia made a sudden gesture toward something behind Liana. "*Ho-gut!*"

Liana looked behind her, saw nothing and Malaxia took the off guard advantage to drive her to the ground, but then, backing up, Malaxia herself tripped and fell over a root. Both rose to face off.

With spells, with branches as broadswords and pikes, then knives, then fists and wrestling, Liana and Malaxia fought in and out of the pool. Malaxia sent fire spells at Liana, who parried them off and sent some back. Both were totally disheveled, Liana's right shoulder bloodied; in the water, Malaxia held up a hand in truce, and Liana stopped her spell from taking flight. The witch swept a fallen coil of hair from her eyes and refastened it atop her head, recommencing the fight with a burst of angry fire from the pool.

They waded ashore.

Liana faced the witch. There was only one choice left. She cast the sky spell with both arms up; Malaxia, the sky/earth spell, one arm up, the other down. Purple white light blinded Liana and the rock cracked beneath Malaxia's feet with a wrenching clap. Their wails joined into one inhuman scream.

On the altar, both candles went out, and the blood-filled chalice evaporated even as it fell over. Malaxia's amulet and Liana's glowing jewel flew from it, over the falls and past the pool into the cascading stream, among the rocks.

A cloud of smoke and shimmering mist filled the glade and rose past the mist of the falls in a huge plume. On the ground below, Liana raised her head and looked for Malaxia. When the mist cleared from the place where she had been, it was empty. Liana peered through the spell mist that hovered about, slowly dissipating till all was clear. Malaxia was gone. Liana went over and searched the ground; there was no trace of the witch, but a wooden shape trampled in the dirt looked familiar—

Maman's angel jar! Sweet herbs and flower petals on the inside, strong boar and stag carved on the outside, it was meant to call the angels down with the fragrances of Heaven, to protect and defend them and their house. Malaxia had even taken that.

Liana picked up the jar and fingered the stag's antlers. It had not protected them very well. Maybe the angels weren't listening that night. Then she pocketed it and went to Jettaret. He moved, began to revive; she gasped, and bent to him so eagerly she knocked him back down.

"Oh!" She drew back and let him sit up. He looked around.

"Malaxia?"

"She's gone."

The Witch's Hand

"All . . . gone?"

Liana checked with the Sight. "Yes. And forever." Liana backed away and attempted a fire spell. Nothing happened. She tried again. "I—I—" Her legs gave out and Jettaret hurried to her.

"Not every day you face something like her. See what being a witch does to you?"

"I'm not a witch anymore. All of it went—with her. Except the Sight, which is mine." She had spent her magic to save them both.

"You didn't want to be a witch—did you? Hmm? Have you anything else of hers? Best to get rid of it.

"She gave me a jewel. I lost it." Liana shed her singed and ragged dress and indicated her ragged shift. "This is mine."

Cold and wet, her powers exhausted, Liana shivered. Jettaret tore a rag from her shift and started to dress her cut shoulder.

"Being an ordinary mortal has its advantages." He put his cloak around her. "I am going to send a message to a certain lady in Lyon—"

"What?"

"I haven't been to Lyon, I was looking for you. I shall send a message telling her I am . . . disinherited, and then she most certainly won't have me. This, I believe, belongs to you." Jettaret drew out Liana's ring. "You pointed me in the right direction with it."

"No I didn't; I don't remember losing it."

"Then maybe that holy water you dipped it helped out." He put it on her left ring finger. "Lady Liana."

"What?" Joy at seeing her ring again masqued what he had said.

"I'll admit that's not quite the way it's done, but—"

"*The witch!*" Marie, Paul, Maxine, Henri, Claire, Alain, Danielle, Robert, and a gaggle of other peasants burst into the glen. Alberge and Domingo entered from opposite sides, Alberge elbowing Robert back to see.

"Hold!" Fortuna Domini flashed with Jettaret's command, and all halted save Alain, who charged forward with a spade. Jettaret dashed the spade away and almost spitted Alain, who retreated in extreme haste.

"Which of you is the leader here?" Jettaret demanded.

Domingo stepped forward. "I am, my son. Domingo, canon regular, and deputy of Rome."

There was an awed murmur from the peasants. Jettaret lowered his sword.

"Give me the witch." Domingo was compassionate, then stern. "Hand her over, or it will go hard with you."

"She's not a witch. She was enchanted by one. And that one has gone to burn forever.

"It's true," Liana spoke up. "I was, but I'm not, now. The real witch is gone."

"Who are you, my son?"

"The Vicomte de Solignac. A returned Crusader." The peasants drew back and several crossed themselves. Jettaret turned to Liana. "Liana, show them."

Jettaret handed Liana his sword. The peasants withdrew further, but Liana could barely lift it. Jettaret took Fortuna Domini back and sheathed it.

"A real witch would have had no trouble. Make fire!"

"But I can't—"

"Make fire!"

Liana tried again and couldn't; Jettaret pointed to Henri.

"Knock him down."

Henri retreated; Liana tried to flatten him with a spell and failed.

"Nothing! She did nothing!" he exclaimed.

"She's just a child." Maxine was in wonderment.

Softly Liana said, "Malaxia lied to me."

"Malaxia?" Domingo had a new alertness "I have read of her. The incarnation of evil. She is dead?"

"I can tell you, Father, what happened, how," she leaned close and whispered, "Please don't burn me!"

"I will hear you. To all here present: it is a known fact that a true witch cannot pray, or withstand the signs of our faith upon her person." Domingo removed his cross and placed it around Liana's neck, and after considering a moment said, "Recite the *Salve Regina.*"

"Everyone knows that," sniffed Claire.

Liana began haltingly, "*Salve Regina . . .*" and was at a loss. Several toughened fists tightened around their farm tools. Jettaret stepped behind and to one side of Domingo, and mouthed the words, "*Mater misericórdiae—*"

"*Mater misericórdiae,*" Liana repeated.

Domingo looked back at Jettaret. Liana remembered, and looked straight at Domingo.

"*Vita, dulcédo et spes nostra, salve.*" Her words accelerated. "*Ad te clamámus éxules fílii Hevae; ad te suspirámus, geméntes et flentes in hac lacrymárum valle—*"

"Enough."

Joyfully running the words together, Liana didn't hear him. "*Eia-ergo-advocáta-nostra-illos-tuos-misericórdes-óculos-ad-nos-convérte—*"

"Enough!" Domingo took his cross back.

"I can't say it that far," Alain admitted.

"There must be a further inquiry, and a full confession," Liana was in trepidation again at Domingo's words. "Do not worry, child. I believe you. And I have some authority in these matters. But a full account must be made to the Church. Vicomte?" Jettaret stepped forward. "I leave her in your care until the official business of this matter is settled. And after, I would speak to you of the Crusade."

"That I would not do, Father."

"Yes, others who have taken the Cross have said the same. It is for a history I am compiling, however, and I would appreciate the facts of your story."

"In time."

"Good. That is all one can ask." He addressed the peasants. "My good people, return to your homes. All is taken care of." In twos and threes, the peasants left down the path.

"I believe I shall take a brisk walk before going back to town." Domingo cleared his throat. "Please be there before dark." He smiled and took one of the other paths through the woods.

Alberge wasn't going anywhere. Jettaret saw him, sighed, and beckoned him over.

"Liana, my former comrade at arms, and very dear friend, Alberge. We have fought together; we know each other's mettle."

"Mam'selle." With a gimpy bow, Alberge kissed Liana's hand.

"Is this how ladies are treated?"

"You'll get used to it, I daresay," Alberge glowered, with a meaningful look at Jettaret. He gimped off down the path that Domingo had taken, singing.

> *Le soleil de la Provence c'est une maman à ses fils*
> *Le soleil de la Provence brille sur à ma vieille ville*
> *Le soleil de la Provence c'est le feu dans mon coeur*
> *Le soleil de la Provence chante mon amour*
> The sun of Provence is a mother to her sons
> The sun of Provence shines over my old town
> The sun of Provence is the fire in my heart
> The sun of Provence sings to my love

Liana took a step after him, and Jettaret made a noise in his throat. Liana turned back toward him. Before her stood the battered soul who had faced down the forces of Hell itself to save her, the betrayed Crusader who still wanted so much to believe, in God, in decency, in faithfulness.

She believed, and met his eyes.

In the woods near the clearing, Alberge met Domingo waiting on the path for him.

"His friend?" Domingo inquired. Alberge nodded. Domingo saw the cross stitched on his tunic. "And a Crusader."

"Not anymore."

"You may find the road to Damascus yet."

"I was on it, priest," Alberge spewed bitter triumph. "And I didn't see St. Paul. Or anyone that looked like Christ Jesus."

"Perhaps not. But his blessing be on you all the same. Whether you like it or not. Loyalty is the second of the high virtues. Only love comes first."

"Somebody had to look after that idiot," growled Alberge. "And you're not the Virgin Mother."

"No. My name is Domingo."

Alberge looked at Domingo's feet. "No shoes? Crazy priest. Your feet are all cut."

"Yes. It helps remind me of the sufferings our Lord went through, and therefore also of His joy."

"Maniac." Alberge started down the path again.

"*Dominus vobiscum.*"

"Drown in your wine, priest."

"God go with you all the same."

"And choke on your Host!" Alberge stumped off down the path.

Domingo raised a hand and moved it down and across in blessing.

The late afternoon sun lit the leaves in the clearing, filling them with light. Liana moved toward Jettaret.

"Jettaret—"

Jettaret held up his hand. "Antoine." He took her in one arm, gently, then they joined in full embrace.

The stream continued its irretrievable cascade down. Liana's fine blue stone, a sad snatch of moonlight beneath the waters, slowly lost its glow and became as the other stones, indistinguishable from among them.

Malaxia's amulet still held among the rocks, though the water was slowly working it loose. It hung there a moment longer, flashed in the sunlight, and was gone.

Brother Domingo was canonized as St. Dominic in 1234, thirteen years after his death.

APPENDIX

Pronunciation of Names

Note: Accented syllables in French are not quite as strong as accented syllables in English.

Malaxia – Mahl-AX-ee-uh
Liana – Lee-AH-nuh
Michel Antoine Jetterat, Vicomte de Solignac – Mee-SHEL An-TWAHN Zheh-tah-REY, Vee-KOHM duh SOLE-in-nyock
Alberge – All-BEARZH

Canonical Hours
The practice of saying prayers at specific times of the day goes back to the earliest days of the Church. By the Middle Ages, there were eight canonical hours. The parenthetically numbered hours are from the Romans' system of time keeping.

1. Matins   (Morning)   Midnight, or early morning
2. Lauds   (Praises)   Dawn; sometimes said with Matins
3. Prime   (1st hour)   6 AM, or sunrise
4. Tierce   (3rd hour)   9 AM
5. Sext   (6th hour)   Noon
6. Nones   (9th hour)   3 PM
7. Vespers   (12th hour)   6 PM, or sunset
8. Compline   7 PM, or after sunset

Matins
    Venue ("O Come"), Psalm 95
    Hymn
    Nocturna (Night Watch) of twelve Psalms
        Three *nocturnas* on Sunday
    Three-part lesson, one from the Bible, two from the Church

Fathers, Sts. Ambrose, Origen, Jerome, Augustine, Chrysostom, Basil, and others
Te Deum

Lauds
    Four Psalms
    A canticle
    Psalms 148-150
    A hymn
    The *Benedictus* (Luke 1:68-79)
    Prayers

Prime, Tierce, Sext, and None (the Little Day Hours)
    A hymn
    Parts of Psalm 119
    Prayer
    On Sundays the Athanasian Creed is said at prime.

Vespers (Evensong)
    Five psalms
    A hymn
    The *Magnificat* (Luke 1:46-55)
    Prayers

Compline (prayers for protection during the darkness)
    General confession
    Four psalms
    A hymn
    The *Nunc dimittis* (Luke 2:29-32)
    Prayers
    Commemoration of the Virgin

Salve Regína
Hail, Holy Queen

Salve, Regína mater misericórdiae, vita, dulcédo et spes nostra, salve. Ad te clamámus, éxules fílii Hevae; ad te suspirámus, geméntes et flentes in hac lacrymárum valle. Eia ergo, advocáta nostra, illos tuos misericórdes óculos ad nos convérte. Et Jesum, benedíctum fructum ventris tui, nobis post hoc exsílium osténde, o clemens, o pia, o dulcis Virgo Maria.

Hail, Holy Queen, mother of mercy, our life, our sweetness and our hope, hail. To you do we cry, poor banished children of Eve; to you do we sigh, mourning and weeping in this valley of tears. Ah then, our advocate, turn your eyes of mercy toward us, and after this our exile, show us the blessed fruit of your womb, Jesus, o clement, o loving, o sweet Virgin Mary.

About the Author

Wendy Joseph vies with her characters for a life of romance and adventure. A deckhand on merchant ships, she has outrun pirates off of Somalia, steered ships large and small through hurricanes and typhoons from the Bering Sea to Singapore, and helped rescue seals on the Pacific coast. Believing history must be lived, she has crewed the 18th century square-rigger Lady Washington and the WWII freighter SS Lane Victory. She has shared her food with starving cats and third world workers. She sings sea shanties, her own songs, and with classical and medieval choirs. Her passion is for works of the imagination, for telling a really good story, and for connecting with the minds and souls of readers and taking them to a magnificent and finer place. Researching *The Witch's Hand* in France, she traced the paths of her characters over the terrain they covered to get the description right, and dug up old documents for historical accuracy. She holds two Master's in English and can splice a twelve strand line. Ashore she holds court with her cats Jean Lafitte and Bijou on the wild coast of Washington State.

ALL THINGS THAT MATTER PRESS ™

FOR MORE INFORMATION ON TITLES AVAILABLE FROM
ALL THINGS THAT MATTER PRESS, GO TO
http://allthingsthatmatterpress.com
or contact us at
allthingsthatmatterpress@gmail.com

Printed in Great Britain
by Amazon